ARENA ONE

SLAVERUNNERS

(BOOK #1 OF THE SURVIVAL TRILOGY)

MORGAN RICE

Also by Morgan Rice

TURNED (Book #1 in the Vampire Journals)
LOVED (Book #2 in the Vampire Journals)
BETRAYED (Book #3 in the Vampire Journals)
DESTINED (Book #4 in the Vampire Journals)
DESIRED (Book #5 in the Vampire Journals)
BETROTHED (Book #6 in the Vampire Journals)
VOWED (Book #7 in the Vampire Journals)

ABOUT MORGAN RICE

Morgan Rice is the #1 Bestselling author of THE VAMPIRE JOURNALS, which has sold over 100,000 copies and has been translated into six languages. Morgan lives in New York City.

ACCLAIM FOR MORGAN RICE'S BOOKS

"Grabbed my attention from the beginning and did not let go....This story is an amazing adventure that is fast paced and action packed from the very beginning. There is not a dull moment to be found."
--Paranormal Romance Guild {regarding *Turned*}

"A great plot, and this especially was the kind of book you will have trouble putting down at night. The ending was a cliffhanger that was so spectacular that you will immediately want to buy the next book, just to see what happens."
--The Dallas Examiner {regarding *Loved*}

"A book to rival *Twilight* and *The Vampire Diaries*, and one that will have you wanting to keep reading until the very last page! If you are into adventure, love and vampires this book is the one for you!"
--vampirebooksite.com {regarding *Turned*}

"An ideal story for young readers. Morgan Rice did a good job spinning an interesting twist on what could have been a typical vampire tale. Refreshing and unique, has the classic elements found in many Young Adult paranormal stories."
--The Romance Reviews {regarding *Turned*}

"Rice does a great job of pulling you into the story from the beginning, utilizing a great descriptive quality that transcends the mere painting of the setting....Nicely written and an extremely fast read, this is a good start to a new vampire series sure to be a hit with readers who are looking for a light, yet entertaining story."
--Black Lagoon Reviews {regarding *Turned*}

"Jam packed with action, romance, adventure, and suspense. This book is a wonderful addition to this series and will have you wanting more from Morgan Rice."
--vampirebooksite.com {regarding *Loved*}

"Morgan Rice proves herself again to be an extremely talented storyteller....This would appeal to a wide range of audiences, including younger fans of the vampire/fantasy genre. It ended with an unexpected cliffhanger that leaves you shocked."
--The Romance Reviews {regarding *Loved*}

"Had I but died an hour before this chance,
I had lived a blessed time; for, from this instant,
There's nothing serious in mortality."

--Shakespeare, *Macbeth*

PART ONE

ONE

Today is less forgiving than most. The wind whips relentlessly, brushing clumps of snow off the heavy pine and right into my face as I hike straight up the mountain face. My feet, crammed into hiking boots a size too small, disappear in the six inches of snow. I slip and slide, struggling to find my footing. The wind comes in gusts, so cold it takes my breath away. I feel as if I'm walking into a living snow globe.

Bree tells me it's December. She likes to count down the days to Christmas, scratching off the numbers each day on an old calendar she found. She does it with such enthusiasm, I can't bring myself to tell her we're nowhere near December. I won't tell her that her calendar is three years old, or that we'll never get a new one, because they stopped making them the day the world ended. I won't deny her her fantasy. That's what big sisters are for.

Bree clings to her beliefs anyway, and she's always believed that snow means December, and even if I told her, I doubt it would change her mind. That's a ten-year-old for you.

What Bree refuses to see is that winter comes early up here. We're high up in the Catskills, and here, there's a different sense of time, a different turn to the seasons. Here, three hours north of what-was-once New York City, the leaves drop by the end of August, scattering across mountain ranges that stretch as far as the eye can see.

Our calendar was current once. When we first arrived, three years ago, I remember seeing the first snow and then checking it in disbelief. I couldn't understand how the page read October. I assumed such early snow was a freak. But I soon learned it wasn't. These mountains are just high enough, just cold enough, for winter to cannibalize Fall.

If Bree would just flip back the calendar, she'd see it right there, the old year, in big, tacky letters: 2117. Obviously, three years old. I tell myself she's just too caught up in her excitement to check closely. This is what I hope. But lately, a part of me is beginning to suspect that she really knows, that she's just chosen to lose herself in fantasy. I can't blame her.

Of course, we haven't had a working calendar for years. Or cell phone, or computer, or TV, or radio, or internet, or technology of any kind—not to mention electricity, or running water. Yet somehow, we've managed to make it, just the two of us, for three years like this. The summers have been tolerable, with fewer hungry days. We can at least fish then, and the mountain creeks always seemed to carry salmon. There are also berries, and even a few wild apple and pear orchards that still, after all this time, bear fruit. Once in a while, we even manage to catch a rabbit.

But the winters are intolerable. Everything is frozen, or dead, and each year I am certain that we will not make it. And this has been the worst winter of all. I keep telling myself that things will turn around; but it's been days now without a decent meal, and Winter has just begun. We are both weak from hunger, and now, Bree is also sick. It doesn't bode well.

As I trudge up the mountain face, retracing the same luckless steps I took yesterday, searching for our next meal, I am beginning to feel our luck has run out. It is only the thought of Bree lying there, waiting at home, that urges me forward. I stop pitying myself and instead hold her face in my mind. I know I can't find her medicine, but I am hoping it's just a passing fever, and that a good meal and some warmth is all she needs. What she really needs is a fire. I never light fires in our fireplace anymore, as it's too dangerous: I can't risk the smoke, the smell, tipping off a slaverunner to our location. But tonight I will surprise her, and just for a little while, take the chance. Bree lives for fires, and it will lift her spirits. And if I can just find a meal to complement it—even something as small as a rabbit—it will complete her recovery. Not just physically. I've noticed her starting to lose hope these last few days—I can see it in her eyes—and I need her to stay strong. I refuse to sit back and watch her slip away, like Mom did.

A new gust of wind slaps me in the face, and this one is so long and vicious I need to lower my head and wait until it passes. The wind roars in my ears, and I would do anything for a real winter coat. I wear only a worn hoodie, one I found years ago by the side of the road. I think it was a boy's, but that's good, because the sleeves are long enough to cover my hands and almost double as gloves. At five six I'm not exactly short, so whoever owned this must have been tall. Sometimes I wonder if he'd care that I'm wearing his clothing. But then I realize he's probably dead. Just like everybody else.

My pants aren't much better: I still wear the same pair of jeans, I'm embarrassed to mote, that I've had on since we escaped the city all those years ago. If there's one thing I regret, it's leaving so hastily. I guess I'd assumed I'd find some clothes up here, that maybe a clothing store would still be open somewhere, or even a salvation army. That was stupid of me: of course, all the clothing stores had long ago been looted. It was as if, overnight, the world went from a place of plenty to a place of scarcity. I'd managed to find a few pieces of clothing scattered in drawers in my Dad's house. These I gave to Bree. I was happy that at least some of his clothes, like his thermals and socks, could keep her warm.

The wind finally stops, and I raise my head and hurry straight up before it can pick up again, forcing myself up at double speed, until I reach the plateau.

I reach the top, breathing hard, my legs on fire, and slowly look around. The trees are more sparse up here and in the distance is a small mountain lake. It's frozen, like all the others, and the sun glares off of it with enough intensity to make me squint.

I immediately look over at my fishing rod, the one I'd left the day before, wedged between two boulders. It sticks out over the lake, a long piece of string dangling from it into a small hole in the ice. If the rod is bent, it means Bree and I will have dinner tonight. If not, I'll know it didn't work—again. I hurry between a cluster of trees, through the snow, and get a good look.

It's straight. Of course.

My heart sinks. I debate walking out onto the ice, using my small axe to chop a hole elsewhere. But I already know it won't make a difference. The problem is not its position—the problem is this lake. The ground is too frozen for me to dig up worms, and I don't even know where to look for them. I'm not a natural hunter, or trapper. If I knew I'd end up where I am now, I would have devoted my entire childhood to outward bound, to survival techniques. But now I find myself useless in most everything. I don't know how to set traps, and my fishing lines have rarely caught a thing.

Being my father's daughter, a Marine's daughter, the one thing that I am good at—knowing how to fight—is useless up here. If I am helpless against the animal kingdom, at least I can handle myself against the two-legged ones. From the time I was young, like it or not, Dad insisted I be his daughter—a Marine's daughter, and proud of it. He also wanted me to be the son he never had. He enrolled me in boxing, wrestling, mixed-martial arts…there were endless lessons on how to use a knife, how to fire a gun, how to find pressure points, how to fight dirty. Most of all, he insisted I be tough, that I never show fear, and that I never cry.

Ironically, I have never had a chance to use a single thing he taught me, and it all couldn't be more useless up here: there is not another person in sight. What I really need is to know how to find food—not to know how to kick someone. And if I do ever run into another person, I'm not going to be flipping him, but asking for help.

I think hard and recall that there is another lake up here somewhere, a smaller one; I saw it once, one summer when I was adventurous and hiked further up the mountain. It's a steep quarter mile, and I haven't tried to go up there since.

I look up and sigh. The sun is already beginning to set, a morose winter sunset cast in a reddish hue, and I'm already weak, tired and frozen. It will take most of what I've got just to make it back down the mountain. The last thing I want is to hike further up. But a small voice inside me urges me to keep climbing. The more time I spend alone these days, the stronger Dad's voice is becoming in my head. I resent it, and I want to block it out, but somehow, I can't.

Stop whining and keep pushing, Moore!

Dad always liked to call me by my last name. Moore. It annoyed me, but he didn't care.

I know that if I go back now, Bree will have nothing to eat tonight. That lake up there is the best I can come up with, our only other source of food. I also want Bree to have a fire, and all the wood down here is soaked. Up there, where the wind is stronger, I might find wood dry enough for kindling. I take one more look straight up the mountain, and decide to go for it. I lower my head, and begin the hike, taking my rod with me.

Each step is painful, a million sharp needles pulsing in my thighs, icy air piercing my lungs. The wind picks up and the snow whips, like sandpaper on my face. A bird caws way up high, as if mocking me. Just when I feel I can't take one more step, I reach the next plateau.

This one, so high up, is different than all the others: it is so densely packed with pine trees, it's hard to see more than ten feet. The sky is shut out under their huge canopy, and the snow is covered with their green needles. The huge tree trunks manage to shut out the wind, too. I feel like I've entered a small private kingdom, hidden from the rest of the world.

I stop and turn, taking in the vista: the view is amazing. I'd always thought we had a great view from Dad's house, halfway up the mountain, but from here, up top, it is spectacular. Mountain peaks soar in every direction, and beyond them, in the distance, I can even see the Hudson River, sparkling. I also see the winding roads that cut their way through the mountain, remarkably intact. Probably because so few people ever come up here. I've never, in fact, seen a car, or any other vehicle. Despite the snow, the roads are remarkably clear; the steep, angular roads, basking in the sun, lend themselves perfectly to drainage, and amazingly, much of the snow has melted off.

I am struck by a pang of worry. I prefer when the roads are covered in snow and ice, when they are impassable to vehicles, because the only people that have cars and fuel these days are slaverunners—merciless bounty hunters that work to feed Arena One. They patrol everywhere, looking for any survivors, to kidnap them and bring them to the arena as slaves. There, I'm told, they make them fight to the death for entertainment.

Bree and I have been lucky. We haven't seen any slaverunners in the years we've been up here—but I think that's only because we live so high up, in such a remote area. Only once did I hear the high-pitched whine of a slaverunner's engine, far off in the distance, on the other side of the river, I think. I know they are down there, somewhere, patrolling. And I don't take any chances—I make sure we keep a low profile, rarely burning wood unless we need to, and keeping a close eye on Bree at all times. Most of the times I take her hunting with me—I would have today if she weren't so sick.

I turn back to the plateau and fix my eyes on the smaller lake. Frozen solid, shining in the afternoon light, it sits there like a lost jewel, hiding between a copse of trees. I approach it, taking a few tentative steps on the ice to make sure it doesn't crack. Once I feel it's solid, I take a few more. I find a spot, remove the small axe from my belt and chop down hard, several times. A crack appears. I remove my knife, take a knee and strike hard, right in the center of the crack. I work the tip of the knife in there and carve a small hole, just big enough to extract a fish.

I hurry back to shore, slipping and sliding, then wedge the fishing rod between two tree branches, unravel the string, and run back out and drop it in the hole. I yank it a few times, hoping that the flash of the metal hook might attract some living creatures beneath the ice. But I can't help feeling it's a futile endeavor, can't help suspecting that anything that ever lived in these mountain lakes died long ago.

It's even colder up here, and I can't just stand here, staring at the line. I have to keep moving. I turn and walk away from the lake, the superstitious part of me telling me I might just catch a fish if I don't stand there staring. I walk in small circles around the trees, rubbing my hands, trying to keep warm. It does little good.

That's when I remember the other reason I hiked up here: dry wood. I look down and search the ground for kindling, but it is a futile task. The ground is covered in snow. I look up at the trees, and see the trunks and branches are mostly covered in snow, too. But there, in the distance, I spot a few wind-swept trees free of snow. I make my way over to them and inspect the bark, running my hand along it. I am relieved to see that some of the branches are dry. I take out my axe and chop one of the bigger branches. All I need is an armful of wood, and this large branch will do perfectly.

I catch it as it comes down, not wanting to let it hit the snow, then brace it against the trunk and chop it again, clean in half. I do this again and again, until I have a small stack of kindling, enough to carry in my arms. I set it down in the nook of a branch, safe and dry from the snow below.

I look around, inspecting the other trunks, and as I look closer, something gives me pause. I approach one of the trees, looking closely, and realize its bark is different than the others. I look up, and realize it's not a Pine. It's a Maple. I am surprised to see a Maple so high up here, and even more surprise that I actually recognize it. In fact, a Maple is probably the only one thing in nature that I *would* recognize. Despite myself, a memory comes flooding back.

Once, when I was young, my Dad got it into his head to take me on a nature outing. God knows why, he decided to take me to tap Maple trees. We drove for hours to some godforsaken part of the country, me carrying a metal bucket, he carrying a spout, and then spent hours more roaming the woods with a guide, searching for the perfect Maples. I remember the look of disappointment on his face after he tapped his first tree and a clear liquid oozed out into our bucket. He had been expecting syrup.

Our guide laughed at him, told him that Maple trees didn't produce syrup—they produced sap. The sap had to be boiled down to syrup. It was a process that took hours, he said. It took about 80 gallons of sap to make a single quart of syrup.

Dad looked down at the overflowing bucket of sap in his hand and turned bright red, as if someone had sold him a rotten bill of goods. He was the proudest man I'd ever met, and if there was anything he hated more than feeling stupid, it was someone making fun of him. When the man laughed, he threw his bucket at him, barely missing him, took my hand, and we stormed off.

After that, he never took me out into nature again.

I didn't mind, though—and actually enjoyed the outing, even though he fumed silently in the car the whole way home. I'd managed to collect a small cup of the sap before he'd taken me away, and I remember secretly sipping it on the car ride home, when he wasn't looking. I loved it. It tasted like sugar water.

Standing here now, before this tree, I recognize it as I would a sibling. This specimen, so high up, is thin and scrawny, and I'd be surprised if it holds any sap at all. But I've got nothing to lose. I take out my knife and strike the tree, again and again, in the same spot. Then I burrow the knife into the hole, pushing deeper and deeper, twisting and turning. I don't really expect anything to happen.

I'm shocked when a drop of sap leaks out. And even more shocked when, moments later it turns into a small, trickling stream. I hold out my finger, touch it, and raise it to my tongue. I feel the sugar rush, and recognize the taste immediately. Just as I remembered. I can't believe it.

The sap leaks out at faster now, and I'm losing much of it as it drips down the trunk. I look around desperately for something to hold it in, a bucket of some sorts—but of course there is none. And then I remember: my thermos. I pull my plastic thermos out of my waistband and turn it upside down, emptying it of water. I can get fresh water anywhere, especially with all this snow—but this sap is precious. I hold the empty thermos flush against the tree, wishing I had a proper spout. I cram the plastic against the trunk as close as I can, and manage to catch much of it. It fills more slowly than I'd like, but within minutes, I've managed to fill half the thermos.

The flow of sap stops. I wait for a few seconds, wondering if it will start again, but it doesn't.

I look around, and spot another Maple, about ten feet in the distance. I rush over to it and raise my knife excitedly and strike hard this time, envisioning myself filling the thermos, envisioning the look of surprise on Bree's face when she tastes it. It might not be nutritious, but it will sure make her happy.

But this time, when my knife strikes the trunk, there is a sharp splitting noise that I don't expect, and this is followed by the groaning of timber. I look up to see the entire tree leaning, and I realize, too late, that this tree, frozen over in a coat of ice, was dead. The plunging of my knife was all it needed to tip it over the edge.

A moment later the entire tree, at least twenty feet, falls over, crashing down to the ground. It stirs up an enormous cloud of snow and pine needles. I crouch down, nervous I might have alerted someone to my presence. I am furious with myself. That was careless. Stupid. I should have examined the tree more carefully first.

But after a few moments my heartbeat settles, as I realize there's no one else up here. I become rational again, realize that trees fall by themselves in the forest all the time, and its crash wouldn't necessarily give away a human presence. And as I look to the place where the tree once stood, I do a double-take. I find myself staring in disbelief.

There, in the distance, hiding behind a grove of trees, built right into the side of the mountain itself, is a small, stone cottage. It is a tiny structure, a perfect square, about fifteen feet wide and deep, built about twelve feet high, with walls made of ancient stone blocks. A small chimney rises from the roof, and there is a small window on each of its walls. The wooden front door, shaped in an arch, is ajar.

This little cottage is so well camouflaged, blends so perfectly with its surroundings, that even while staring at it, I can barely pick it out. Its roof and walls are covered in snow, and the stone that's exposed blends perfectly into the landscape. The cottage looks ancient, as if it were built hundreds of years ago. I can't understand what it's doing here, who would have built it, or why. Maybe it was built for a caretaker for a state park. Maybe it was home to a recluse. Or a survival nut.

It looks like it hasn't been touched in years. I carefully scan the forest floor, looking for footprints, or animal prints, in or out. But there are none. I think back to when the snow started falling, several days ago, and do the math in my head. No one has been in or out of here for at least three days.

My heart races at the thought of what could be inside. Food, clothing, medicine, weapons, materials—*anything* would be a godsend.

I move cautiously across the clearing, checking over my shoulder as I go just to make sure no one is watching. I move quickly, leaving big, conspicuous snow prints. As I reach the front door, I turn and look one more time, then stand there and wait for several seconds, listening. There is no sound but that of the wind and a nearby stream, which runs just a few feet in front of the house. I reach out and slam the back of my axe handle hard on the door, a loud reverberating noise, to give any animals that might be hiding inside a final warning.

There is no response.

I quickly shove open the door, pushing back the snow, and step inside.

It is dark in here, lit only by the last light of day streaming in through the small windows, and it takes my eyes a moment to adjust. I wait, standing with my back against the door, on guard in case any animals might be using this space as shelter. But after several more seconds of waiting, my eyes fully adjust to the dim light and it is clear that I'm alone.

The first thing I notice about this little house is its warmth. Perhaps it is because it is so small, with a low ceiling, and built right into the stone mountain itself; or perhaps because it is protected from the wind. Even though the windows are wide open to the elements, even though the door is still ajar, it must be at least fifteen degrees warmer in here—much warmer than Dad's house ever is, even with a fire going. Dad's house was built cheaply to begin with, with paper-thin walls and vinyl siding, built on a corner of a hill that always seems to be in the wind's direct path.

But this place is different. The stone walls are so thick and well-built, I feel snug and safe in here. I can only imagine how warm this place could get if I shut the door, boarded up the windows, and had a fire in the fireplace—which looks to be in working shape. The inside consists of one large room, maybe fifteen by fifteen feet, and I squint into the darkness as I

24

comb the floor, looking for anything, anything at all, that I can salvage. Amazingly, this place looks like it's never been entered since the war. Every other house I've seen has smashed windows, debris scattered all over the place, clearly picked clean of anything that might be useful, down to the copper wires for the light bulbs. But not this one. It is pristine and clean and tidy, as if its owner just got up one day and walked away. I wonder if it was before the war even began. Judging from the cobwebs on the ceiling, and its incredible location, hidden so well behind the trees, I am guessing it was. That no one's been here in decades.

I see the outline of an object against the far wall, and I make my way towards it, hands in front of me, groping in the darkness. When my hands touch it, I realize it is a chest of drawers. I run my fingers over its smooth, wood surface and can feel them covered in dust. I run my fingers over small knobs—drawer handles. I pull delicately, opening them one at a time. It is too dark to see, so I reach into each drawer with my hand, combing the surface. The first drawer yields nothing. Neither does the second. I open them all, quickly, my hopes falling—when suddenly, at the fifth drawer, I stop. There, in the back, I feel something. I slowly pull it out.

I hold it up to the light, through the open window, and at first I can't tell what it is; but then I feel the telltale aluminum foil, and I realize: it's a chocolate bar. A few bites were taken out of it, but it is still wrapped in its original wrapping, and mostly preserved. I unwrap it just a bit and hold it to my nose and smell it. I can't believe it: real chocolate. We haven't had chocolate since the war.

The smell brings a sharp hunger pang, and it takes all my willpower not to tear it open and devour it. I force myself to remain strong, carefully re-wrapping it and stowing it in my pocket. I will wait until I am with Bree to enjoy it. I smile, anticipating the look on her face when she takes her first bite. It will be priceless.

I quickly rummage through the remaining drawers, now hopeful I'll find all sorts of treasure. But everything else comes up empty. I turn back to the room and walk through its width and breadth, along the walls, to all four corners, looking for anything at all. But the place is empty.

Suddenly, I step on something soft. I kneel down and pick it up, holding it to the light. I am amazed: a teddy bear. It is worn, and missing an eye, but still, Bree loves teddy bears, and misses the one she left behind. She will be ecstatic when she sees this. It looks like this is her lucky day.

I cram the bear in my belt, and as I get up, I feel my hand brush something soft on the floor. I grab it and hold it up, and am delighted to realize it's a scarf. It's black and covered in dust, so I couldn't see it in the darkness, and as I hold it to my neck and chest, I can already feel its warmth. I hold it out the window and shake it hard, removing all the dust. I look at it in the light: it is long and thick—not even any holes. It is like pure gold. I immediately wrap it around my neck and tuck it under my shirt, and already feel much warmer. I sneeze.

The sun is setting, and as it seems I've found everything I'm going to, I begin to exit. As I head for the door, suddenly, I stub my toe into something hard, metal. I stop and kneel down, feeling for it in case it's a weapon. It's not. It's a round, iron knob, attached to the wooden floor plank. Like a knocker. Or a handle.

I yank it left and right. Nothing happens. I try twisting it. Nothing. Then I take a chance and stand off to the side and pull it hard, straight up.

A trap door opens, raising a cloud of dust.

I look down and discover a crawlspace, about four feet high, with a dirt floor. My heart soars at the possibilities. If we lived here, and there was ever trouble, I could always hide Bree down here. This little cottage becomes even more valuable in my eyes.

And not only that. As I look down, I catch sight of something gleaming. I push back the heavy wooden door all the way, and quickly scramble down the ladder. It is black down here, and I hold my hands in front of me, groping my way. As I take a step forward, I feel something. Glass. Shelves are built into the wall, and lined up on them are glass jars. Mason jars.

I pull one down and hold it up to the light. Its contents are red and soft. It looks like jam. I quickly unscrew the tin lid, hold it to my nose and smell it. The pungent smell of raspberries hits me like a wave. I stick a finger in, scoop it and hold it tentatively to my tongue. I can't believe it: raspberry jam. And it tastes as fresh as if it were made yesterday.

I quickly tighten the lid, cram the jar into my pocket, and hurry back to the shelves. I can already feel, in the blackness, that there are dozens more. I grab the closest one, rush back to the light, and hold it up. It looks like pickles.

I am in awe. This place is a gold mine.

I wish I could grab it all, but my hands are freezing, I don't have anything to carry it with, and it's getting dark out. So I put the jar of pickles back where I found it, scramble up the ladder, and, as I make it back to the main floor, close the trap door firmly behind me. I wish I had a lock; I feel nervous leaving all of that down there, unprotected. But then I remind myself that this place hasn't been touched in years—and that I probably never would have even noticed it if that tree didn't fall.

As I leave, I close the door all the way, feeling protective, already feeling as if this is our home.

Pockets full, I hurry back towards the lake—but suddenly freeze as I sense movement and hear a noise. At first I worry someone has followed me; but as I slowly turn, I see it is something else. A deer is standing there, ten feet away, staring back at me. It is the first deer I've seen in years. Its large, black eyes lock onto mine, then it suddenly turns and bolts.

I am speechless. I'd spent month after month searching for a deer, hoping I could get close enough to one to throw my knife at it. But I'd never been able to find one, anywhere. Maybe I wasn't hunting high enough. Maybe up here is where they've lived all along.

I resolve to return, first thing in the morning, and wait all day if I have to. If it was here once, maybe it will come back. The next time I see it, I will kill it. That deer would be enough food to feed us for a week.

I am filled with new hope as I hurry to the lake. As I approach and check my rod, my heart leaps to see that it's bent nearly in half. Shaking with excitement, I scurry across the ice, slipping and sliding. I grab the line, which is shaking wildly, and pray that it holds.

I reach over and yank it firmly. I can feel the force of a large fish yanking back, and I silently will the line not to snap, the hook not to break. I give it one final yank, and the fish comes flying out of the hole. It is a huge Salmon, the size of my arm. It lands on the ice and flip-flops every which way, sliding across. I run to it and reach down and grab it, but it slips right through my hands, and plops back on the ice. My hands are too slimy to grab a hold of it, so I lower my sleeves and reach down and grab it more firmly this time. It flops and squirms in my hands for a good thirty seconds, until finally, it settles down, dead.

I am amazed. It is my first catch in months.

I am ecstatic as I slide across the ice and set it down on the shore, packing it in the snow, afraid it will somehow come back to life and jump back into the lake. I take down the rod and line and hold it one hand, then grab the fish in the other. I can feel the mason jar of jam in one pocket, and the thermos of sap in the other, crammed in with the chocolate bar, and the teddy bear on my waist. Bree will have an abundance of riches tonight.

There is just one thing left to grab. I walk over to the stack of dry wood, balance the rod in my arm, and with my free hand grab as many logs as I can hold. I drop a few, and can't take as many as I'd like, but I'm not complaining. I can always come back for the rest of it in the morning.

Hands, arms and pockets full, I slip and slide down the steep mountain face in the last light of day, careful not to drop any of my treasure. As I go, I can't stop thinking about the cottage. It's perfect, and my heart beats faster at the possibilities. This is exactly what we need. Our Dad's house is too conspicuous, built on a main road. I've been worrying for months that we're too vulnerable being there. All we'd need is one random slaverunner to pass by, and we'd be in trouble. I've been wanting to move us for a long time, but just had no idea where. I haven't seen any other houses up here at all.

That little cottage, so high up, so far from any road—and built literally into the mountain—is so well camouflaged, it's almost as if it were built just for us. No one would ever be able to find us there. And even if they did, they couldn't come anywhere near us with a vehicle. They'd have to hike up on foot, and from that vantage point, I'd spot them a mile away.

The house also has a fresh water source, a running stream right in front of its door; I wouldn't have to leave Bree alone every time I go hiking to bathe and wash our clothes. And I wouldn't have to carry buckets of water one at a time all the way from the lake every time I prepare a meal. Not to mention that, with that huge canopy of trees, we would be concealed enough to light fires in the fireplace every night. We would be safer, warmer, in a place teeming with fish and game—and stocked with a basement full of food. My mind is made up. I'm going to move us there tomorrow.

It's like a weight off my shoulders. I feel reborn. For the first time in as long as I can remember, I don't feel the hunger gnawing away, don't feel the cold piercing my fingertips. Even the wind, as I climb down, seems to be at my back, helping me along, and I know that things have finally turned around. For the first time in as long as I can remember, I know that now, we can make it.

Now, we can survive.

TWO

By the time I reach Dad's house it is twilight, the temperature dropping, the snow beginning to harden and crunch beneath my feet. I exit the woods and see our house sitting there, perched so conspicuously on the side of the road, and am relieved to see that all looks undisturbed, exactly as I left it. I immediately check the snow for any footprints—or animal prints—in or out, and find none.

There are no lights on inside the house, but that is normal. I would be concerned if there were. We have no electric, and lights would only mean that Bree has lit candles—and she wouldn't without me. I stop and listen for several seconds, and all is still. No noises of struggle, no cries for help, no cries of sickness. I breathe a sigh of relief.

A part of me is always afraid I will return to find the door wide open, the window shattered, footprints leading into the house, Bree abducted. I've had this nightmare several times, and always wake up sweating, and walk into the other room to make sure Bree is there. She always is, safe and sound, and I reprimand myself. I know I should stop worrying, after all these years. But for some reason, I just can't shake it: every time I have to leave Bree alone, it's like a little knife in my heart.

Still on alert, sensing everything around me, I examine our house in the fading light of day. It was honestly never nice to begin with. A typical mountain ranch, it sits as a rectangular box with no character whatsoever, festooned with cheap, aqua vinyl siding, which looked old from day one, and which now just looks rotted. The windows are small and far and few between and made of a cheap plastic. It looks like it belongs in a trailer park. Maybe fifteen feet wide by about thirty feet deep, it should really be a one bedroom, but whoever built it, in their wisdom, carved it into two small bedrooms and an even smaller living room.

I remember visiting it as a child, before the war, when the world was still normal. Dad, when he was home, would bring us up here for weekends, to get away from the city. I didn't want to be ungrateful, and I always put on a good face for him, but silently, I never liked it: it always felt dark and cramped, and had a musty smell to it. As a kid, I remember being unable to wait for the weekend to be over, to get far away from this place. I remember silently vowing that when I was older, I would never come back here.

Now, ironically, I am grateful for this place. This house saved my life—and Bree's. When the war broke out and we had to flee from the city, we had no options. If it weren't for this place, I don't know where we would have gone. And if this place weren't as remote and high up as it is, then we would have probably been captured by slaverunners long ago. It's funny how you can hate things so much as a kid that you end up appreciating as an adult. Well, almost adult. At 17, I consider myself an adult, anyway. I've probably aged more than most of them, anyway, in the last few years.

If this house wasn't built right on the road, so exposed—if it were just a bit smaller, more protected, deeper in the woods, I don't think I'd worry so much. Of course, we'd still have to put up with the paper-thin walls, the leaking roof, and the windows that let in the wind. It would never be a comfortable, or a warm house. But at least it would be safe. Now, every time I look at it, and look out at the sweeping vista beyond it, I can't help but think it's a sitting target.

My feet crunch in the snow as I approach our vinyl door, and barking erupts from inside. Sasha, doing what I trained her to do: protect Bree. I am so grateful for her. She watches over

Bree so carefully, barks at the slightest noise; it allows me just enough peace of mind to leave her when I hunt. Although at the same time, her barking also sometimes worries me that she'll tip us off: after all, a barking dog usually means humans. And that's exactly what a slaverunner would listen for.

I hurriedly step into the house and quickly silence her. I close the door behind me, juggling the logs in my hand, and step into the blackened room. Sasha quiets, wagging her tail and jumping up on me. A chocolate lab, six years old, Sasha is the most loyal dog I could ever imagine—and the best company. If it weren't for her, I think Bree would have fallen into a depression long ago. I might have, too.

Sasha licks my face, whining, and seems even more excited than usual; I can tell from her sniffing at my waistline, at my pockets, that she already senses I've brought home something special. I set down the logs so that I can pet her, and as I do, I can feel her ribs. She's way too skinny. I feel a fresh pang of guilt. Then again, Bree and I are, too. We always share with her whatever we forage, so the three of us are a team of equals. Still, I wish I could give her more.

She pokes her nose at the fish, and as she does, it flies out of my hand and onto the floor. Sasha immediately pounces on it, her claws sending it sliding across the floor. She jumps on it again, this time biting it. But she must not like the taste of raw fish, so she lets it go. Instead, she plays with it, pouncing on it again and again as it slides across the floor.

"Sasha, stop!" I say quietly, not wanting to wake Bree. I also fear that if she plays with it too much, she might tear it open and waste some of the valuable meat. Obediently, Sasha stops. I can see how excited she is, though, and I want to give her something. I reach into my pocket, twist open the tin lid to the mason jar, scoop out some of the raspberry jam with my finger, and hold it out to her.

Without missing a beat she licks my finger, and in three big licks, she has eaten the whole scoop. She licks her lips and stares back at me wide-eyed, already wanting more.

I stroke her head, give her a kiss, then rise back to my feet. Now I wonder whether it was kind to give her some, or just cruel to give her so little.

The house is dark as I stumble through, as it always is at night. Rarely will I set a fire. As much as we need the heat, I don't want to risk attracting the attention. But tonight is different: Bree has to get well, both physically and emotionally, and I know a fire will do the trick. I also feel more open to throwing caution to the wind, given that we will move out of here tomorrow.

I cross the room to the cupboard and remove a lighter and candle. One of the best things about this place was its huge stash of candles, one of the very few good byproducts of my Dad's being a Marine, of his being such a survival nut. When we'd visit as kids, the electricity would go out during every storm, and so he'd stockpile candles, determined to beat the elements. I remember I used to make fun of him for it, call him a hoarder when I discovered his entire closet full of candles. Now that I'm down to the last few candles, I wish he'd hoarded more.

I've been keeping our only lighter alive by using it sparingly, and by siphoning off a tiny bit of gas from the motorcycle once every few weeks. I thank God every day for Dad's bike, and I am also grateful that he fueled it up one last time: it is the one thing we have that makes me think we still have an advantage, that we have something really valuable, some way of surviving if things go to hell. Dad always kept the bike in the small garage attached to the house, but when we first arrived, after the war, the first thing I did was remove it and roll it up the hill, into the woods, hiding it beneath bushes and branches and thorns so thick that no one could ever possibly find it. I figured, if our house is ever discovered, the first thing they'd do is check the garage.

I'm also grateful that Dad taught me how to drive it when I was young, despite Mom's protests. He told me it was harder to learn than most bikes, because of the attached sidecar. I remember back when I was twelve, terrified, learning to ride the bike while Dad sat in the sidecar, barking orders at me every time I stalled. I learned on these steep, unforgiving mountain roads, and I remember feeling like we were going to die. I remember looking out over the edge, seeing the drop, and crying, insisting that he drive. But he refused. He sat there stubbornly for over an hour, until I finally stopped crying and tried again. And somehow, I learned to drive it. That was my upbringing in a nutshell.

I haven't touched the bike since the day I hid it, and I don't even risk going up to look at it except when I need to siphon off the gas— and even that I will only do at night. I imagine that if ever one day we're in trouble and need to get out of here fast, I'll put Bree and Sasha in the sidecar and drive us all off to wherever we need to go. But in reality, I have no idea where else we'd possibly go. From everything I've seen and heard, the rest of the world is a wasteland, filled with violent criminals, gangs, and few survivors. The violent few who've managed to survive have congregated in the cities, kidnapping and enslaving whoever they can find, either for their own ends, or to service the death matches in the arenas. I am guessing that Bree and I are among very few survivors who still live freely, on our own, outside the cities. And among the very few who haven't yet starved to death.

I light the candle, and Sasha follows as I walk slowly through the darkened house. I assume Bree is asleep, and this worries me: she normally doesn't sleep this much. I stop before her door, debating whether to wake her. As I stand there, I look up and am startled by my own reflection in the small mirror. I look much older, as I do every time I see myself. My face, thin and angular, is flush from the cold, my light brown hair falls down, framing my face, to my shoulders, and my steel-grey eyes stare back at me as if they belong to someone I don't recognize. They are hard, intense eyes. Dad always said they were the eyes of a wolf. Mom always said they were beautiful. I wasn't sure who to believe.

I quickly look away, not wanting to see myself. I reach out and turn the mirror backwards, so that it won't happen again.

I slowly open Bree's door. The second I do, Sasha charges in and rushes to Bree's side, lying down and resting her chin on Bree's chest as she licks her face. It never ceases to amaze me how close those two are—sometimes I feel like they are even closer than we are.

Bree slowly opens her eyes, and squints into the darkness.

"Brooke?" she asks.

"It's me," I say, softly. "I'm home."

She sits up and smiles as her eyes light up with recognition. She lies on a cheap mattress on the floor, and throws off her thin blanket and begins to get out of bed, still in her pajamas. She is moving more slowly than usually, and it is obvious she is still sick.

I lean down and give her a hug.

"I have a surprise for you," I say, barely able to contain my excitement.

She looks up wide-eyed, then closes her eyes and opens her hands, waiting. She is so believing, so trusting, it amazes me. I debate what to give her first, then settle on the chocolate. I reach into my pocket and pull out the bar, and place it slowly in her palm. She opens her eyes and looks down at her hand, squinting in the light, unsure. I hold the candle up to it.

"What is it?" she asks.

"Chocolate," I answer.

She looks up as if I'm playing a trick on her.

"Really," I say.

"But where did you get it?" she asks, uncomprehending. She looks down as if an asteroid has just landed in her hand. I don't blame her: there are no stores anymore, no people around, and no place within a hundred miles of here that I could conceivably find such a thing.

I smile down at her. "Santa gave it to me, for you. It's an early Christmas present."

She wrinkles her brows. "No, *really*," she insists.

I take a deep breath, realizing it's time to tell her about our new home, about leaving here tomorrow. I try to figure the best way to phrase it. I hope she will be as excited as I am—but with kids, you never know. A part of me worries she might be attached to this place, and not want to leave.

"Bree, I have some big news," I say, as I lean down and hold her shoulders. "I discovered the most amazing place today, high up. It's a small, stone cottage, and it's perfect for us. It's cozy, and warm, and safe, and it has the most beautiful fireplace, which we can light every night. And best of all, it has all kinds of food right there. Like this chocolate."

Bree looks back down at the chocolate, studying it, and her eyes open twice as wide as she realizes it's real. She gently pulls back the wrapper, and smells it. She closes her eyes and smiles, then leans in to take a bite—but suddenly stops herself. She looks up at me in concern.

"What about you?" she asks. "Is there only one bar?"

That's Bree, always so considerate, even if she's starving. "You go first," I say. "It's okay."

She pulls the wrapper back, and takes a big bite. Her face, hollowed-out from hunger, crumbles in ecstasy.

"Chew slowly," I warn. "You don't want to get a stomach ache."

She slows down, savoring each bite. She breaks off a big piece and puts it in my palm. "Your turn," she says.

I slowly put it into my mouth, taking a small bite, letting it sit on the tip of my tongue. I suck on it, then chew it slowly, savoring every moment. The taste and smell of chocolate fills my senses. It is quite possibly the best thing I've ever had.

Sasha whines, pushing her nose close to the chocolate, and Bree breaks off a chunk and gives it to her. Sasha snaps it out of her fingers and swallows it in a single gulp. Bree laughs, delighted by her, as always. Then, in an impressive show of self-restraint, Bree wraps up the remaining half of the bar, rationing it. She reaches up and wisely places it way up high on the dresser, out of Sasha's reach. She still looks weak, but I can see her spirits starting to return.

"What's that?" she asks, pointing at my waist.

For a moment I don't realize what she's talking about, then I look down and see the teddy bear. In all the excitement, I'd almost forgotten. I reach down and hand it to her.

"I found it in our new home," I say. "It's for you."

Bree's eyes open wide in excitement as she clutches the bear, wrapping it to her chest and rocking it back and forth.

"I love it!" Bree exclaims, her eyes shining. "When can we move? I can't wait!"

I am relieved. Before I can respond, Sasha leans in and sticks her nose in Bree's new teddy bear, sniffing it; Bree rubs it playfully in Sasha's face, and Sasha snatches it and runs out the room.

"Hey!" Bree yells, erupting in hysterical laughter as she chases after her.

They both run into the living room, already immersed in a tug-of-war over the bear. I'm not sure who enjoys it more.

I follow them in, cupping the candle carefully so that it doesn't blow out, and bring it right to my pile of kindling. I grab a few of the smaller twigs, place them in the fireplace, then grab a handful of dry leaves from a basket beside the fireplace. I'm glad I collected these last Fall and stored them here, knowing they would serve as great fire-starters. They work like a charm. I place the dry leaves beneath the twigs, light them, and the flame soon reaches up and licks the wood. I keep feeding leaves into the fireplace, until eventually, the twigs are fully caught. I blow out the candle, saving it for another time.

"We're having a fire?" Bree yells excitedly.

"Yes," I say. "Tonight's a celebration. It's our last night here."

"Yay!" Bree screams, jumping up and down, and Sasha barks beside her, joining in the excitement. Bree runs over and grabs some of the kindling, helping me as I place it over fire. We place them carefully, allowing space for air, and Bree blows on it, fanning the flames. Once the kindling catches, I place a thicker log on top. I keep stacking bigger logs, until finally, we have a roaring fire.

In moments, the room is alight, and I can already feel its warmth. I stand beside the fire, as do Bree and Sasha, and hold out my hands, rubbing them, letting the warmth penetrate my fingers. Slowly, the feeling starts to return. I feel myself gradually thaw out from the long day outdoors, and I start to feel myself again.

"What's that?" Bree asks, pointing across the floor. "It looks like a fish!"

She runs over to it and grabs it, picking it up, and it slips right out of her hands. She laughs, and Sasha, not missing a beat, pounces on it with her paws, sliding it across the floor. "Where did you catch it!?" Bree yells.

I reach over and pick it up before Sasha can do more damage, open the door, and throw it outside, into the snow, where it will be better preserved and out of harm's way, before closing the door behind me.

"That was my other surprise," I say. "We're going to have dinner tonight!"

Bree runs over and gives me a big hug. Sasha barks, as if understanding. I hug her back.

"I have two more surprises for you," I announce with a smile. "They're for desert. Do you want me to wait till after dinner? Or do you want them now?"

"Now!" she yells, excited.

I smile, excited, too. At least it will hold her over for dinner.

I reach into my pocket and extract the jar of jam. Bree looks at it funny, clearly uncertain, and I unscrew the lid and place it under her nose. "Close your eyes," I say.

She does. "Now, inhale."

She breathes deeply, and a smile crosses her face. She opens her eyes.

"It smells like raspberries!" she exclaims.

"It's jam. Go ahead. Try it."

Bree reaches in with two fingers, takes a big scoop, and eats it. Her eyes light up.

"Wow," she says, as she reaches in, takes another big scoop, and holds it up to Sasha, who runs over and without hesitation gulps it down. Bree laughs hysterically, and I tighten the lid and set it up high on the mantle, away from Sasha.

"Is that also from our new house?" she asks.

I nod, relieved to hear that she already considers it our new home.

"And there is one last surprise," I say. "But this one I'm going to have to save for dinner."

I extract the thermos from my belt and place it higher up on the mantle, out of her sight, so she can't see what it is. I can see her craning her neck, and I hide it well. "Trust me," I say. "It's gonna be good."

*

I don't want the house to stink like fish, so I decide to brave the cold and prepare the fish outside. I bring my knife and set to work on it, propping it on a tree stump as I kneel down beside it in the snow. I don't really know what I'm doing, but I know enough to realize you don't eat the head or the tail. So I begin by chopping these off.

Then I figure that we're not going to eat the fins either, so I chop these off—or the scales, either, so I slice these off as best I can. Then I figure it has to be opened to eat it, so I slice what's left of it clean in half. It reveals a thick, pink inside, filled with lots of small bones. I don't know what else to do, so I figure it's ready to cook.

Before I head in, I feel the need to wash my hands. I just reach down, grab a handful of snow, and rinse my hands with it, grateful for the snow—usually, I have to hike to the closest stream, since we don't have any running water. I rise, and before going inside, I stop for a second and take in my surroundings. At first I am listening, as I always do, for any signs of noise, of danger. After several seconds, I realize the world is as still as can be. Finally, slowly, I relax, breathe deep, feel the snowflakes on my cheeks, take in the perfect quiet, and realize how utterly beautiful my surroundings are. The towering pines are covered in white, snow falls endlessly from a purple sky, and the world seems perfect, like a fairytale. I can see the glow of the fireplace through the window, and from here, it looks like the coziest place in the world.

I come back inside the house with the fish, closing the door behind me, and it feels good to come into a place so much warmer, with the soft light of the fire reflecting off of everything.

Bree has tended the fire well, as she always does, adding logs expertly, and now it roars to even greater heights. She is preparing place settings on the floor, beside the fireplace, with knives and forks from the kitchen. Sasha sits attentively beside her, watching her every move.

I carry the fish over to the fire. I don't really know how to cook it, so I figure I'll just put it over the fire for a while, let it roast, turn it over a few times, and hope that works. Bree reads my mind: she immediately heads to the kitchen and returns with a sharp knife and two long skewers. She slices the fish clean in half, sticks one skewer in one and one in the other, handing it to me, and reaches out and roasts her portion over the flame. I follow her lead. Bree's domestic instincts have always been superior to mine, and I'm grateful for her help. We have always been a good team.

We both stand there, staring at the flames, transfixed, holding our half of the fish over the fire until our arms grow heavy. The smell of fish fills the room, and after about ten minutes I get a pain in my stomach and grow impatient with hunger. I decide mine is done; after all, I figure people eat raw fish sometimes, so how bad could it be? Bree seems to agree, and we each put our portion on our plate and sit on the floor, beside each other, our backs to the couch and our feet to the fire.

"Careful," I warn. "There are still lots of bones inside."

I pull out the bones, and Bree does the same. Once I clear enough of them, I take a small chunk of the pink fish meat, hot to the touch, and eat it, bracing myself.

It actually tastes good. It could use salt, or some kind of seasoning, but at least it tastes cooked, and fresh as can be. I can feel the much-needed protein enter my body. Bree wolfs hers down, too, and I can see the relief on her face. Sasha sits beside her, staring, licking her lips, and Bree chooses a big chunk, carefully de-bones it and feeds it to Sasha. Sasha chews it thoroughly and swallows it, then licks her chops and stares back, eager for more.

"Sasha, here," I say.

She comes running over, and I take a portion of my fish, de-bone it, and feed her; she swallows it down in seconds. Before I know it, my portion is gone—as is Bree's—and I am surprised to feel my stomach growling again. I already wish I had caught more. Still, this was a bigger dinner than we'd had in weeks, and I try to force myself to be content with what we have.

Then I remember the sap. I jump up, remove the thermos from its hiding place and hold it out to Bree.

"Go ahead," I smile, "the first sip is yours."

"What is it?" she asks, unscrewing it and holding it to her nose. "It doesn't smell like anything."

"It's maple sap," I say. "It's like sugar water. But better."

She tentatively sips, then looks at me, eyes open wide in delight. "It's delicious!" she cries. She takes several big sips, then stops and hands it to me. I can't resist taking several big sips myself. I feel the sugar rush. I lean over and carefully pour some into Sasha's bowl; she laps it all up and seems to like it, too.

But I am still starving. In a rare moment of weakness, I think of the jar of jam and figure, why not? After all, I assume there's lots more of it in that cottage on the mountaintop—and if this night isn't cause to celebrate, then when is?

I bring down the mason jar, unscrew it, reach in with my finger, and take out a big heaping. I place it on my tongue and let it sit in my mouth as long as I can before swallowing. It's heavenly. I hold out the rest of the jar, still half-full, to Bree. "Go ahead," I say, "finish it. There's more in our new house."

Bree's eyes open wide as she reaches out. "Are you sure?" she asks. "Shouldn't we save it?"

I shake my head. "It's time to treat ourselves."

Bree doesn't need much convincing. In moments, she eats it all, sparing just one more heaping for Sasha.

We lie there, propped against the couch, our feet to the fire, and finally, I feel my body start to relax. Between the fish, the sap and the jam, finally, slowly, I feel my strength return. I look over at Bree, who's already dozing off, Sasha's head on her lap, and while she still looks sick, for the first time in a while I detect hope in her eyes.

"I love you, Brooke," she says softly.

"I love you, too," I answer.

But by the time I look over, she is already fast asleep.

*

Bree lies on the couch opposite the fire, while I now sit in the chair beside her; it is a habit we've become accustomed to over the months. Every night before bed, she curls up on the couch, too scared to fall asleep alone in her room. I keep her company, waiting until she dozes off, after which I'll carry her to bed. Most nights we don't have the fire, and we just sit there anyway. Tonight, Bree wakes from her place on the floor and climbs immediately to the couch, awake, but still very sleepy.

Bree always has nightmares. She didn't use to: I remember a time, before the war, when she fell asleep so easily. In fact, I'd even tease her for this, call her "bedtime Bree" as she'd fall asleep in the car, on a couch, reading a book in a chair—anywhere. But now, it's nothing like that; now, she'll be up for hours, and when she does sleep, it's restless. Most nights I hear her whimpers or screams through the thin walls. Who can blame her? With the horror we've seen, it's amazing she hasn't completely lost it. There are too many nights when I can barely sleep myself.

The one thing that helps her is when I read to her. Luckily, when we escaped, Bree had the presence of mind to grab her favorite book. *The Giving Tree*. Every night, I read it to her. I know it by heart now, and when I am tired, sometimes I close my eyes and just recite it from memory. Luckily, it's short.

As I lean back in the chair, feeling sleepy myself, I turn back the worn cover and begin to read. Sasha lies on the couch beside Bree, ears up, and sometimes I wonder if she's listening, too.

"Once, there was a tree, and she loved a little boy. And every day the boy would come, and he would gather her leaves, and make them into crowns and play king of the forest."

I look over and see that Bree, on the couch, is fast asleep already. I'm relieved. Maybe it was the fire, or maybe the meal. Sleep is what she needs most now, to recover. I remove my new scarf, wrapped snugly around my neck, and gently drape it over her chest. Finally, her little body stops trembling.

I put one final log on the fire, sit back in my chair, and turn, staring into the flames. I watch it slowly die and wish I'd carried more logs down. It's just as well. It will be safer this way.

A log crackles and pops as I settle back, feeling more relaxed than I have in years. Sometimes, after Bree falls asleep, I'll pick up my own book and read for myself. I see it sitting there, on the floor: *Lord of the Flies*. It is the only book I have left and is so worn from use, it looks like it's a hundred years old. It's a strange experience, having only one book left in the world. It makes me realize how much I'd taken for granted, makes me pine for the days when there were libraries.

Tonight I'm too excited to read. My mind is racing, filled with thoughts of tomorrow, of our new life, high up on the mountain. I keep running over in my head all of the things I will need to transport from here to there, and how I will do it. There are our basics—our utensils, matches, what's left of our candles, blankets, and mattresses. Other than that, neither of us have much clothes to speak of, and aside from our books, we have no real possessions. This house was pretty stark when we arrived, so there are no mementos. I would like to bring this couch and chair, although I will need Bree's help for that, and I'll have to wait until she's feeling well enough. We'll have to do it in stages, taking the essentials first, and leaving the furniture for last. That's fine; as long as we're up there, safe and secure, that is what matters most.

I start thinking of all the ways I can make that little cottage even safer than it is. I will definitely need to figure out how to create shutters for its open windows, so I can close them when I need to. I look around, surveying our house for anything I can use. I would need hinges to make the shutters work, and I eye the hinges on the living room door. Maybe I can remove these. And while I'm at it, maybe I can use the wooden door, too, and saw it into pieces.

The more I look around, the more I begin to realize how much I can salvage. I remember that Dad left a tool chest in the garage, with a saw, hammer, screwdriver, even a box of nails. It is one of the most precious things we have, and I make a mental note to take that up first.

After, of course, the motorcycle. That is dominant in my mind: when to transport it, and how. I can't bear the thought of leaving it behind, even for a minute. So on our first trip up there I'll bring it. I can't risk starting it and attracting all that attention—and besides, the mountain face is too steep for me to drive it up. I will have to walk it up, straight up the mountain. I can already anticipate how exhausting that will be, especially in the snow. But I see no other way. If Bree wasn't sick, she could help me, but in her current state, she won't be carrying anything—and I suspect, I may even need to carry her. I realize we have no choice but to wait until tomorrow night, for the cover of darkness, before we move. Maybe I'm just being paranoid—I realize the chances of anyone watching us are remote, but still, it's better to be cautious. Especially because I know that there are other survivors up here. I am sure of it.

I remember the first day we arrived. We were both terrified, lonely, and exhausted. That first night, we both went to bed hungry, and I remember wondering how we were ever going to survive. I wondered if I'd made a mistake to leave Manhattan, abandon our mother, leave all that we knew behind.

And then our first morning, I woke up, opened the door, and was shocked to find it, sitting there: the carcass of a dead deer. At first, I was terrified. I took it as a threat, a warning, assuming someone was telling us to leave, that we were not welcome there. But after I got over my initial shock, I realized that wasn't the case at all: it was actually a gift. Someone, some other survivor, must have been watching us. He must have seen how desperate we looked, and in an act of supreme generosity, he must have decided to give us his kill, our first meal, enough meat to last for weeks. I can't imagine how valuable it must have been for him.

I remember walking outside, looking all around, up and down the mountain, peering into all the trees, expecting some person to pop out and wave. But no one ever did. All I saw were trees, and even though I waited for minutes, all I heard was silence. But I knew, I just knew, I was being watched. I knew then that other people were up here, surviving just like us.

Ever since then, I've felt a kind of pride, felt we were part of a silent community of isolated survivors that live in these mountains, keeping to themselves, never communicating with each other for fear of being seen, for fear of becoming visible to a slaverunner. I assume that is how the others have survived as long as they have: by taking nothing to chance. At first, I didn't understand it. But now, I appreciate it. And ever since then, while I never see anyone, I've never felt alone.

But it also made me more vigilant; these other survivors, if they are still alive, must surely by now be as starving and desperate as we. Especially in the winter months. Who knows if starvation, if a need to fend for their families, has pushed any of them over the line to desperation, if their charitable mood has been replaced by pure survival instinct. I know the thought of Bree, Sasha and myself starving has sometimes lead me to some pretty desperate thoughts. So I won't leave anything to chance. We'll move at nighttime.

Which works out perfectly, anyway. I need to take the morning to climb back up there, alone, to scout it out first, to make sure one last time that no one has been in or out. I also need to go back to that spot where I found the deer and wait for it. I know it's a longshot, but if I can find it again, and kill it, it can feed us for weeks. I wasted that first deer that was given to us, years ago, because I didn't know how to skin it, or carve it up, or preserve it. I made a mess of it, and managed to squeeze just one meal out of it before the entire carcass went rotten. It was a terrible waste of food, and I'm determined to never do that again. This time, especially with the snow, I will find a way to preserve it.

I reach into my pocket and take out the pocket knife Dad gave me before he left; I rub the worn handle, his initials engraved and the

Marine Corps logo emblazoned on it, as I've done every night since we arrived here. I tell myself he is still alive. Even after all these years, even though I know the chances of our seeing him again are slim to none, I can't quite bring myself to let this idea go.

I wish every night that Dad had never left, had never volunteered for the war at all. It was a stupid war to begin with. I never really fully understood how it all began, and I still don't now. Dad explained it to me, several times, and I still didn't get it. Maybe it was just because of my age, maybe I just wasn't old enough to realize how senseless the things are that adults can do to each other.

The way Dad explained it, it was a second American civil war—this time, not between the North and the South, but between political parties. Between the Democrats and Republicans. He said it was a war that was a long time coming. Over the last hundred years, he said, America was drifting into a land of two nations: those on the far right, and those on the far left. Over time, positions hardened so deeply, it became a nation of two different, opposing, ideologies. He said that the people on the left, the Democrats, wanted a nation that was run by a bigger and bigger government, one that raised taxes to 70%, and could be involved in every aspect of people's lives. He said the people on the right, the Republicans, kept wanting a smaller and smaller government, one that would abolish taxes altogether, get out of people's hair, and allow people to fend for themselves. He said that over time, these two different ideologies, instead of compromising, just kept drifting further apart, getting more extreme—until they reached a point where they couldn't see eye to eye on anything.

Worsening the situation, he said, was that America had gotten so crowded, it had become harder than ever for any politician to get national attention—and politicians in both parties began to realize that the only way they could get the attention they needed was to take extreme positions. It was the only way that they could get the air time—and that was what they needed to rise to the top for their own personal ambition.

As a result, the most prominent people of both parties were the ones who were most extreme, each taking more and more extreme positions to outdo the other, positions, he said, that they didn't even truly believe in themselves but that they were backed into a corner to take. Naturally, when the two parties debated, they could only collide with each other—and they did so with harsher and harsher words. At the beginning, it was just name calling and personal attacks. But over time, the verbal warfare escalated. And then one day, it crossed a point of no return.

One day, about ten years ago, a fateful tipping point came when one political leader threatened the other with one fateful word: "secession." He said that if the Democrats tried to raise taxes even one more cent, his party would secede from the union. He said that every village, every town, every state would be divided in two. Not by land, but by ideology. Adding to this, his timing couldn't have been worse: at that time, the nation was struggling with a depression, and there were enough malcontents out there, fed up with the loss of jobs, to gain him popularity. The media loved the ratings he got, and they fed him more and more air time. Soon his popularity grew. Eventually, with no one to stop him, with the Democrats unwilling to compromise, and with momentum carrying itself, his idea hardened. His party proposed their nation's own flag, and even their own currency.

That was the first tipping point. If someone had just stepped up and stopped him then, it may all have stopped. But no one did. So he pushed further.

Emboldened, this politician took it further: he proposed that the new union also have its own police force, its own courts, its own state troopers—and its own military. That was the second tipping point.

If the Democratic President at the time had been a good leader, he might have stopped things then. But he worsened the situation by making one bad decision after another. Instead of trying to calm things, to address the core needs that lead to such discontent, he instead decided that the only way to quash what he called "the Rebellion" was to take a hard line: he accused the entire Republican leadership of sedition. He declared martial law, and one night, during the middle of the night, had them all arrested.

That escalated things, and rallied their entire party. It also rallied half the military. People were divided, within every home, every town, every military barracks; slowly, tension built in the streets, and neighbor hated neighbor. Even families were divided.

One night, those in the military leadership loyal to the Republicans followed secret orders and instituted a coup, breaking them out of prison. There was a standoff. And on the steps of the Capitol building, the first fateful shot was fired. A young soldier thought he saw an officer reach for a gun, and he fired first. And once the first soldier fell, there was no turning back. The final line had been crossed. An American had killed an American. A firefight ensued, with dozens of officers dead. The Republican leadership was whisked away to a secret location. And from that moment on, the military split into. The government split in two. Towns, villages, counties, and states all split in two. This was known as the First Wave.

During the first few days, crisis managers and government factions desperately tried to make peace. But it was too little, too late. Nothing seemed able to stop the coming storm. A faction of hawkish generals took matters into their own hands, wanting the glory, wanting to be the first in war, wanting the advantage of speed and surprise. They figured that crushing the opposition immediately was the best way to put an end to all of this.

The war began. Battles ensued on American soil. Pittsburgh became the new Gettysburg, with two hundred thousand dead in a week. Tanks mobilized against tanks. Planes against planes. Every day, every week, the violence escalated. Lines were drawn in the sand, military and police assets were divided, and battles ensued in every state in the nation. Everywhere, everyone fought against each other, friend against friend, brother against brother. It reached a point where no one even knew what they were fighting about anymore. The entire nation was spilled with blood. And no one seemed able to stop it. This became known as the Second Wave.

Up to that moment, as bloody as it was, it was still conventional warfare. But then came the Third Wave, the worst of all. The President, in desperation, operating from a secret bunker, decided there was only one way to quell what he still insisted on calling "the Rebellion." Summoning his best military officers, they advised him to use the strongest assets he had to quell the rebellion once and for all, before it engulfed the entire nation. They advised him to use local, targeted nuclear missiles. He consented.

The next day nuclear payloads were dropped in strategic places across America, strategic Republican strongholds. Hundreds of thousands died on that day, in places like Nevada, Texas, Mississippi. Millions died on the second.

The Republicans responded. They seized hold of their own assets, ambushed NORAD, and launched their own nuclear payloads, onto Democratic strongholds. States like Maine and New Hampshire were mostly eviscerated. Within the next ten days, nearly all of America was destroyed, one city after another. It was wave after wave of sheer devastation, and those who weren't killed by direct attack died soon after from the toxic air and water. Within a matter of a month, there was no one left to even fight. Streets and buildings emptied out one at a time, as people were marched off to fight against former neighbors.

But Dad didn't even wait for the draft—and that is why I hate him. He left way before. He'd been an officer in the Marine Corps for twenty years before any of this broke out, and he'd seen it all coming sooner than most. Every time he watched the news, every time he saw two politicians screaming at each other in the most disrespectful way, always upping the ante, Dad would shake his head and say, "This will lead to war. Trust me."

And he was right. Ironically, Dad had already served his time and had been retired from Corps for years before this happened; but when that first shot was fired, on that day, he re-enlisted. Before there was even talk of a full-out war. He was probably the very first person to volunteer, and for a war that hadn't even started yet.

And that is why I'm still mad at him. Why did he have to do this? Why couldn't he have just let everyone else kill each other? Why couldn't he have stayed home, protected us? Why did he care more about his country than his family?

I still remember, vividly, the day he left us. I came home from school that day, and before I even opened the door, I heard shouting coming from inside. I braced myself. I hated it when Mom and Dad fought, which seemed like all the time, and I thought this was just another one of their arguments.

I opened the door and knew right away that this was different. That something was very, very wrong. Dad stood there in full uniform. It didn't make any sense. He hadn't worn his uniform in years. Why would he be wearing it now?

"You're not a man!" Mom screamed at him. "You're a coward! Leaving your family. For what? To go and kill innocent people?"

Dad's face turned red, as it always did when he got angry.

"You don't know what you're talking about!" he screamed back. "I'm doing my duty for my country. It's the right thing to do."

"The right thing for *who*?" she spat back. "You don't even know what you're fighting for. For a stupid bunch of politicians?"

"I know exactly what I'm fighting for: to hold our nation together."

"Oh, well, excuse me, Mister America," she screamed back at him. "You can justify this in your head anyway you want, but the truth is, you're leaving because you can't stand me. Because you never knew how to handle domestic life. Because you're too stupid to make something of your life after the Corps. So you jump up and run off at the first opportunity—"

Dad stopped her with a hard slap across the face. I can still hear the noise in my head.

I was shocked; I'd never seen him lay a hand on her before. I felt the wind rush out of me, as if I'd been slapped myself. I looked at him, and almost didn't recognize him. Was that really my father? I was so stunned that I dropped my book, and it landed with a thud.

They both turned and looked at me, alerted to my presence. Mortified, I turned and ran down the hall, to my bedroom, and slammed the door behind me. I didn't know how to react to it all, and just had to get away from them.

Moments later, there was a soft knock on my door.

"Brooke, it's me," Dad said in a soft, remorseful voice. "I'm sorry you had to see that. Please, let me in."

"Go away!" I yelled back.

A long silence followed. But he still didn't leave.

"Brooke, I have to leave now. I'd like to see you one last time before I go. Please. Come out and say goodbye."

I started to cry.

"Go away!" I snapped again. I was so overwhelmed, so mad at him for hitting Mom, and even more mad at him for leaving us. And deep down, I was so scared that he would never come back.

"I'm leaving now, Brooke," he said. "You don't have to open the door. But I want you to know how much I love you. And that I'll always be with you. Remember, Brooke, you're the tough one. Take care of this family. I'm counting on you. Take care of them."

And then I heard my father's footsteps, walking away. They grew softer and softer. Moments later I heard the front door open, then close.

And then, nothing.

Minutes—it felt like days—later, I slowly opened my door. I already sensed it. He was gone. And I already regretted it; I wished I'd said goodbye. Because I already sensed, deep down, that he was never coming back.

Mom sat there, at the kitchen table, head in her hands, crying softly. I knew that things had changed permanently that day, that they would never be the same—that *she* would never be the same. And that I wouldn't, either.

And I was right. As I sit here now, staring into the embers of the dying fire, my eyes heavy, I realize that since that day, nothing has ever been the same again.

*

I am standing in our old apartment, in Manhattan. I don't know what I'm doing here, or how I got here. Nothing seems to make sense, because the apartment is not at all as I remember. It is completely empty of furniture, as if we had never lived in it. I'm the only one here.

There is a sudden knock on the door, and in walks Dad, in full uniform, holding a briefcase. He has a hollow look to his eyes, as if he has just been to hell and back.

"Daddy!" I try to scream. But the words don't come out. I look down and realize that I am glued to the floor, hidden behind a wall, and that he can't see me. As much as I struggle to break free, to run to him, to call out his name, I cannot. I'm forced to watch helplessly, as he walks into the empty apartment, looking all around.

"Brooke?" he yells out. "Are you here? Is anybody home?"

I try to answer again, but my voice won't work. He searches room to room.

"I said I'd come back," he says. "Why didn't anyone wait for me?"

Then, he breaks into tears.

My heart breaks, and I try with all I have to call out to him. But no matter how hard I try, nothing comes out.

He finally turns and leaves the apartment, gently closing the door behind him. The click of the handle reverberates in the emptiness.

"DADDY!" I scream, finally finding my voice.

But it is too late. I know he is gone forever, and somehow it is all my fault.

I blink, and the next thing I know I am back in the mountains, in Dad's house, sitting in his favorite chair beside the fire. Dad is sitting there, on the couch, and he leans forward, head down, playing with his Marine Corps knife. I am horrified to notice that half his face is melted away, all the way to the bone; I can actually see half his skull.

He looks up at me, and I am afraid.

"You can't hide here forever, Brooke," he says, in a measured tone. "You think you're safe here. But they'll come for you. Take Bree and hide."

He rises to his feet, comes over to me, grabs me by the shoulders and shakes me, his eyes burning with intensity. "DID YOU HEAR ME, SOLDIER!?" he screams.

He disappears, and as he does, all the doors and windows crash open at once, in a cacophony of shattered glass.

Into our house rush a dozen slaverunners, guns drawn. They're dressed in their signature all-black uniforms, from head to toe, with black facemasks, and they race to every corner of the house. One of them grabs Bree off the couch and carries her away, screaming, while another runs right up to me, digs his fingers into my arm and aims his pistol right to my face.

He fires.

I wake screaming, disoriented.

I feel fingers digging into my arm, and confused between my dream state and reality, I am ready to strike. I look over and see that it's Bree, standing there, shaking my arm.

I am still sitting in Dad's chair, and now the room is flooded with sunlight. Bree is crying, hysterical.

I blink several times as I sit up, trying to get my bearings. Was it all just a dream? It had felt so real.

"I had a scary dream!" Bree cries, still gripping my arm.

I look over and see the fire has gone out long ago. I see the bright sunlight, and realize it must be late morning. I can't believe I have fallen asleep in the chair—I have never done this before.

I shake my head, trying to get the cobwebs out. That dream felt so real, it's still hard to believe it didn't happen. I've dreamt of Dad before, many times, but never anything with such immediacy. I find it hard to conceive that he's not still in the room with me now, and I look around the room again, just to make sure.

Bree tugs on my arm, inconsolable. I have never seen her quite like this, either.

I kneel down and give her a hug. She clings to me.

"I dreamed these mean men came and took me away! And you weren't here to save me!"

Bree cries, over my shoulder. "Don't go!" she pleads, hysterical. "Please, don't go. Don't leave me!"

"I'm not going anywhere," I say, hugging her tight. "Shhh…. It's OK…. There's nothing to worry about. Everything is fine."

But deep down, I can't help feeling that everything is *not* fine. On the contrary. My dream really disturbs me, and Bree's having such a bad dream, too—and about the same thing— doesn't give me much solace. I'm not a big believer in omens, but I can't help wondering if it's all a sign. But I don't hear any kind of noise or commotion, and if there was anybody with a mile of here, surely I would know.

I lift Bree's chin, wiping her tears. "Take a deep breath," I say.

Bree listens, slowly catching her breath. I force myself to smile. "See," I say. "I'm right here. Nothing's wrong. It was just a bad dream. Okay?"

Slowly, Bree nods.

"You're just overtired," I said. "And you have a fever. So you had bad dreams. It's all going to be fine."

As I kneel there, hugging Bree, I realize that I need to get going, to climb the mountain and scout out our new house, and to find us food. My stomach drops as I consider breaking the news to Bree, and how she'll react. Clearly, my timing couldn't be worse. How can I possibly tell her that I need to leave her now? Even if only for an hour or two? A part of me wants to stay here, to watch over her all day; yet I also know that I need to go, and that the sooner I get it over with, the safer we will be. I can't just sit here all day and do nothing, waiting for nightfall. And I can't risk changing the plan and moving us during daylight, just because of our silly dreams.

I pull Bree back, stroking her hair out of her face, smiling as sweetly as I can. I muster the strongest, most adult voice that I can.

"Bree, I need you to listen to me," I say. "I need to go out now, just for a little while—"

"NO!" she wails. "I KNEW it! It's just like my dream! You're going to leave me! And you're never going to come back!"

I hold her shoulders firmly, trying to console her.

"It's not like that," I say firmly. "I just need to go for an hour or two. I just need to make sure our new house is safe for our move tonight. And I need to hunt for food. Please, Bree, understand. I would bring you with me, but you are too sick right now, and you need to rest. I'll be back in just a few hours. I promise. And then tonight, we'll go up there together. And do you know what the best part is?"

She looks up at me slowly, still crying, and eventually shakes her head.

"Starting tonight, we'll be up there together, safe and sound, and have a fire every night, and all the food you want. And I can hunt and fish and do everything I need to right there, in front of the cottage. I'll never have to leave you again."

"And Sasha can come, too?" she asks, through her tears.

"And Sasha, too," I say. "I promise. Please, trust me. I'll be back for you. I would never leave you."

"Do you promise?" she asks.

I muster all the solemnity I can, and look her dead in the eyes.

"I promise," I reply.

Bree's crying slows and eventually, she nods, seeming satisfied.

It breaks my heart, but I quickly lean in, plant a kiss on her forehead, then get up, cross the room and walk out the door. I know that if I stay for just one second more, I'll never summon the resolve to leave.

And as the door reverberates behind me, I just can't shake the sickening feeling that I'll never see my sister again.

THREE

I hike straight up the mountain in the bright light of morning, an intense light shining off the snow. It is a white universe. The sun shines so strongly, I can barely see in the glare. I would do anything for a pair of sunglasses, or a baseball cap.

Today is thankfully windless, warmer than yesterday, and as I hike, I hear the snow melting all around me, trickling in small streams downhill and dropping in big clumps off of pine branches. The snow is softer, too, and walking is easier.

I check back over my shoulder, survey the valley spread out below, and see that the roads are partially visible again in the morning sun. This worries me, but then I chide myself, annoyed that I am allowing myself to be disturbed by omens. I should be tougher. More rational, like Dad.

My hood is up, but as I lower my head to the wind, which grows stronger the higher I get,

I wish I'd worn my new scarf. I bunch my hands and rub them, wishing for gloves, too, and double my speed. I am resolved to get there quickly, scout out the cottage, search for that deer, and hurry back down to Bree. Maybe I'll salvage a few more jars of jam, too; that will cheer Bree up.

I follow my tracks from yesterday, still visible in the melting snow, and this time, the hike is easier. Within about twenty minutes, I'm back to where I was the day before, rounding the highest plateau.

I am sure I am in the same place as yesterday, but as I look for the cottage, I can't find it. It is so well hidden that, even though I know where to look, I still can't see it. I start to wonder if I'm in the right place. I continue on, following my footsteps, until I get to the exact spot I stood the day before. I crane my neck, and finally, I spot it. I'm amazed at how well-concealed it is, and am even more encouraged about living here.

I stand and listen. All is silent save for the sound of the trickling stream. I check the snow carefully, looking for any signs of prints going in or out (aside from mine), since yesterday. I find none.

I walk up to the door, stand in front of the house and do a 360, scanning the woods in every direction, checking the trees, looking for any signs of disturbance, any evidence that anyone else has been here. I stand for at least a minute, listening. There is nothing. Absolutely nothing.

Finally, I am satisfied, relieved that this place is truly ours, and ours alone.

I pull back the heavy door, jammed by the snow, and bright light floods the interior. As I duck my head and enter, I feel as if I'm seeing it for the first time in the light. It is as small and cozy as I remember. I see that it has original, wide-plank wood flooring, which looks to be at least a hundred years old. It is quiet in here. The small, open windows on either side let in a good deal of light, too.

I scan the room in the light, looking for anything I might have overlooked—but find nothing. I look down and find the handle to the trap door, kneel down and yank it open. It opens up with a whirl of dust, which swims in the sunlight.

I scramble down the ladder, and this time, with all the reflected light, I have a much better view of the stash down here. There must be hundreds of jars. I spot several more jars of raspberry jam, and grab two of them, cramming one in each pocket. Bree will love this. So will Sasha.

I do a cursory scan of the other jars, and see all sorts of foods: pickles, tomatoes, olives, sauerkraut. I also see several different flavors of jams, with at least a dozen jars of each. There is even more in the back, but I don't have time to look carefully. Thoughts of Bree are weighing heavily on my mind.

I scramble up the ladder, close the trap door and hurry out the cottage, closing the front door tight behind me. I stand there and survey my surroundings again, bracing myself for anyone who may have been watching. I am still afraid this is all too good to be true. But once again, there is nothing. Maybe I've just become too on-edge.

I head off in the direction where I spotted the deer, about thirty yards away. As I reach it, I take out Dad's hunting knife, and hold it at my side. I know it's a long shot for me to see it again, but maybe this animal, like me, is a creature of habit. If I should be lucky enough to see it again, there's no way I'm fast enough to chase it down, or quick enough to pounce—nor do I have a gun or any real hunting weapons. But the way I see it, I do have one chance, and that is my knife. I've always been proud of my ability to hit a bull's-eye thirty yards away. Knife-throwing was the one skill of mine that Dad always seemed impressed by—at least impressed enough to never try to correct or improve me. Instead, he took credit for it, saying my talent was due to him. In reality, though, he couldn't throw a knife half as well as I could.

I kneel in the place I was before, hiding behind a tree, watching the plateau, holding the knife in my hand, waiting. Praying. All I hear is the sound of the wind.

I run through in my head what I will do if I see it: I will slowly stand, take aim, and throw the knife. I first think I will aim for its eye, but then decide to aim for its throat: if I miss by a few inches, then there will still be a chance of hitting it somewhere. If my hands aren't too frozen, and if I'm accurate, I figure that maybe, just maybe, I can wound it. But I realize those are all big "ifs."

Minutes pass. It feels like ten, twenty, thirty…. The wind dies, then reappears in gusts, and as it does, I feel the fine flakes of snow being blown off the trees and into my face. As more time passes, I grow colder, more numb, and I begin to wonder if this is a bad idea. I get another sharp hunger pain, though, and know that I have to try. I will need all the protein I can get to make this move happen—especially if I'm going to push that motorcycle uphill.

But after nearly an hour of waiting, I am utterly frozen. I debate whether to just give it up and head back down the mountain. Maybe, instead, I should try to fish again.

I decide to get up and walk around, to circulate my limbs and keep my hands nimble; if I had to use them now, they'd probably be useless. As I rise to my feet my knees and back ache from stiffness. I begin to walk in the snow, starting with small steps. I lift and bend my knees, twist my back left and right. I stick the knife back in my belt, then rub my hands over each other, blowing on them again and again, trying to restore the feeling.

Suddenly, I freeze. In the distance, a twig snaps, and I sense motion.

I turn slowly. There, over the hilltop, a deer comes into view. It steps slowly, tentatively, in the snow, gently lifting its hooves and placing them down. It lowers its head, chews on a leaf, then slowly takes another step forward.

My heart pounds with excitement. It is exactly what I'd been praying for. I rarely feel that Dad is with me, but today, I do. I can hear his voice in my head now: *Steady. Breathe slowly. Don't let it know you're here. Focus.* If I can bring down this animal, it will be food—real food—for Bree and Sasha and I for at least a week. We *need* this.

It takes a few more steps into the clearing and I get a better view of it: a large deer, it stands maybe thirty yards away. I'd feel a lot more confident if it were standing ten yards away, or even twenty. I don't know if I can hit it at this distance. If it were warmer out, and if it wasn't moving, then yes. But my hands are numb, the deer is moving, and there are so many trees in the way. I just don't know. I do know that if I miss it, it will never come back here again.

I wait, studying it, afraid to spook it. I will for it to come closer. But it doesn't seem to want to.

I debate what to do. I can charge it, getting as close as I can, then throw. But I realize that would be stupid: after just one yard, it would surely bolt. I wonder if I should try to creep up on it. But I doubt that will work, either. The slightest noise, and it will be gone.

So I stand there, debating. I take one small step forward, positioning myself to throw the knife, in case I need to. And that one small step is my mistake.

A twig snaps beneath my feet, and the deer immediately lifts its head and turns to me. We lock eyes. I know that it sees me, and that it's about to bolt. My heart pounds, as I know this is my only chance. My mind freezes up.

Then I burst into action. I reach down, grab the knife, take a big step forward, and drawing on all my skills, I reach back and throw it, aiming for its throat.

Dad's heavy Marine Corps knife tumbles end over end through the air, and I pray it doesn't hit a tree first. As I watch it tumbling, reflecting light, it is a thing of beauty. In that same moment, I see the deer turn and begin to run.

It is too far away for me to see exactly what happens, but a moment later, I could swear I hear the sound of the knife entering flesh. The deer takes off, though, and I can't tell if it's wounded.

I take off after it. I reach the spot where it was, and am surprised to see bright red blood in the snow. My heart flutters, encouraged.

I follow the trail of blood, running and running, jumping over rocks, and after about fifty yards, I find it: there it is, collapsed in the snow, lying on its side, legs twitching. I see the knife lodged in its throat. Exactly in the spot I was aiming for.

The deer is still alive, and I don't know how to put it out of its misery. I can feel its suffering, and I feel terrible. I want to give it a quick and painless death, but don't know how.

I kneel and extract the knife, then lean over, and in one swift motion, slice it deeply across the throat, hoping that will work. Moments later, blood comes rushing out, and within about ten more seconds, finally, the deer's legs stop moving. Its eyes stop fluttering, too, and finally, I know it's dead.

I stand over, staring down, holding the knife in my hand, and feel overwhelmed with guilt. I feel barbaric, having killed such a beautiful, defenseless creature. In this moment, it's hard for me to think of how badly we needed this food, of how lucky I was to catch it at all. All I can think of is that, just a few minutes before, it was breathing, alive like me. And now, it's dead. I look down at it, lying so perfectly still in the snow, and despite myself, I feel ashamed.

That is the moment when I first hear it. I dismiss it at first, assume I must be hearing things, because it is just not possible. But after a few moments, it rises a tiny bit louder, more distinct, and I know it's real. My heart starts pounding like crazy, as I recognize the noise. It is a noise I've heard up here only once before. It is the whine of an engine. A car engine.

I stand there in astonishment, too frozen to even move. The engine grows louder, more distinct, and I know a car engine up here can only mean one thing. Slaverunners. No one else would dare drive this high up, or have any reason to.

I break into a sprint, leaving the deer, charging through the woods, past the cottage, down the hill. I can't go fast enough. I think of Bree, sitting there, alone in the house, as the engines grow louder and louder. I try to increase my speed, running straight down the snowy slope, tripping as I go, my heart pounding in my throat.

I run so fast that I fall, face-first, scraping my knee and elbow, and getting the wind knocked out of me. I struggle back to my feet, noticing the blood on my knee and arm, but not caring. I force myself back into a jog, then into a sprint.

Slipping and sliding, I finally reach a plateau, and from here, I can see all the way down the mountain to our house. My heart leaps into my throat: I see distinctive car tracks in the snow, leading right to our house. Our front door is open. And most ominous of all, I don't hear Sasha barking.

I run, further and further down, and as I do, I get a good look at the two vehicles parked outside our house: slaverunner cars. All black, built low to the ground, they look like muscle cars on steroids, with enormous tires and bars on all the windows. Emblazoned on their hoods is the emblem of Arena One, obvious even from here—a diamond with a jackal in its center. They are here to feed the arena.

I sprint further down the hill. I need to get lighter. I reach into my pockets, pull out the jars of jam and throw them to the ground. I hear the glass smash behind me, but I don't care. Nothing else matters now.

I am barely a hundred yards away when I see the vehicles start up, begin to leave my house. They head back down the winding country road. I want to break into tears as I realize what has happened.

Thirty seconds later I reach the house, and run past it, right to the road, hoping to catch them. I already knowing the house is empty.

I'm too late. The car tracks tell the story. As I look down the mountain, I can see them, already a half-mile away, and gaining speed. There's no way I can ever catch them on foot.

I run back to the house, just in case, by some remote chance, Bree has managed to hide, or they left her. I burst through the open front door, and as I do, I am horrified by the sight before me: blood is everywhere. On the ground lies a dead slaverunner, dressed in his all-black uniform, blood pouring from his throat. Beside him lies Sasha, on her side, dead. Blood pours out her side from what looks like a bullet wound. Her teeth are still embedded in the corpse's throat. It becomes clear what happened: Sasha must have tried to protect Bree, lunging at the man as he entered the house and lodging her teeth in his throat. The others must have shot her. But still, she did not let go.

I run through the house, room to room, screaming Bree's name, hearing the desperation in my own voice. It is no longer I voice I recognize: it is the voice of a crazy person.

But every door is wide open, and everything is empty.

The slaverunners have taken my sister.

FOUR

I stand there, in the living room of my Dad's house, in shock. On the one hand, I've always feared that this day would come; yet now that it has, I can hardly believe it. I am overcome with guilt. Did last night's fire tip us off? Did they see the smoke? Why couldn't I have been more cautious?

I also hate myself for leaving Bree alone this morning—especially after we'd both had such bad dreams. I see her face, crying, pleading with me not to leave. Why didn't I listen to her? Trust my own instinct? Looking back, I can't help feeling that Dad really did warn me. Why didn't I listen? None of that matters now, and I only pause for a moment. I am in action mode, and in no way prepared to give up and let her go. I am already running through the house, preparing to not lose any precious time in chasing down the slaverunners and rescuing Bree.

I run over to the corpse of the slaverunner and examine him quickly: he is dressed in their signature all-black, military uniform, with black combat boots, black military fatigues, and a long-sleeved black shirt covered by a tightly-fitting black bomber coat. He still wears a black face mask with the insignia of Arena One—the hallmark of a slaverunner—and also wears a small black helmet. Little good that did him: Sasha still managed to lodge her teeth into his throat. I glance over at Sasha and choke up at the sight. I'm so grateful to her for putting up such a fight. I feel guilty for leaving her alone, too. I glance at her corpse, and vow to myself that after I get Bree back, I will return and give her a proper burial.

I quickly strip the slaverunner's corpse for valuables. I begin by taking his weapons belt and clipping it around my own waist, fastening it tight. It contains a holster and a handgun, and I pull it out and check it quickly: filled with ammo, it appears to be in perfect working order. This is like gold—and now it is mine. Also on the belt are several backup clips of ammo.

I remove his helmet and see his face: I'm surprised to see he is much younger than I'd thought. He can't be older than 18. Not all slaverunners are merciless bounty hunters; some of them are pressed into service, at the mercy of the Arena makers, who are the real power-holders. Still, I don't feel any sympathy for him. After all, pressed into service or not, he'd come up here to take my sister's life—and mine, too.

I want to just run out and chase them down, but I discipline myself to stop and salvage what I can first. I know that I will need it out there, and that another minute or two spent here can end up making the difference. So I reach down and try his helmet on and am relieved to see that it fits. Its black visor will come in handy in blocking out the blinding light off the snow. I raid his clothing next, which I desperately need. I strip his gloves, made of an ultra-light, padded material, and am relieved to see they fit my hands perfectly. My friends always teased me about my big hands and feet and I always felt embarrassed by it—but now, for once, I am glad. I strip his jacket next and am relieved to see that it fits too, just a tad too big. I look down and see how small his frame is, and realize I am lucky. We are nearly the same size. The jacket is thick and padded, lined with some sort of down material. I have never worn anything as warm and luxurious in my life, and I am so grateful. Now, finally, I can brave the cold.

I look down and know I should strip his shirt, too—but I just can't bring myself to wear it. Somehow, it's too personal.

I hold my feet up to his, and am thrilled to see we are the same size. I waste no time stripping my old, worn boots, a size too small, then stripping his and putting them on my feet. I stand. They are a perfect fit, and feel amazing. Black combat boots with steel-tip toes, the inside lined with fur, they climb all the way up my shin. They are a thousand times warmer—and more comfortable—than my current boots.

Wearing my new boots, coat, gloves, and with his weapons belt snug around me, gun and ammo inside, I feel like a new person, ready for battle. I glance down at Sasha's corpse and then look over and, nearby, see Bree's new teddy bear, on the floor and covered in blood. I fight back tears. A part of me wants to spit in this slaverunner's face before I walk out the door, but I simply turn and run out the house.

I moved quickly, managing to strip him and dress myself in under a minute, and now I race out of the house at breakneck speed, making up for lost time. As I burst out the front door, I can still hear the distant whine of their engines. They can't have more than a mile on me, and I'm determined to close that gap. All I need is a small stroke of luck—for them to get stuck in just one snow bank, to hit one bad turn—and maybe, just maybe, I can catch them. And with this gun and ammo, I might even be able to give them a run for their money. If not, I will go down fighting. There is absolutely no way that

I'm ever coming back here without Bree by my side.

I run up the hill, into the woods, as fast as I can, racing for my Dad's motorcycle. I glance over and see that the garage doors were blown open, and realize the slaverunners must have searched it for a vehicle. I am so grateful I had the foresight to hide the bike long ago.

I scramble up the hill in the melting snow, and hurry to the bushes concealing the bike. The new gloves, thickly padded, come in handy: I am able to grab hold of thorny branches and tear them out of my way. Within moments, I clear a path, and see the bike. I am relieved to find it's still there, and well-sheltered from the elements. Without wasting a beat, I tighten my new helmet, grab the key from its hiding place in the spoke, and jump onto the bike. I turn the ignition, and kickstart it.

The engine turns over, but doesn't catch. My heart plummets. I haven't started it in years. Could it be dead? I try to start it, kicking and revving it again and again. It makes noise, louder and louder, but still nothing. I feel more and more frantic. If I can't get this started, I have no chance of catching them. Bree will be gone to me forever.

"Come on, COME ON!" I scream, my entire body shaking.

I kick it again and again. Each time it makes more and more noise, and I feel like I'm getting closer.

I raise my head back to the sky.

"DAD!" I scream. "PLEASE!"

I kick it again, and this time, it catches. I am flooded with relief. I rev it several times, louder and louder, and small black clouds of exhaust exit the tailpipe.

Now, at least, I have a fighting chance.

*

I turn the heavy handlebars and walk the bike back a few feet; it is almost more weight than I can manage. I turn the handlebars again and give it just a little bit of gas, and the bike starts rolling down the steep mountain, still covered in snow and branches.

The paved road is about fifty yards ahead of me, and going down the mountain, through these woods, is treacherous. The bike slips and slides, and even when I hit the brakes, I can't really control it. It is more of a controlled slide. I slide by trees, barely missing them, and get jolted as the bike falls into large holes in the dirt, then bumps hard over rocks. I pray that I don't blow a tire.

After about thirty seconds of the roughest, bumpiest ride I can imagine, finally, the bike clears the dirt and lands onto the paved road with a bang. I turn and give it gas, and it is responsive: it flies down the steep, paved mountain road. Now, I am rolling.

I gain some real speed, the engine roaring, wind racing over my helmet. It is freezing, colder than ever, and I am grateful I stripped the gloves and coat. I don't what I would have done without them.

Still, I can't go too fast. This mountain road twists sharply and there is no shoulder; one turn too sharp and I will plummet, dropping hundreds of feet straight down the cliff. I go as fast as I can, yet slow before each turn.

It feels great to be driving again; I had forgotten what real freedom felt like. My new coat flaps like crazy in the wind. I lower the black visor, and the bright white of the snowy landscape changes to a subdued gray.

If I have one advantage over the slaverunners, it is that I know these roads better than anyone. I've been coming up here since I was a kid, and I know where the road bends, how steep it is, and shortcuts that they could never possibly know. They're in *my* territory now. And even though I'm probably a mile or more behind them, I feel optimistic I can find a way to catch them. This bike, as old as it is, must be at least as fast as their muscle cars.

I also feel confident I know where they're going. If you want back on the highway—which they surely do—then there's only one way out of these mountains, and that's Route 23, heading east. And if they're heading for the city, then there's no other way but to cross the Hudson via the Rip Van Winkle Bridge. It's their only way out. And I'm determined to beat them to it.

I'm getting used to the bike and gaining good speed, good enough that the whine of their engines is becoming louder. Encouraged, I gun the motorcycle faster than I should: I glance down and see I am doing 60. I know it's reckless, since these hairpin turns force me to slow down to about 10 miles an hour if I want any chance of not wiping out in the snow. So I accelerate, and then decelerate, turn after turn. I finally gain enough ground that I can actually see, about a mile in the distance, the bumper of one of their cars, just disappearing around a bend. I am encouraged. I'm going to catch these guys—or die trying.

I take another turn, slowing down to about 10 and getting ready to speed up again, when suddenly, I almost run into a person, standing there in the road, right in front of me. He appears out of nowhere, and it's too late for me to even react.

I'm about to hit him, and I have no choice but to slam on the brakes. Luckily I'm not going fast, but my bike still slides in the snow, unable to gain traction. I do a 360, spinning twice, and finally come to a stop as my bike slams against the granite face of the mountainside.

I'm lucky. If I had spun the other way, I would have spun right off the cliff.

It all happened so fast, I am in shock. I sit there on the bike, gripping the bars, and turn and look up the road. My first instinct is that the man is a slaverunner, placed in the road to derail me. In one quick move, I kill the ignition and draw the gun, aiming it right at the man, who is still standing there, about twenty feet from me. I release the safety and pull back the pin, like Dad taught me so many times in the firing range. I aim it right for his heart, instead of his head, so if I miss, I'll still hit him somewhere.

My hands are shaking, even with the gloves on, and I realize how nervous I am to pull the trigger. I've never killed anyone before.

The man suddenly raises his hands, high into the air, and takes a step towards me.

"Don't shoot!" he yells.

"Stay where you are!" I yell back, still not quite prepared to kill him.

He stops in his tracks, obedient.

"I'm not one of them!" he yells. "I'm a survivor. Like you. They took my brother!"

I wonder if it's a trap. But then I raise my visor and look him up and down, see his worn jeans, filled with holes, just like mine, see that he's only wearing one sock. I look closer and see that he has no gloves, and that his hands are blue; he has no coat either and wears only a worn, grey thermal shirt, with holes in it. Most of all, I see that his face is emaciated, more hollowed-out than mine, and I notice the dark circles under his eyes. He hasn't shaved in a long time, either. I also can't help noticing how strikingly attractive he is, despite all of this. He looks to be about my age, maybe 17, with a big shock of light brown hair, and large, light blue eyes.

He's obviously telling the truth. He's not a slaverunner. He's a survivor. Like me.

"My name is Ben!" he yells out.

Slowly, I lower the pistol, relaxing just a bit, but still feeling on edge, annoyed that he stopped me, and feeling an urgency to continue on. Ben has lost me valuable time, and almost made me wipe out.

"You almost killed me!" I scream back. "What were you doing standing in the road like that?"

I turn the ignition and kickstart the bike, ready to leave.

But Ben takes several steps towards me, waving his hands frantically.

"Wait!" he screams. "Don't go! Please! Take me with you! They have my brother! I need to get him back. I heard your engine and I thought you were one of them, so I blocked the road. I didn't realize you were a survivor. Please! Let me come with you!"

For a moment, I feel sympathy for him, but my survival instinct kicks in, and I am unsure. On the one hand, having him might be helpful, given there is strength in numbers; on the other hand, I don't know this person at all, and I don't know his personality. Will he fold in a fight? Does he even know how to fight? And if I let him ride in the sidecar, it will waste more fuel, and slow me down. I pause, deliberating, then finally decide against it.

"Sorry," I say, closing my visor, and preparing to pull out. "You'll only slow me down."

I begin to rev the bike, when he screams out again.

"You owe me!"

I stop for a second, confused by his words. *Owe* him? For what?

"That day, when you first arrived," he continues. "With your little sister. I left you a deer. That was a week's worth of food. I gave it to you. And I never asked for a thing back."

His words hit me hard. I remember that day like it was yesterday, and how much that meant to us. I'd never imagined I'd run into the person who left it. He must have been here, all this time, so close—hiding in the mountains, just like us. Surviving. Keeping to himself. With his little brother.

I do feel indebted to him. And I reconsider. I don't like owing people. Maybe, after all, it is better to have strength in numbers. And I know how he feels: his brother was taken, just like my sister. Maybe he is motivated. Maybe, together, we can do more damage.

"*Please*," he pleads. "I need to save my brother."

"Get in," I say, gesturing to the sidecar.

He jumps in without hesitating.

"There's a spare helmet inside."

A second later, he is sitting and fumbling with my old helmet. I don't wait a second longer. I tear out of their fast.

The bike feels heavier than it did, but it also feels more balanced. Within moments, I'm back up to 60 again, straight down the steep mountain road. This time, I won't stop for anything.

*

I race down the winding country roads, twisting and turning, and as I turn a corner, a panoramic view of the valley opens up before me. I can see all the roads from here, and I see the two slaverunner cars in the distance. They are at least two miles ahead of us. They must have hit Route 23 to be gaining that kind of speed, which means they are off the mountain and on a wide, straight road. It burns me to think that Bree is in the back of one of those cars. I think of how frightened she must be. I wonder if they're restraining her, if she's in pain. The poor girl must be in hysterics. I pray she didn't see Sasha die.

I gun the bike with newfound energy, twisting and turning way too sharply, and I look over and notice that Ben is gripping the edge of the sidecar, looking terrified, hanging on for his life. After several more hairpin turns, we get off the country road and go flying onto 23. Finally, we are on a normal highway, on flat land. Now, I can gun the bike for all it has.

And I do. I shift, and turn the grip, giving it as much gas as it can handle. I've never driven this bike—or anything—this fast in my life. I watch it pass 100, then 110, then 120…. There is still snow on the road, and it comes flying up into my face, bouncing off the visor; I feel the flakes brushing against the skin on my throat. I know I should slow down, but I don't. I have to catch these guys.

130…140…. I can barely breathe we are going so fast, and I know that if for some reason I need to break, I won't be able. We would spin and tumble so fast, there's no way we would make it. But I have no choice. 150...160....

"SLOW DOWN!" Ben screams. "WE ARE GOING TO DIE!"

I'm feeling the same exact thing: we *are* going to die. In fact, I feel certain of it. But I no longer care. All these years of being cautious, of hiding from everyone, have finally gotten to me. Hiding is not in my nature; I prefer to confront things head on. I guess I'm like Dad in that way: I'd rather stand and fight. Now, finally, after all these years, I have a chance to fight. And knowing that Bree is up there, just ahead of us, so close, has done something to me: it's made me mad. I just can't bring myself to slow down. I see the vehicles now, and I'm encouraged. My speed is working and I'm definitely gaining ground. They're less than a mile away, and for the first time, I really feel I'm going to catch them.

The highway curves, and I lose sight of them, but as I curve around, I see them again. But this time, they are not on the highway; they seem to have disappeared. I am confused, until I look up and see what has happened. And it makes me hit the brakes hard.

In the distance, a huge tree has been felled and lies across the highway, blocking it. Luckily,

I still have time to brake. I see the slaverunners' tracks, veering off the main road, and around the tree. As we come to a near stop before the tree, veering off the road, following the slaverunners' tracks, I notice the bark is freshly cut. And I realize what happened: someone must have just felled it. A survivor, I am guessing, one of us. He must have seen what happened, seen the slaverunners, and he felled a tree to stop them. To help us.

The gesture surprises me, and warms my heart. I'd always suspected there was a silent network of us hiding out here in the mountains, watching each other's backs. Now I know for sure. Nobody likes a slaverunner. And nobody wants to see it happen to them.

The slaverunners' tracks are distinct, and I follow them as they turn along the shoulder and make a sharp turn back onto the highway. Soon I am back on 23, and I can see them clearly now, about half a mile up ahead. I have gained some distance. I gun it again, as fast as the bike can handle, but they are flooring it now, too. They must see me. An old, rusted sign reads "Cairo: 2." We are close to the bridge. Just a few miles

It is more built-up down here, and as we fly by I see the crumbling structures along the side of the road. Abandoned factories. Warehouses. Strip malls. Even houses. Everything is the same: burnt-out, looted, destroyed. There are even abandoned vehicles, just shells. It's as if there is nothing left in the world that's working.

On the horizon, I see their destination: the Rip van Winkle bridge. A small bridge, just two lanes wide, encased by steel beams, it spans the Hudson River, connecting the small town of Catskill on the west with the larger town of Hudson on the east. A little-know bridge, once used by locals, now only slaverunners use it. It suits their purposes perfectly, leading them right to Route 9, which takes them to the Taconic Parkway and then, after 90 miles or so, right into the heart of the city. It is their artery.

But I've lost too much time, and no matter how much gas I give it, I just can't catch up. I won't be able to beat them to the bridge. I am closing the gap, though, and if I gain enough speed, maybe I can overtake them before they cross the Hudson.

A former toll-keeper's building sits at the base of the bridge, forcing vehicles to line up in a single lane and pass a toll booth. At one time there was a barricade that prevented cars from passing, but that has long since been rammed. The slaverunners fly through the narrow passageway, a sign hanging over them, rusted and dangling, that reads "E-Z PASS."

I follow them through it and race onto the bridge, now lined with rusted streetlamps that haven't worked in years, their metal twisted and crooked. As I gain speed, I notice one of the vehicles, in the distance, screech to a stop. I'm puzzled by this—I can't understand what they're doing. I suddenly see one of the slaverunners jump out of the car, plant something on the road, then jump back in his car and take off. This gains me precious time. I'm closing in on their car, a quarter mile away, and feel like I'm going to catch them. I still can't understand why they stopped—or what they planted.

Suddenly, I realize—and I slam on the brakes.

"What are you doing?" Ben yells. "Why are you stopping!?"

But I ignore him as I slam harder on the brakes. I brake too hard, too fast. Our bike can't gain traction in the snow, and we begin to spin and slide, around and around in big circles. If there were no railings, we'd slide right off the bridge and plunge to the icy river. Luckily, there are metal railings, and we slam into these hard instead.

We spin back towards the middle of the bridge. Slowly, we are braking, our speed reducing, and I only hope we can stop in time. Because now I realize—too late—what they've dropped on the road.

There is a huge explosion. Fire shoots into the sky as their bomb goes off.

A wave of heat comes right at us, and shrapnel goes flying everywhere. The explosion is intense, flames shooting everywhere, and the force of it hits us like a tornado, blowing us back. I can feel the heat, scorching my skin, even through the clothing. The heat and shrapnel engulf us. Hundreds of bits of shrapnel bounce off my helmet, the loud sound echoing in my head.

The bomb blew such a big hole that it cut the bridge in two, creating a ten yard gap between the sides. Now there is no way to cross it. And worse, we are still siding right to a hole that will send us plunging hundreds of feet below. It is lucky I slammed on the brakes when I did, and that the explosion is still fifty yards ahead. But our bike won't stop sliding, bringing us right towards it.

Finally, our speed drops to thirty, then down to twenty, then ten…. But the bike won't fully stop on this ice, and I can't stop the sliding, right towards the center of the bridge—now just a gaping chasm.

I pull on the brakes as hard as I possibly can, trying everything. But I realize that none of that will do any good now, as we keep sliding, uncontrollably, to our deaths.

And the last thing I think, before we plunge, is that I hope Bree has a better death than I do.

PART II

FIVE

Fifteen feet...ten...five.... The bike is slowing, but not enough, and we are just a few feet away from the edge. I brace myself for the fall, hardly conceiving that this is how I am going to die.

Then, the craziest thing happens: I heard a loud thump, and I am jolted forwards, as the bike slams into something and comes to a complete stop. A piece of metal, ripped in the explosion, juts up from the bridge, and has lodged itself in the spoke of our front wheel, stopping us.

I'm in a state of shock as I sit there, on the bike. I slowly look down and my heart drops as I realize that I'm dangling in the air, over the edge of the chasm. There is nothing under me at all. Hundreds of feet below I see the white ice of Hudson. I'm confused as to why I am not plunging.

I turn and see that the other half of my bike—the sidecar—is still lodged on the bridge.

Ben, looking more dazed than I, still sits in it. He lost his helmet somewhere along the way, and his cheeks are covered in soot, charred form the explosion. He looks over at me, then down at the chasm, then back up at me in disbelief, as if amazed I'm still alive.

I realize that his weight, in the sidecar, is the only thing balancing me out, keeping me from falling. If I hadn't have taken him, I'd be dead right now.

I need to do something before the entire bike tips over. Slowly, delicately, I pull my aching body off the bike, and climb over onto the sidecar, on top of Ben. I then climb over him, set my feet down on the pavement, and slowly pull back the bike.

Ben sees what I'm doing and gets out and pulls it, too. Together, we pull it back off the edge, and get the whole bike back onto safe ground.

He looks at me with his big blue eyes, and looks as if he's just been through a war.

"How did you know it was a bomb?" he asks.

I shrug. Somehow, I just knew.

"If you didn't slam on the brakes when you did, we'd be dead," he says, grateful.

"If you weren't sitting in the sidecar, I'd be dead," I respond.

Touché. We each owe each other.

We both look down, at the chasm in the bridge. I look up, and in the distance, spot the slaverunners' cars crossing the bridge and making it to the other side.

"Now what?" he asks.

I look everywhere, frantic, weighing our options. I look down at the river again. It is completely white, frozen with ice and snow. I look up and down the expanse of the river, looking for any other bridges, any other crossings. I see none.

At this moment, I realize what I must do. It is risky. In fact, it probably will mean our deaths. But I have to try. I vowed to myself. I will not give up. No matter what.

I jump back onto the bike. Ben follows, jumping into the sidecar. I put back on my helmet and gun it, back in the direction from which we came.

"Where are you going?" he calls out. "We're going the wrong way!"

I ignore him, gunning it across the bridge, back to our side of the Hudson. As soon as I clear the bridge I make a left onto Spring Street, heading towards the town of Catskill.

I remember coming here as kid with Dad, and a road that led right to the river's edge. We used to fish there, pull right up to it and never even have to leave our truck. I remember being amazed that we could drive right up to the water. And now, a plan formulates in my mind. A very, very risky plan.

We pass a small, abandoned church and cemetery on our right, and I see the gravestones sticking up out of the snow, so typical for a New England town. It amazes me that, with the whole world looted and destroyed, the cemeteries remain, seemingly untouched. It is as if the dead rule the earth.

The road comes to a tee, and I make a right on Bridge Street, and go down a steep hill. After a few blocks, I come to the ruins of a huge marble building, "Greene County Court House" still emblazoned across its portico, and make a left onto Main Street and speed down what was once the sleepy river town of Catskill. It is lined with stores on either side, burnt-out shells, crumbled buildings, broken windows, and abandoned vehicles. There's not a soul in sight. I race down the center of Main Street, the electricity out, past stoplights that no longer work. Not that I'd stop if they did.

I pass the ruins of the Post Office on my left, and swerve around a pile of rubble in the street, ruins of a townhouse that must have collapsed at some point. The street continues downhill, twisting, and the road thins out. I pass the rusted hulls of boats, now beached on the land, their bodies destroyed. Behind them are the immense, rusted structures of what were once fuel depots, circular, rising a hundred feet high.

I make a left, towards the waterfront park, now covered in weeds. What's left of a sign reads "Dutchman's Landing." The park juts out, right into the river, and the only thing separating the road from the water are a few boulders, with gaps in between them. I aim for one of those gaps, lower my visor, and gun the bike for all it's worth. It's now or never. I can already feel my heart racing.

Ben must realize what I'm doing. He sits bolt upright, gripping the sides of the bike in terror.

"STOP!" he screams. "WHAT ARE YOU DOING!?"

But there's no stopping now. He enlisted for this ride, and there is no turning back. I'd offer to let him out, but there is no more time to lose; besides, if I stopped, I might not get up the nerve again to do what I'm about to do.

I check the speedometer: 60…70…80….

"YOU'RE GOING TO DRIVE US RIGHT INTO THE RIVER!" he screams.

"IT'S COVERED IN ICE!" I scream back.

"THE ICE WON'T HOLD!" he screams back.

90…100…110….

"WE'LL FIND OUT!" I respond.

He's right. The ice might not hold. But I see no other way. I have to cross that river, and I have no other ideas.

120...130...140....

The river is coming up on us fast.

"LET ME OUT!" he screams, desperate.

But there is no time. He knew what the signed up for.

I gun it one last time.

And then our world turns white.

SIX

I drive the bike in the narrow gap between the rocks, and next thing I know, we go flying. For a second we are airborne, and I wonder if, when we hit the ice, it will hold—or whether we will crash right through it and plummet into the icy water, to a certain and brutal death.

A second later my entire body is jolted, as we hit something hard.

Ice.

We hit it at 140, faster than I can even imagine, and as it hits, I lose control. The tires can't gain traction, and my driving becomes more like a controlled slide; I do my best to just steer the handlebars, which sway wildly. But, to my surprise and relief, at least the ice is holding. We go flying across the solid sheet of ice that is the Hudson River, veering left and right, but at least heading in the right direction. As we do, I pray to God that the ice holds.

Suddenly I hear the horrific noise behind me of cracking ice, even louder than the roar of my engine. I check back over my shoulder, and as I do, an enormous crack opens in the river, following the trail of our bike. The river opens up right behind us, revealing water. Our only saving grace is that we are going so fast, the cracking isn't quite fast enough to catch us, always a foot behind. If our engine and tires can just hold, just for a few more seconds, maybe, just maybe, we can outrace it.

"HURRY!" screams Ben, eyes wide open with fear as he looks back over his shoulder.

I gun it as fast as I possibly can, just topping 150. We are thirty yards away from the opposite shore, and closing in.

Come on, come on! I think. All we need is a few more yards.

The next thing I know there is a tremendous crash, and my entire body is jerked front and back. I hear Ben groan out in pain. My whole world shakes and spins, and it is then I realize that we have arrived on the opposite shore. We slam into it doing 150, hitting the steep bank hard, which snaps our heads back on impact. But after a few vicious bumps, we clear the bank.

We made it. We are back on dry land.

Behind us, the river is now entirely split open, cracked in half, water spilling onto the ice. I don't think we could have made it a second time.

There is no time to think about that now. I try to gain control of the bike again, to slow it down, as we are going faster than I would like. But the bike is still fighting me, its tires still trying to gain traction—and suddenly we drive over something incredibly hard and uneven, which sends my jaw smashing into my teeth. It feels like we drove over rocks.

I look down: train tracks. I'd forgotten. There are still old tracks here, right along the river, from when trains used to run. We hit them hard as we cross the river, and as we jump them, the metal shakes the bike so violently, I almost lose hold of the grips. Amazingly, the tires still hold, and we cross the tracks on a country road, running parallel to the river, and I am finally able to slow the bike, dropping down to 70. We pass the rusted hull of an old, huge train, lying on its side, burnt out, and I bang a sharp left on a country road with an old sign that reads "Greendale." It is a narrow country lane with a sharp ascent uphill, away from the river.

We lose speed as we drive nearly straight up. I pray that the bike will make it in the snow and not slide back down. I gun it, as the speed drops. We are down to about 20 miles an hour, when finally, we clear the hilltop. We even out on level land, and I gain speed again as we fly down this narrow country road, taking us alternately through woods, then farmland, then woods again, then past an old, abandoned firehouse. It continues, dipping and rising, twisting and turning, taking us past abandoned country houses, past herds of deer and flocks of geese, even over a small country bridge spanning a creek.

Finally, it merges into another road, Church Road, aptly named, as we pass the remnants of a huge Methodist church on our left and adjoining graveyard—of course, still intact. I know there is only one way the slaverunners can go. If they want the Taconic, which they must, then there's no way there without taking Route 9. They are heading North to South—and we are heading West to East. My plan is to cut them off. And now, finally, *I* have the advantage. I crossed the river about a mile further south than they. If I can just go fast enough, I can beat them to the punch. Finally, I am feeling optimistic. I can cut them off—and they will never expect it. I will hit them perpendicularly and maybe I can take them out.

I gun the bike again, pushing it past 140.

"WHERE ARE YOU GOING?" Ben yells out.

He still looks shell-shocked, but I have no time to explain: in the distance, I suddenly spot their cars. They are exactly where I thought they'd be. They don't see me coming. They don't see that I am lined up to smash right into them.

Their cars ride single file, one about twenty yards behind the other, and I realize I can't take them both out. I am going to need to choose one. I decide to aim for the one in front: if I can run it off the road, perhaps it will cause the one behind it to slam on the brakes, or spin out and crash, too. It is a risky plan: the impact may very well kill us. But I don't see any other way. I can't exactly ask them to stop. I only pray that, if I am successful, Bree survives the crash.

I increase speed, closing in on them. I am a hundred yards away...then 50...then 30....

Finally, Ben realizes what I'm about to do.

"WHAT ARE YOU DOING!?" he screams, and I can hear the fear in his voice. "YOU'RE GOING TO HIT THEM!"

Finally he gets it. That's exactly what I'm hoping to do.

I rev it one last time, topping 150, and barely catch my breath as we go racing at top speed on the country road. Seconds later, we go flying onto Route 9—and smash directly into the first vehicle. It is a perfect hit.

The impact is tremendous. I feel the crash of metal on metal, feel my body jerking to a stop, then feel myself go flying off my bike and through the air. I see a world of stars, and as I'm flying, I realize that this is what it feels like to die.

SEVEN

I go flying through the air, head over heels, and finally feel myself land in the snow, the impact crushing my ribs and knocking the wind out of me. I go tumbling, again and again. I roll and roll, unable to stop, bumped and bruised in every direction. The helmet is still fastened to my head, and I am grateful for it as I feel my head crack against rocks in the ground. Behind me, there is the loud sound of crashing metal.

I lay there, frozen, wondering what I have done. For a moment, I am unable to move. But then I think of Bree, and force myself to. Gradually, I move my leg, then raise an arm, testing it. As I do, I feel excruciating pain on my right, in my ribs, enough to take my breath away. It feels like I've cracked one of them. With a supreme effort, I am able to turn over to my side. I lift my visor, look over and take in the scene.

It looks like I hit the first car with such force that I knocked it on its side; it lays there, its wheels spinning. The other vehicle has spun out, but is still upright; it sits in a ditch on the side of the road, about fifty yards ahead of us. Ben still sits in the sidecar; I can't tell if he's dead or alive. It seems I am the first one to regain consciousness. There seems to be no other signs of life from anyone.

I don't waste any time. I feel more achy than ever—as if I've just been run over by a Mack Truck—but I think again of Bree, and somehow summon the energy to move. I have the advantage now, while everyone else is recovering.

Limping, feeling a throbbing pain in my ribs, I hobble over to the car on its side. I pray that Bree is in there, that she's unhurt, and that I can get her out of here somehow. I reach down and take out the gun as I approach, holding it cautiously in front of me.

I look in and see that both slaverunners are slumped in their seats, covered in blood. One's eyes are open, clearly dead. The other appears to be dead, too. I quickly check the backseats, hoping to see Bree.

But she's not there. Instead, I find two other teenagers—a boy and a girl. They sit there, frozen with fear. I can't believe it. I hit the wrong car.

I immediately look over to the car on the horizon, the one in the ditch, and as I do, it suddenly revs its engine and its wheels spin. It is trying to get out. I prepare to sprint towards it, to reach it before it pulls out. My heart thumps in my throat, knowing Bree is right there, barely fifty yards away.

Just as I'm about to burst into action, I suddenly hear a voice.

"HELP ME!"

I look over and see Ben, sitting in the sidecar, trying to get out. I look behind him and see flames spreading on the bike, behind the gas tank. My bike is on fire. And Ben is stuck. I stand there, torn, looking back and forth between Ben and the car that holds my sister. I need to go and rescue her. But at the same time, I can't let him die. Not like this.

Furious, I run to him. I grab him, feeling the heat from the flames behind him, and yank on him, trying to get him out. But the metal of the sidecar has bent in on his legs, and it's not easy. He tries to help, too, and I yank, again and again, the flames growing higher. I am sweating, grunting, as I yank with all I have. Finally, I pry him loose.

And just as I do, suddenly, the bike explodes.

EIGHT

The explosion sends us both flying back through the air, and I land hard on my back in the snow. For the third time this morning, the wind is knocked out of me.

I look up at the sky, seeing stars, trying to clear my head. I can still feel the heat on my face from the force of the flames, and my ears ring from the noise.

As I struggle to my knees, I feel a searing pain in my right arm. I look over and see that a small piece of shrapnel is sticking through the edge of my bicep, maybe two inches long; it looks like a piece of twisted metal. It hurts like crazy.

I reach over and, without thinking, in one quick motion grab the end of it, grit my teeth and yank. For a moment, I am in the worst pain of my life, as the metal goes completely through my arm and out the other side. Blood rushes down my arm and into the snow, staining my coat.

I quickly take off one sleeve of the coat and can see the blood on my shirt. I tear off a piece of the sleeve with my teeth and take a strip of cloth and tie it tight over the wound, then put my coat back on. I hope it will staunch the flow of blood. I manage to sit up, and as I look over, I see what was once my Dad's bike: now it is just a heap of useless metal, on fire. It will clearly never run again. Now we're stuck.

I look over at Ben. He looks dazed, too, on his hands and knees, breathing hard, his cheeks black with soot. But at least he is alive.

I hear the roar of an engine, and look over and see that in the distance, the other car has caught traction. It is already taking off down the highway, gaining speed, with my sister inside. I am furious at Ben for making me lose her. I have to catch them.

I turn to the slaverunner car before me, still on its side, and wonder if it runs. I run over to it, determined to try.

I push it for all I have, trying to get it back on all four tires. But it's too heavy, barely rocking.

"Help me!" I yell to Ben.

He gets up and hurries to my side, limping. He takes position beside me, and together, we push with all we have. The car is heavier than I imagine, weighed down by all its iron bars. It rocks more and more, and finally, after one big heave, we get it back onto all four tires. It lands in the snow with a crash.

I waste no time. I open the driver's side door and reach in and grab the dead driver with both hands by the shirt and yank him out of the seat. His torso is covered in blood, and my hands turn red as I throw him into the snow.

I lean in and examine the slaverunner in the passenger seat. His face is covered in blood, too, but I am not certain he is dead. In fact, as I look closer, I detect some signs of movement. Then he shifts in his seat. He's alive.

I lean across the car and grab him by his shirt, tight in a fist. I hold my gun to his head and shake him roughly. Finally, his eyes bat open. He blinks, disoriented.

I assume the other slaverunners are heading to Arena One. But I need to know for sure. They have such a big head start on us, that I need to know. I lean in close.

He turns and looks at me, and for a moment, I am stunned: half his face is melted away. It is an old wound, not from the accident, which means he must be a Biovictim. I've heard rumors of these people, but I've never seen one up close. When the nuclear payloads were dropped in the cities, those few who survived a direct attack carried the scars, and were rumored to be more sadistic and aggressive than others. We call them the Crazies.

I have to be extra careful with this one. I tighten my grip on the gun.

"Where are they taking her?" I demand, through gritted teeth.

He looks back blankly, as if trying to comprehend. I feel certain, though, that he understands.

I shove the barrel tight against his cheek, letting him know I mean business. And I do. Every passing moment is precious, and I can feel Bree getting further away from me.

"I said, where are they taking her?"

Finally, his eyes open in what seems to be fear. I think he gets the message.

"The arena," he finally says, his voice raspy.

My heart flutters, my worst fears confirmed.

"Which one?" I snap.

I pray he does not say *Arena One*.

He pauses, and I can see he is debating whether or not to tell me. I jab the pistol tighter against his cheekbone.

"Tell me now or you're wasted!" I yell, surprising myself with the anger in my voice.

Finally, after a long pause, he answers: "Arena One."

My heart pounds, my worst fears confirmed. Arena One. Manhattan. It is rumored to be the worst of them all. That can only mean one thing: a certain death for Bree.

I feel a fresh rage towards this man, this bottom feeder, this slaverunner, the lowest rung of society, who has come up here to kidnap my sister, and God knows who else, to feed the machine, just so that others can watch helpless people kill each other. All this senseless death, just for their own entertainment. It is enough to make me want to kill him on the spot.

But I pull the gun back, and loosen my grip. I know that I should kill him, but a part of me can't bring myself to. He answered my questions, and somehow I feel killing him now wouldn't be fair. So instead, I decide I will abandon him here. I will kick him out of the car and leave him here, which will mean a slow death by starvation. There is no way a slaverunner can survive alone in nature. They are city dwellers—not survivors like us.

I lean back to tell Ben to yank this slaverunner out of the car, when suddenly, I detect motion out of the corner of my eye. I suddenly stop and see the slaverunner is reaching for his belt. He is moving faster than I thought he was capable of. He has tricked me: he is actually in fairly good shape.

He pulls out a gun faster than I could have ever thought possible. Before I can even register what's happening, he is already raising it in my direction. Stupidly, I've underestimated him.

Some instinct in me takes over, perhaps some instinct inherited from Dad, and without even thinking clearly, I raise my gun, and right before he shoots, I fire.

NINE

The gunshot is deafening, and a moment later, the car is splattered in blood. I am so overcome by adrenaline, I don't even know who fired first.

I am shocked as I look down and realize that I shot him in the head.

A screaming erupts. I look to the back seat and see that the young girl sitting behind the driver's side is shrieking. She suddenly leans forward, pulls herself out from the back, jumps out, and hits the snow running.

For a moment, I debate whether to chase her down—she is clearly in shock, and in her state, who knows if she even knows where she's going. In this weather, and in this remote location, I doubt she can survive long.

But I think of Bree, and have to stay focused. She is what matters most now. I can't afford to waste time tracking this girl down. I turn and watch her run, and it feels odd to think of her as being so much younger than I am. In truth, she is probably close to my age.

I check the reaction of the captured boy in the backseat, maybe twelve. But he just sits there, staring, frozen. He looks to me like he's in a catatonic state. He's not even blinking. I wonder if he's had some kind of psychotic break. I stand and look over at Ben, who still stands there, staring down at the dead corpse. He doesn't say a word.

The gravity of what I have done suddenly hits me: I have just killed a man. Never in my life did I think I would. I have always felt bad even killing an animal, and I realize I should feel awful.

But I am too numb. Right now, all I feel is that I did what I had to to defend myself. He was a slaverunner after all, and he came up here to hurt us. I realize I should feel more remorse—but I don't. That frightens me. I can't help but wonder if I'm more like Dad than I care to admit.

Ben is useless, still standing there, staring, so I run around to his side of the car, open the passenger side door and begin to yank out the body. It is heavy.

"Help me!" I snap. I am annoyed by his inaction—especially while the other slaverunners are getting away.

Finally, Ben hurries over and helps me. We drag it out, the blood staining our clothes, walk it a few feet, then throw it into the snow, which turns red. I reach down and quickly strip the corpse of its gun and ammo, realizing Ben is too passive, or isn't thinking clearly.

"Take his clothes," I say. "You'll need them."

I don't waste any more time. I run back to our car, open the driver's side door and jump in. I go to turn the keys, when I suddenly look down and check the ignition. They are missing.

My heart drops. I check the floor of the car frantically, then the seats, then the dash. Nothing. The keys must have fallen out in the crash.

I look outside, at the snow, and notice some unusual markings that might indicate a trail from the keys. I get down, kneeling in the snow, and comb frantically through it, searching. I feel more and more desperate. It is like finding a needle in a haystack.

But suddenly, a miracle happens: my hand strikes something small. I comb the snow more carefully, and am flooded with relief to see it's the keys.

I jump back in the car, turn the ignition, and the car roars to life. This vehicle is some kind of modified muscle car, something like an old Camaro, and the engine roars way too loud; I can already tell it will be a fast ride. I only hope it's fast enough to catch the other one.

I am about to put it into gear and take off when I look over and see Ben, still standing there, staring down at the corpse. He still hasn't stripped the corpse's clothing, even though he is standing there, freezing. I guess seeing the death affected him more than it did me. I have lost all patience and for a moment I debate just taking off; but then I realize that it wouldn't be fair to leave him here alone, especially since he—or his body weight, at least—saved me back there on the bridge.

"I'M LEAVING!" I shriek at him. "GET IN!"

That snaps him out of it. He comes running over, jumps in and slams the door. Just as I am about to gun it, he turns and looks in the backseat.

"What about him?" he asks.

I follow his gaze and see, in the backseat, the catatonic boy, still sitting there and staring.

"You want out?" I ask the boy. "Now's your chance."

But he keeps staring straight ahead, not responding. I don't have the luxury of time to figure it out; there have been too many delays already. If he won't decide, I'll decide for him. Coming along with us might kill him—but leaving him here will definitely kill him. He's coming with us.

I peel out, getting back onto the highway with a thud. I am pleased to see the car is still running, and is faster than I could imagine. I am also pleased to see it handles well on the snowy highway. I hit the clutch and give it gas and shift to second gear, then to third, then fourth.... I am grateful Dad taught me how to drive stick—another manly thing I probably never should have learned as a teenage girl, and another thing I resented at the time but am thankful for now. I watch the speedometer climb: 80...90...100...110...120.... I am unsure how hard to push it. I worry that if I go too fast I'll lose control in the snow, especially since this highway hasn't been maintained in years—and because, with the snow covering, I can't even see the potholes. If we hit just one big hole, or one patch of ice, we could be off the road. I get it up just a bit more, to 130, and decide to hold it there.

I look over at Ben and see he has just finished buckling his seatbelt and is now gripping the dash, his knuckles white, looking straight ahead at the road in fear.

"You killed him," he says.

I can barely hear him over the roar of the engine, and I wonder if I just imagined it, or if it was my conscience speaking. But Ben turns and looks at me, and repeats it:

"You killed that man," he says louder, as if amazed such a thing could happen.

I'm not sure how to respond.

"Yes I did," I say finally, annoyed. I don't need him reminding me of it. "Do you have a problem with that?"

Slowly, he shakes his head. "I've just never seen a man killed before."

"I did what I had to do," I snap back, defensive. "He was reaching for a gun."

I give it more gas, hitting 135, and as we turn the bend, I am relieved to spot the other car on the horizon. I am catching up, speeding faster than they dare to. At this rate, in a few minutes I might just catch them. I am encouraged.

I am sure they spot us—I just hope they don't realize it's us. Maybe they think the other slaverunners got their car back on the road. I don't think they saw our encounter.

I give it even more gas, hitting 140, and the distance starts to close.

"What are you going to do when you catch them?" Ben suddenly screams, and I can hear the panic in his voice.

That is exactly what I have been wondering. I don't know yet. I just know I need to catch up to them.

"We can't shoot at their car, if that's what you're thinking," he says. "The bullet might kill my brother—or your sister."

"I know," I reply. "We're not going to shoot. We're going to run them off the road," I say, suddenly deciding.

"That's crazy!" he yells, gripping the dashboard tighter as we close the gap even more. Snow is bouncing off our windshield like crazy, and I feel like I'm in one of those videogames going out of control. The Taconic twists, narrowing as we go.

"That could kill them!" he yells. "What good will that do? My brother will die in there!"

"My sister is in there, too!" I shout back. "You think I want her dead?"

"So then what are you thinking!?" he screams.

"You have any other ideas!?" I shout back. "You expect me to just pull up and ask them to pull over?"

He is silent.

"We *have* to stop them," I continue. "If they reach the city, we'll never get them back. That's a certain death. At least this gives them a chance."

Just as I get ready to floor it one more time, suddenly, the slaverunners surprise me, and slow down. They slow so much that in moments I pull up beside them. At first I can't understand why they are doing this, and then I realize: they think we are their partners. They still don't realize it's us.

We pull up, and just as I prepare to turn hard on the wheel, to smash into them, their tinted passenger-side window lowers. The grinning face of a slaverunner appears, his facemask raised; he still assumes I am one of his.

I lower my window, scowling back: I want him to have one good look at me before I send him to hell.

His smile suddenly drops, as his expression morphs into one of shock. I still have the element of surprise, and am about to turn hard on the wheel, when suddenly, I am distracted: as I look over, I catch a glimpse of Bree in the backseat. She is alive. She looks back at me, and I can see the fear in her eyes.

Suddenly, we hit a pothole. The sound is deafening, and our car shakes as if a bomb has gone off. It jolts me so hard that my head slams into the metal ceiling, and my teeth smash into each other. I feel as if I've lost a filling. Our car swerves wildly, and it takes me several seconds to regain control and straighten it out. It was a close call. It was stupid of me: I never should have taken my eyes off the road. We've lost speed, and the other vehicle has sped up, and is now a good fifty yards ahead of us. Worse, now they know we're not one of theirs.

I floor it again: 130…140…. I step on the gas until the pedal is touching the floor, but it won't go any further. The speedometer hits 150. I assume the car in front of me has the capacity to go as fast, but they, clearly, are being more sensible. The icy conditions on this road are risky at even 80 miles an hour, and they are not willing to take the extra risk. But I have nothing to lose. If I lose Bree, I have nothing left to live for anyway.

We are closing in on them again. They are thirty yards away…twenty.

Suddenly, their passenger window rolls down, and light reflects off of something shiny. I realize, too late, what it is: a gun.

I slam on the brakes, just as they fire several times. I duck as the bullets bounce off our hood and windshield, and the metallic sound of ricocheting bullets fills our ears. At first I think we're finished, but then I realize the bullets haven't penetrated: this car must be bulletproof.

"You're going to get us killed!" Ben yells. "Stop this! There has to be another way!"

"There's no other way!" I scream back, more to assure myself than him.

I have crossed some sort of line inside, and I absolutely refuse to back down.

"There is no other way," I repeat quietly to myself, my eyes locked on the road.

I step on it one more time, swerving to the side, then floor it, coming up alongside them. With one strong pull on the wheel, I smash into them hard, just as the slaverunner is reaching out with his gun again. My front fender hits their rear wheel. Their car swerves wildly, and so does mine. For a moment, we are both all over the road. They smash into a metal railing, then bounce back and smash into me. I smash into the metal railing on my side.

The highway opens up and the railings disappear, and there is flat farmland on either side of us. It is perfect. I know I can take them out now. I floor it one more time, preparing to swerve again. I have them perfectly in my sights, and reach up to turn the wheel.

Suddenly, there is a gleam of metal as the slaverunner reaches out again, gun in hand.

"WATCH OUT!" Ben yells.

But it is too late. Gunshots ring out, and before I can swerve, the bullets rip into our front tires. I lose complete control of the car. Ben screams, as we go flying across the road. So, despite myself, do I.

My universe is upside down, as the car tumbles, and we spin again and again.

My head smashes against the metal roof. I feel the sharp tug of the seatbelt digging into my chest, and the world is just a blur through the windshield. There is the sound of metal crunching in my ears, so loud, I can hardly think.

The last thing I remember is wishing my Dad were here to see me now, to see how close I had come. I wonder if he would be proud.

And then, after one final crash, my world goes black.

TEN

I don't know how long I'm out. I peel open my eyes, and wake to a tremendous pain in my head. Something is wrong, and I can't figure out what.

Then I realize: the world is upside down.

I feel blood rushing to my face. I look about, trying to figure out what happened, where I am, if I'm even still alive. And then, slowly, I begin to take it all in.

The car is sitting upside down, the engine has stopped, and I'm still buckled in the driver's seat. It's silent. I wonder how long I've been sitting here like this. I reach over, slowly moving my arm, trying to feel for injuries. As I do, I feel a sharp pain in my arms and shoulders. I don't know if I'm injured, or where, and I can't tell as long as I'm hanging upside down in the seat. I realize I need to unbuckle myself.

I reach over and, unable to see the buckle, feel along the strap until I reach something cold and plastic. I dig my thumb into it. At first, it doesn't give.

I push harder.

Come on.

There is a sudden click, and the belt snaps off and I go plummeting down, landing right on my face, against the metal roof; the drop must be a foot, and makes my headache far worse.

It takes a few seconds to get my wits back about me, and slowly, I get to my knees. I look over and see Ben there beside me; he is still buckled in, too, also hanging upside down. His face is covered in blood and blood drips slowly from his nose, and I can't tell if he's alive or dead. But his eyes are closed, and I take that as a good sign—at least they're not open and unblinking.

I check the backseat for our passenger, the boy—and as soon as do, I regret it. He lies on the bottom of the car, his neck twisted in an unnatural position, eyes open and frozen. Dead.

I feel responsible. Maybe I should have forced him out of the car earlier. Ironically, this boy might have been better off if he stayed with the slaverunners than me. But there's nothing I can do about it now.

Seeing this boy dead reinforces the gravity of the accident; I check my body again for injuries, not even knowing where to look, since everything hurts. But as I twist, I feel a searing pain in my side, my ribs, and as I take a deep breath, it hurts to breathe. I reach over, and it's sensitive to the touch. It feels like I've cracked another rib.

I can move, but it hurts like hell. I also still have the burning pain in my arm from the shrapnel of our previous accident. My head feels heavy, as if it's in a vice, my ears are ringing, and I have a pounding headache that just won't quit. I probably have a concussion.

But there's no time to dwell on that now. I need to see if Ben is alive. I reach over and shake him. He doesn't respond.

I debate the best way to get him out and realize there's no easy way to do it. So I reach over and push hard on his seatbelt release button. The strap flies off and Ben plummets down and lands hard, face first, on the metal roof. He grunts loudly, and I'm flooded with relief: he's alive.

He lays there, curled up, groaning. I reach over and shove him hard, again and again. I want to wake him, see how badly he's hurt. He squirms, but still doesn't seem fully conscious.

I have to get out of this car: I feel claustrophobic in here, especially being so close to the dead boy, still staring at me with his unmoving eyes. I reach over, searching for the door handle. My vision is a bit blurry, and it's hard to find, especially with everything upside down. I use two hands, groping the door, and finally, I find it. I pull on it, and nothing happens. Great. The door must be jammed shut.

I yank on it again and again, but still, nothing happens.

So I lean back, bring my knees to my chest, and kick the door as hard as I can with both feet. There is a crash of metal and a burst of cold air rushes in, as the door goes flying open.

I roll out into the snow, into a world of white. It is snowing again, and it is coming down as hard as ever. It feels good to be out of the car, though, and I get to my knees, and slowly stand. I feel a rush of blood to my head, and for a moment, the world spins. Slowly, my headache lessens, and it feels good to be upright, back on my feet, breathing fresh air. As I try to stand straight, the pain in my ribs worsens, as does the pain in my arm. I roll my shoulders back and feel stiff, bruised all over. But I don't feel that anything else is broken, and I don't see any blood. I'm lucky.

I hurry over to the passenger side door, get to one knee, and yank it open. I reach in and grab Ben by the shirt and try to yank him out. He is heavier than I suspect, and I have to yank hard; I pull slowly but firmly, and finally get him out into the fresh snow. He enters the snow face first, and finally, that wakes him. He rolls onto his side, wiping the snow off his face. He then gets to his hands and knees and opens his eyes, staring at the ground, breathing hard. As he does, blood drips from his nose into the white snow, staining it.

He blinks several times, disoriented, and turns and looks up at me, holding up a hand to shield his eyes from the falling snow.

"What happened?" he asks, his speech slurred.

"We had an accident," I answer. "You okay?"

"I can't breathe," he says, sounding nasally, cupping his hands beneath his nose to catch the blood. As he leans back, I can finally see: he has a broken nose.

"Your nose is busted," I say.

He looks back at me, slowly comprehending, and his eyes flood with fear.

"Don't worry," I say, going over to him. I reach up with both hands, and place them on his nose. I remember when Dad taught me how to set a broken nose. It was late one night, after he'd come home from a bar fight. I couldn't believe it. He made me watch, said it would be good for me to learn something useful. He stood there in the bathroom as I watched, leaned into the mirror, and reached up and did it. I still remember the cracking noise it made.

"Hold still," I say.

In one quick motion, I reach up and push hard on both sides of his crooked nose, setting it straight. He screams out in pain, and I feel badly. But I know this is what he needs to get it back into place, and to staunch the flow of blood. I reach down and hand him a clump of snow, putting into his hands and guiding it up, so that he holds it against his nose.

"This will stop the blood, and reduce the swelling," I say.

Ben holds the clump of snow to his nose, and within moments, it turns red. I look away.

I step back and survey our car: it sits there, upside down, its chassis visible to the sky. Its three intact tires are still spinning, very slowly. I turn and look back towards the highway. We're about thirty yards off the road—we must've really tumbled far. I wonder how big of a lead they have on us.

It's amazing, I realize, that we're even still alive, especially given our speed. Surveying this stretch of highway, I realize we got lucky: if we had tumbled back there, we would have plunged off a cliff. And if the thick snow hadn't sheltered us, I'm sure the impact would have been worse.

I survey our car, wondering if there's any way we can get it running again. I realize it's doubtful. Which means I'll never find Bree, and which means we'll be stranded here, in the middle of nowhere, and probably dead within a day. We have no choice: we *have* to find a way to get it working.

"We have to flip it over," I say, with sudden urgency. "We have to get it back on its wheels and see if it still works. I need your help."

Ben slowly registers what I'm saying, then hurries over to my side, stumbling at first. The two of us stand beside each other, on one side of the car, and both begin to push.

We manage to rock it, and then, using our momentum, push it again and again. It takes all that I have, and I can feel myself slipping in the snow, feel the pain tearing through my bicep, through my ribs.

The car rocks in bigger and bigger swings, and just as I wonder if I can go on, we give it one final heave. I reach up, above my head, pushing and pushing it, walking forward in the snow as I do.

It is just enough. The car reaches a tipping point, on its side, then suddenly lands with a crash on all four wheels. A huge cloud of snow rises up. I stand there catching my breath, as does Ben.

I survey the damage. It is extensive. The hood and roof and trunk look as if they've been worked over by a sledgehammer. But amazingly, the bones of it are still in shape. However, there is one glaring problem. One of the tires—the one that was shot out—is in such bad shape that there's no way we can drive on it.

"Maybe there's a spare," Ben says, reading my mind. I look over and he's already hurrying over to the trunk. I'm impressed.

I hurry over to it, too. He pushes the button several times, but it doesn't open.

"Look out," I say, and as he steps back I raise my knee and kick down hard with my heel. The trunk pops open.

I look down and am relieved to see a spare tire sitting there. Ben reaches in and grabs it, and I pull back the lining, and beneath it, find a jack and wrench. I grab it and follow Ben, who carries the spare to the front. Without missing a beat, Ben takes the jack, jams it under the chassis, then takes the wrench and starts cranking it up. I'm impressed by how comfortable he is with the tools, and how quickly he gets the car jacked up. He removes all the bolts and pulls off the useless tire and chucks it into the snow.

He puts in the new tire, and I hold it steady as he puts the bolts back in, one by one. He tightens them and lowers the car, and as we step back and look, it's like having a brand-new tire. Ben has surprised me with his mechanical skills; I never would have expected that from him.

I waste no time opening the driver's side door, jumping back in the car, and turning the keys. But my heart drops as I hear silence. The car is dead. I try the ignition again and again. But nothing. Nothing at all. It seems the accident destroyed the car somehow. A hopeless feeling sets in. Was this all for nothing?

"Pop the hood," Ben says.

I pull the lever and Ben hurries around to the front, and I get out and join him. I stand over him as he reaches in and starts fiddling with several wires, knobs and switches. I am surprised by his dexterity.

"Are you a mechanic?" I ask.

"Not really," he answers. "My Dad is. He taught me a lot, back when we had cars."

He holds two wires together, and there is a spark. "Try it now," he says.

I hurry back in and turn the ignition, hoping, praying. This time, the car roars to life.

Ben slams closed the hood, and I see a proud smile on his face, which is already swelling up from the broken nose. He hurries back and opens his door and is about to get back in, when suddenly he freezes, staring into the backseat.

I follow his gaze, and I remember. The boy in the back.

"What should we do with him?" Ben asks.

There's no more time to waste. I get out, reach in and yank him out, trying not to look. I drag him several feet, in the snow, over to a large tree, and lay him down beneath it. I look at him for just a moment, then turn and run back to the car.

Ben still stands there.

"That's it?" he asks, sounding disappointed.

"What do you expect?" I snap. "A funeral service?"

"It just seems…a bit callous," he says. "He died because of us."

"We don't have time for this," I say, at my wit's end. "We're all going to die anyway!"

I jump back into the running car, my thoughts fixed on Bree, on how far the other slaverunners have gone. While Ben is still closing his door, I peel out.

Our car goes flying across the snowy field, up a steep bank and with a bang, back onto the highway. We skid, then catch traction. We are rolling again.

I step on the gas, and we start to gain real speed. I am amazed: this car is invincible. It feels as good as new.

In no time, we are doing over 100. This time, I'm a bit more cautious, shell-shocked from the accident. I bring it up to 110, but don't press it past that. I can't risk wiping out again.

I figure they're probably at least ten minutes ahead of us, and we might not be able to catch them. But anything can happen. All I need is for them to hit one bad pothole, for just one mishap to happen to them.... If not, I'll just have to follow their tracks, and hope I can find them.

"We have to find them before they reach the city," Ben says, as if reading my mind. He has an annoying habit of doing that, I notice. "If they get there before us, we'll never find them again."

"I know," I respond.

"And if we enter the city, we'll never make it out. You know that, don't you?"

The very same thought has been going through my mind. He's right. From everything I've heard, the city is a deathtrap, filled with predators. We're hardly equipped to fight our way out.

I step on it, giving it a bit more gas. The engine roars, and we are now cruising at 120. The snow hasn't slowed, and bounces off the windshield. I think of the dead boy in the backseat, see his face, his unblinking eyes; I remember how close we came to death, and a part of me wants to slow down. But I have no choice.

As we drive, time feels like it's crawling, going forever. We must drive twenty miles, then thirty, then forty...on and on, forever into the snow. I'm gripping the steering wheel with both hands, leaning forward, watching the road more carefully than I have in my life. I'm swerving to avoid potholes left and right, like a videogame.

Which is hard to do in this speed, and in this snow. Still, I manage to miss nearly all of them. Once or twice I don't, though, and we pay the price dearly, my head slamming into the roof, and my teeth smashing into each other. But no matter what, I keep going.

As we round the bend, I spot something in the distance that worries me: the tracks of the slaverunner's car seem to veer off the road, into a field. It doesn't make any sense, and I wonder if I am seeing things correctly, especially in this blizzard.

But as we get closer, the more certain I become. I slow dramatically.

"What are you doing?" Ben asks.

My sixth sense tells me to slow down, and as we get close, I'm glad I do.

I slam on the brakes, and luckily I'm only doing 50 when I do. We slip and slide for about 20 yards, and finally, we come to a stop.

Just in time. The highway comes to an abrupt stop. It ends in a huge crater, plunging deep into the earth. If I hadn't stopped, we would surely be dead right now.

I look down, over the edge of the precipice. It is a massive crater, probably a hundred yards in diameter. It looks like a huge bomb had been dropped on this highway at some point during the war.

I turn the wheel and follow the slaverunner's tracks, which take me though a snowy field, then onto winding local roads. After several minutes, it leads us back onto the highway. I pick up speed again, this time bringing it up to 130.

I drive and drive and drive, and feel like I'm driving to the end of the earth. I probably cover another 40 miles and I begin to wonder how much further this highway can go. The snowy sky begins to grow darker, and soon it will be nightfall. I feel the need to push, and get the car up to 140. I know it's risky, but I need to catch up to them.

As we go, we pass some of the old signs for the major arteries, still hanging, rusting away: the Sawmill Parkway; the Major Deegan; 287; the Sprain.... The Taconic forks, and I merge onto the Sprain Parkway, then the Bronx River Parkway, following the slaverunner's tracks. We are getting closer to the city now, open sky gradually replaced by tall, crumbling buildings. We are in the Bronx.

I feel the need to catch them and push the car up to 150. It becomes so loud that I can barely hear.

As we round another bend, my heart leaps: there, in the distance, I see them, a mile ahead.

"That's them!" Ben screams.

But as we close the gap, I suddenly see what they're going for. A crooked sign reads "Willis Avenue Bridge." It is a small bridge, encased in metal beams, barely wide enough for two lanes. At its entrance sit several Humvees, slaverunners sitting on the hoods, machine guns mounted and aimed towards the road. More Humvees sit on the far side of the bridge.

I gun it, pushing the gas pedal as far as it will go, and we top 150. The world flies by in a blur. But we are not catching up: the slaverunners are speeding up, too.

"We can't follow them in!" Ben yells. "We'll never make it!"

But we have no choice. They've got at least a hundred yards on us, and the bridge is maybe a hundred yards away. We're not going to beat them there. I am doing all I can, and our car is already shaking from the speed. There's no way around it: we're going to have to enter the city.

As we approach the bridge, I wonder if the guards realize we aren't one of theirs. I only hope we can get through fast enough, before they catch on and fire on us.

The slaverunner car flies between the guards, racing over the bridge. We follow, fifty years behind, and as we do, the guards still don't realize. Soon, we are thirty yards away…then 20…then 10….

As we race onto the entrance, we are close enough that I can see the horrified expressions on the guards' faces. Now, they realize.

I look up, and the guards raise their machineguns our way.

A second later, shots ring out.

We are covered in automatic machine gun fire, bouncing off the hood and windshield, bullets spraying everywhere. I duck.

Worse, something starts to fall, impeding our way, and I see it is a spiked iron gate. It is being lowered on the bridge, to block our entrance to Manhattan.

We're going too fast, and I can't possibly stop in time. The gate is falling too fast, and I realize, too late, that in just a few moments, we will smash into it, and it will tear our car to pieces.

I prepare for impact.

ELEVEN

I brace myself as we head for the descending gate. It's too late to turn back now, and too late to slam on the brakes. From the looks of those heavy, reinforced iron bars, with spikes at the end, I don't see how we can possibly drive through it. I figure our only chance is to outrace it, to go fast enough to slip through before it completely descends. So I floor it, the car roaring and shaking. As we get within feet of it, the guards jump out of the way, and I brace myself for impact.

There is the awful noise of metal smashing into metal, along with the noise of broken glass. It is deafening, as if a bomb has exploded right beside my car. It sounds like one of those huge car wrecking machines, crunching a car until it's flat.

Our car jerks violently on the impact, and for a moment, I feel as if I'm going to die. Shattered glass goes flying everywhere, and I do the best I can to hold it steady, while raising a hand to my eyes. And then, a second later, it's over. To my shock, we are still driving, flying over the bridge, into Manhattan.

I try to figure out what happened. I look up at our roof, and check back over my shoulder, and realize we outraced the bars—though they managed to lower just enough to slice open our roof. Our roof is now perforated, sliced into bits. It looks as if it's been put through a bread slicer. It sliced the top of our windshield, too, cracking it badly enough that my vision is impaired. I can still drive, but it's not easy.

Bits of shattered glass are everywhere, as are bits of torn metal. Freezing air rushes in and I can feel snowflakes landing on my head.

I look over and see that Ben is shaken, but unhurt. I saw him duck at the last second, just like I did, and that probably saved his life. I check over my shoulder and see the group of guards scrambling to rally and come after us; but the iron gate is all the way down, and they don't seem able to get it up again. We are going so fast, we have a big lead on them anyway. Hopefully by the time they get their act together we'll be far gone.

I turn back to the road ahead and in the distance, maybe a quarter-mile ahead, I see the other slaverunners, speeding through Manhattan. I realize that we have passed the point of no return. I can hardly conceive that we are now on the island of Manhattan, have actually crossed the bridge—probably the only bridge still working in or out of here. I realize now there is no way back.

Up to this point, I had envisioned rescuing Bree and bringing her home. But now, I'm not so sure. I'm still determined to rescue her—but I'm not sure how to get us out of here. My feeling of dread is deepening. I am increasingly feeling this is a mission of no return. A suicide mission. But Bree is all that matters. If I have to go down trying, I will.

I floor the gas again, bringing it up past 140. But the slaverunners floor it, too, still intent on evading us. They have a good head start, and unless something goes wrong, catching up to them won't be easy. I wonder what their destination is. Manhattan is vast, and they could be going anywhere. I feel like Hansel and Gretel heading into the woods.

The slaverunners make a sharp right onto a wide boulevard, and I look up and see a rusted sign which reads "125th Street." I follow them, and realize they're heading west, crosstown. As we go, I look around and see that 125th is like a postcard for the apocalypse: everywhere are abandoned, burnt-out cars, parked crookedly in the middle of the street. Everything has been stripped down and salvaged. The buildings have all been looted, the retail spaces smashed, leaving nothing but piles of glass on the sidewalks. Most buildings are just shells, burnt-out from the bomb-dropping campaigns. Others have collapsed. As I drive, I have to swerve around random piles of rubble. Needless to say, there are no signs of life.

The slaverunners make a sharp left, and as I follow them, a sign, upside down, reads "Malcolm X Boulevard." It is another wide street, and we head south, right through the heart of Harlem. Downtown. I wonder where they are heading. We turn so fast that our tires screech, burning rubber, the sound louder than ever now that our roof is open to the elements. There is still snow on the streets, and our car slides a good ten feet until it straightens out again. I take the turn faster than the slaverunners, and gain a few seconds' time.

Malcolm X Boulevard is as bad as 125th: everywhere is destruction. Yet this has something else, too: abandoned military tanks and vehicles. I spot a Humvee, turned on its side, just a shell now, and I wonder what battles took place here. A huge, bronze statue lies on its side, in the middle of the road. I swerve around it, then around a tank, driving on the sidewalk, taking out a mailbox with a huge crash. The box goes flying over our roof, and Ben ducks.

I swerve back onto the road and gun it. I'm getting closer. They are now only a hundred yards ahead of us. They swerve, too, avoiding rubble, potholes, shells of cars. They have to slow each time, but all I have to do is follow their tracks, so I can maintain speed. I'm gaining on them, and am starting to feel confident I can catch them.

"Take out their tires!" I yell to Ben, over the roar of the engine. I take the extra handgun from my waist, reach over and cram it into Ben's ribs, keeping my eyes on the road all the while.

Ben holds up the gun, examining it, and it's clear that he's never used one before. I can feel his anxiety.

"Aim low!" I say. "Make sure you don't hit the gas tank!"

"I'm not a good shot!" Ben says. "I might hit my brother. Or your sister!" he screams back.

"Just aim low!" I scream. "We have to try. We have to stop them!"

Ben swallows hard as he reaches over and opens his window. A tremendous noise and cold air races into the car as Ben leans out the window and holds out the gun.

We are closing in on them, and Ben is just beginning to take aim—when suddenly we hit a tremendous pothole. Both of us jump, and my head slams into the ceiling. I look over and see the gun go flying from Ben's hand, out the window—and then hear it clattering as it lands on the pavement behind us. My heart drops. I can't believe he has dropped the gun. I am furious.

"You just lost our gun!" I scream.

"I'm sorry!" he yells back. "You hit that pothole! Why didn't you watch the road?"

"Why didn't you hold it with both hands!?" I scream back. "You've just lost our one chance!"

"You can stop and go back for it," he says.

"There's no time!" I snap.

My face reddens. I'm starting to feel that Ben is completely useless, and regret taking him it all. I force myself to think of how he helped me with his mechanical skills, fixing the car, and of how he saved me with his body weight, back on the motorcycle, on the bridge. But it is hard to remember. Now, I'm just furious. I wonder if I can trust him with anything.

I reach into my holster, pull out my gun, and stick it into his ribs.

"This one's mine," I say. "You drop it, I'm kicking *you* out."

Ben holds it tight, with both hands, as he leans out the window again. He takes aim.

But at just that moment a park appears before us, and the slaverunners disappear right into it.

I can't believe it. Central Park lies right in front of us, marked by a huge, felled tree blocking its path. The slaverunners swerve around it and enter the park, and at the last second, I do, too. Ben leans back into the car, his chance lost—but at least he still holds the gun.

Central Park is nothing like what I remember. Covered in waist high weeds that emerge from the snow, it has been left to grow wild these past years, and now looks like a forest. Trees have fallen sporadically in all different places. Benches are empty. Statues are smashed or toppled, leaning on their sides. There are also signs of battle: tanks and Humvees, burnt out, upside down, lie throughout the park. All of this is blanketed by snow, giving it the feel of a surreal winter wonderland.

I try to take my eyes off it all, and focus instead on the slaverunners before me. They must know where they're going, as they stay on a twisting and turning service road which cuts through the park. I follow them closely as they zigzag their way through. On our right, near 110th street, we pass the remnants of a vast, empty pool. Soon after we pass the remains of a skating rink, now just an empty shell, its small outbuilding smashed and looted.

They make a sharp turn onto a narrow road, really just a trail. But I am right behind them as we go into the heart of a thick forest, narrowly missing trees, dipping and rising up and down hills. I had never realized that Central Park could be so primitive: with no sight of the skyline, I feel like I could be in a forest anywhere.

Our car slips and slides in the snowy, dirt trails, but I am able to stay with them. Soon we reach a large hilltop, and the park opens up. I see it all laid out before me. We go flying over the hilltop, and are airborne for a few seconds until we land with a crash. They race downhill, and I am right behind them, closing the gap.

We race through what were once massive ball fields. One after the other, we drive right down the center of the fields. The bases are no longer there—or if they are, they are hidden in the snow, but I can still spot what remains of the rusted, chained fences that once marked their dugouts. It is a field of white, and our car slips and slides as we follow them. We are definitely closing in, now just 30 yards away. I wonder if their engine was affected, or if they are slowing on purpose. Either way, now is our chance.

"What are you waiting for!?" I scream to Ben. "Shoot!"

Ben opens his window and leans out, clutching the pistol with both hands and taking aim.

Suddenly, the slaverunners jerk hard to the left, making a sharp turn. And then I realize, too late, why they slowed: right before me is a pond, barely frozen. Their slowing had been a trap: they had been hoping I'd drive right into the water.

I tug the wheel hard at the last second, and we just manage to miss plunging into the water. But the turn was too sharp and too fast, and our car spins out in the field of snow, spinning in large circles again and again. I feel dizzy as the world spins around and around, in a blur, and I pray we don't crash into anything.

Luckily, we don't. There are no structures anywhere around us—if there were, we surely would have crashed. Instead, after a few more 360s, we finally stop spinning. I sit there for a moment, the car stopped, breathing hard. It was a close call.

These slaverunners are smarter than I thought. It was a bold move, and they must know this terrain well. They know exactly where they're going. I'm guessing no one else has ever managed to follow them as far as we have. I look over and see that Ben has managed to hold onto the gun this time; another lucky break. I shake out the cobwebs, put it back in gear, and floor it.

Suddenly, there is a loud beeping noise, and I look down to see a red light flashing on the dash: GAS LOW.

My heart drops. Not now. Not after all we've been through. Not when we're this close.

Please God, just give us enough gas to catch them.

The beeping continues incessantly, loud in my ear, like a death knoll, as I follow them across the snowy fields. I've lost sight of them, and have to resort to following their tracks. As I follow their tracks up a hill, I come to an intersection and see tracks crisscrossing in every direction. I'm not sure which way to fork, and it feels like it might be another trap. I decide to stay the course, straight ahead, but even as I do, I have a sinking feeling that these tracks are old, and that they might've turned off somewhere.

Suddenly, the sky opens up, and I find myself driving on a narrow lane, beside what was once the Central Park Reservoir. I look over at it, and am shocked by the site: it is like a huge crater in the Earth, now empty of water and lined with snow. Huge weeds grow up from its bottom. This lane is narrow, and barely fits the width of my car, and as I look to my left, I see a steep drop-off down the hill. But to my right, there is an even steeper drop-off to the bottom of the reservoir. One wrong move in either direction, and we are toast. I look ahead, wondering why the slaverunners would choose such a perilous route. But I still can't see any signs of their car.

Suddenly, there is a crash, and my head snaps forward. At first I'm confused, and then I realize: we've been hit from behind.

I look in the rearview and see they're right behind us. I can see the sadistic smiles on both of their faces. Their facemasks are lifted, and I can see that they're both Biovictims, with grotesque, unnatural faces, misshapen, and huge buck teeth. I can see the sadism, the joy they take as they speed up and ram us again from behind. My neck snaps forward on the impact. They are much smarter than I thought: somehow, they managed to get behind us, and now, they have the advantage. I had not expected this. I have no room to maneuver, and I can't slam on the brakes.

They smash into us again, this time angling the car as they do, and our car slips to the side. We smash into the steel railing of the reservoir, then slide over the other way and almost fall off the cliff. They've got us in a bad position. If they smash us again like that, we will roll downhill and be finished.

I step on the gas, realizing the only way out is to outrun them. But they are going just as fast, and they hit us again. This time, we smash into the metal divider and slide further, about to go over the cliff. Luckily, we smash into a tree and it saves us, keeps us back on the road.

I'm feeling increasingly desperate. I look over, and see that Ben seems stunned, too, looking more pale than before. Suddenly, I have an idea.

"Shoot them!" I scream.

He immediately opens his window and leans out with the gun.

"I can't hit their tires from here!" he screams over the wind. "They're too close! The angle is too steep!"

"Aim for the windshield!" I scream back. "Don't kill the driver. Take out the passenger!"

I can see in my rearview that they copy our idea: the passenger is lowering his window, taking out his gun, too. I only pray that Ben hits them first, that he's not afraid to fire. Suddenly, several shots ring out, deafening even above the noise.

I flinch, half-expecting to feel a bullet hit me in the head.

But I am surprised to realize that it is Ben who has fired. I check the rearview, and can't believe what I see: Ben's aim was perfect. He hit the passenger's side of the windshield several times—so many times, in the same spot, that he seems to have actually punctured the bulletproof glass. I see the red splattering the inside of the windshield, and that can only mean one thing. Blood.

I can't believe it: Ben has managed to shoot the passenger. Ben. The boy who just minutes ago was traumatized to see a dead body. I can't believe he actually hit him, and at this speed.

It works. Their car suddenly slows down dramatically, and I use the opportunity to floor it.

Moments later, we are out of the reservoir, and back into open fields. Now, the game has changed: they have a man down, and we are caught up to them. Now, finally, we have the advantage. If only the "low gas" gauge would stop beeping, I would actually feel optimistic.

Their car comes flying out behind us, and I slow, pull up beside them, and spot the worried look on the driver's face. That is the confirmation I need: I am relieved to know that it was, indeed, the passenger who was hit, and not Bree. As I look over, I catch a glimpse of Bree, alive, in the backseat, and my heart soars with hope. For the first time, I feel I can really do this. I can get her back.

We're now racing side-by-side, in the open field, and I pull hard on the wheel and smash into them. Their car goes flying across the field, swerving wildly. But it doesn't go down. And without missing a beat, their driver comes right back at me, smashing into us. Now we go swerving wildly. This guy just won't quit.

"Shoot!" I scream again to Ben. "Take out the driver!"

I realize their car will crash, but we have no choice. And if it has to crash anywhere, this open field, surrounded by trees, is the best place.

Ben immediately lowers his window and takes aim, more confident this time. We're driving alongside him, perfectly lined up, and we have a direct line of fire to the driver. This is our moment.

"SHOOT!" I scream again.

Ben pulls the trigger, and suddenly, I hear a sound that makes my stomach drop.

The click of an empty gun. Ben pulls the trigger again and again, but it is nothing but clicks. He used all of our ammo back at the reservoir.

I spot an evil, victorious smile on the slaverunner's face, as he suddenly swerves right into us. He smashes us hard, and we go flying across the snowy field, onto a grassy hill, and suddenly I look up and see a wall of glass. Too late.

I brace myself as we drive through the glass wall, shattering like a bomb all around us, raining down shards of glass through the holes in the roof. It takes a moment until I realize where we are: the Metropolitan Museum of Art. The Egyptian Wing. We have just driven through its glass wall.

I look over and can tell that nothing is left in the museum, looted long ago; but I do see the huge pyramid, still in the room. I finally manage to swerve away, and stop driving through glass. The other slaverunner gained some distance, and is now about 50 yards ahead, to my right, and once again, I step on it.

I follow him as he continues racing south through the park, up and down rolling hills. I worriedly check the gas gauge, which won't stop beeping. We pass the remnants of an amphitheater, beside a pond, in the shadow of the Belvedere Castle, now sitting as a ruin atop the hill. The theater is now just covered in snow and weeds, its bleachers rusted.

We race across what was once the Great Lawn, and I follow his tracks in the snow, weaving, avoiding holes. I feel so bad for Bree as I think of what she must be going through. I only pray this hasn't traumatized her too much. I pray that some part of our Dad is with her, keeps her strong and tough through all of this.

Suddenly, I have a lucky break: up ahead, they hit a huge pothole. His car shakes, then swerves violently, and he loses control, doing a wide 360. I find myself flinching with them, hoping that Bree doesn't get hurt.

Their car is OK. After a couple of spins, it regains traction, and they begin speeding again. But now I have closed the gap, and am closing in fast. In just a few more seconds, I'll be right behind him.

But I've been staring at his vehicle, and stupidly, I take my eyes off the road. I look back just in time, and find myself freezing up: there is a huge animal right in front of us.

I swerve, but too late. It hits us square against the windshield, splattering, and tumbles over the roof. There are blood stains all over the glass, and I run the wipers, grateful they still work. The thick blood smears, and I can barely see.

I check the rearview, wondering what the hell it was, and see a huge, dead ostrich behind us. I am bewildered. But I have no time to process this, because suddenly, I am amazed to see a lion in front of us.

I swerve hard, barely missing it. I do a double take, and am shocked to see it's real. It is lean and looks malnourished. I am even more baffled. Then, finally, I spot the source of it: there, on my left, is the Central Park zoo, its gates and doors and windows all wide open. Milling nearby are a few animals, and lying in the snow are the dead carcasses of several more, their bodies long ago picked clean.

I step on the gas, trying not to look, as I follow the slaverunner's tracks. They lead us up a small hill, then down a steep hill, right into a crater. I realize this was once a skating rink. A large sign hangs crookedly, its letters worn away, and reads "Trump."

In the distance, I finally see that the park is coming to an end. He turns hard to the left, and I follow him, and we both race up a hill. Moments later, we both burst out of Central Park—at the same time, side by side—exiting on 59th Street and Fifth Avenue. I go flying over the hill, and for a moment my car is airborne. We land with a crash, and I momentarily lose control, as we slide into a statue, toppling it.

Before us is a huge circular fountain; I swerve out of the way at the last second, and chase him around the circle. He jumps up onto the sidewalk, and I follow him, and he heads right for a massive building. The Plaza Hotel. Its former façade, once immaculate, is now covered in grime and neglect. Its windows all smashed, it looks like a tenement.

He smashes into the rusted rods holding the awning, and as he does, it comes crashing down, bouncing off his hood. I swerve out of the way, then follow him as he makes a sharp left and cuts across Fifth Avenue, clearly trying to shake me. He races up a small stone staircase, and I follow, our car shaking violently with each step.

I look up and see that he heads for the huge, glass box of what was once the Apple Store. Amazingly, its façade is still intact. It is, in fact, the only intact thing I've seen anywhere since the war began.

Not anymore. At the last second he swerves out of the way, and it is too late for me to turn. Our car smashes right into the façade of the Apple box. There's a tremendous explosion of glass, and it rains down through the holes in our roof as I ride right through the Apple Store. I feel a little guilty to have destroyed the one thing left standing—but then again, I think of how much I paid for an iPad back in the day, and my guilt lessens.

I regain control and follow him as he makes a left down Fifth Avenue. He's got about thirty yards on me, but I won't give up, like a dog chasing a bone. I just hope our gas holds.

As I drive down Fifth Avenue, I am amazed at what it has become. This famed avenue, once the beacon of prosperity and materialism, is now, like everything else, just an abandoned, dilapidated, shell, its stores looted, its retail spaces destroyed. Huge weeds grow right down the middle of it, and it looks like a marshland. Bergdorf's flies by, on my right, its floors completely empty, no windows left, like a ghost house. I swerve around abandoned cars, and as we hit 57th Street, I spot what was once

Tiffany's. This place, once the hallmark of beauty, is now just another haunted mansion, like everything else. Not a single jewel remains in its empty windows.

I step on the gas and we cross 55th, then 54th, then 53rd Streets…. I pass a cathedral, Saint Patrick's, on my left, its huge arched doors torn off long ago, now lying flat, face down, on its staircase. I can see right into its open structure, right to the stained glass on the other side.

I have taken my eyes off the road too long, and suddenly the slaverunner makes a sharp right onto 48th Street. I'm going too fast, and when I try to make the turn I skid out, doing a 360. Luckily I don't hit anything.

I come back around and follow him, but his tricky move has gained him some distance. I follow him across 48th, heading west, crosstown, and I find myself what was once Rockefeller Center. I remember coming here with Dad, at Christmas time, remember thinking how magical it was. I can't believe it now: everywhere is rubble, crumbling buildings. Rock Center has become a massive wasteland.

Again, I take my eyes off the road too long, and as I look back, I slam on the brakes, but there isn't time. Right in front of me, lying on its side, is the huge Rockefeller Christmas tree. We are going to hit it. Right before we make impact, I can see some lights and ornaments still left on it. The tree is brown, and I wonder how long it's been laying here.

I smash right into it, doing 120. I hit it with such force, the entire tree shifts on the snow, and I'm pushing it, dragging it along. Finally, I manage to swerve hard to the right, getting around the narrow tip of it. Thousands of pine needles sprinkle down through the gaping holes in our roof. A bunch more stick to the blood still matted to our windshield. I can't imagine what our car looks like from the outside.

This slaverunner knows the city too well: his smart moves have gained him another advantage, and he is now out of sight. But I still see his tracks and up ahead, I see he's made a left on Sixth Avenue. I follow him.

Sixth Avenue is another wasteland, it streets filled with abandoned tanks and Humvees, most upside down, all stripped of anything that might be useful, including the tires. I swerve in and out of these as I see the slaverunner up ahead. I wonder for the millionth time where he could be heading. Is he crisscrossing the city just to lose me? Does he have a destination in mind? I think hard, trying to remember where Arena One is located. But I have no idea. Up until today, I was never even sure it really existed.

He guns it down Sixth and so do I, finally gaining speed. As we cross 43rd, on my left, I catch a glimpse of Bryant Park, and the rear of what was once the New York Public Library. My heart drops. I used to love going into that magnificent building. Now, it is nothing but rubble.

The slaverunner makes a sharp right on 42nd street, and this time I'm right behind him. We both skid, then straighten out. We race down 42nd, heading West, and I wonder if he's heading for the West Side highway.

The street opens up, and we are in Times Square. He bursts into the square and I follow, entering the vast intersection. I remember coming here as a kid, being so overwhelmed by the size and scope of it, by all the people. I remember being dazzled by all the lights, the flashing billboards. Now, like everything else, it is a ruin. Of course, none of the lights work, and there is not a single person in sight. All the billboards that used to hang so proudly now either dangle precariously in the wind, or lie face down on the street below. Huge weeds cover the intersection. In its center, where there was once an army recruiting center, now, ironically, lie the shells of several tanks, all twisted and blown up. I wonder what battle took place here.

Suddenly, the slaverunner makes a sharp left, heading down Broadway. I follow, and as I do, I am shocked by what I see before me: an enormous cement wall, like a prison wall, rises high into the sky, topped with barbed wire. The wall stretches as far as I can see, blocking off Times Square from whatever lies south of it. As if trying to keep something out. There is an opening in the wall, and the slaverunners drive right through it; as they pass through, a massive iron gate suddenly slams down behind them, shutting them off from me.

I slam on the brakes, screeching the car to a halt right before we smash into it. In the distance, I see the slaverunners taking off. It is too late. I have lost them.

I can't believe it. I feel numb. I sit there, frozen, in the silence, our car stopped for the first time in hours, and feel my body trembling. I hadn't foreseen this. I wonder why this wall is here, why they would wall off a part of Manhattan. What they would need protection from.

And then, a moment later, I have my answer.

An eerie noise rises up all around me, the sound of screeching metal, and the hair raises on the back my neck. I turn and see people rise up from the earth, popping up from manholes in every direction. Biovictims. All throughout Times Square. They are emaciated, dressed in rags, and look desperate. The Crazies.

They really do exist.

They rise from the earth, all around us, and head right for us.

TWELVE

Before I can even react, I sense movement high above, and look up. Standing up high, atop the wall, are several slaverunners, wearing their black face masks, holding machine guns. They aim them down towards us.

"DRIVE!" Ben screams, frantic.

I'm already stepping on the gas, tearing out of there, as the first gunshots ring out. A hail of fire pours down on the car, bouncing off the roof, off the metal, off the bulletproof glass. I only pray that it doesn't slip between the cracks.

Simultaneously, the crazies rush us from all sides. One of them reaches back and throws a glass bottle with a burning rag on it. A Molotov cocktail lands right before our car and explodes, the flames rising before us. I swerve just in time, and the flames graze the side of our car.

Another comes running up and jumps on the windshield. He grabs on and won't let go, his face snarling at me through the glass, inches away. I swerve again, scraping against a pole, and it knocks him off.

Several more jump on the hood and trunk, weighing us down. I floor it, trying to shake them, as I continue west across 42nd.

But three of them manage to hold onto our car. One of them is dragging on the cement, and another is crawling his way up the hood, towards us. He raises a crow bar and prepares to bring it down, right on the windshield.

I make a sharp turn sharp left on Eighth Avenue, and that does it. The three of them go flying off the car, and sliding across the snow on the ground.

It was a close call. Too close.

I race down Eighth Avenue, and as I do, spot another opening in the wall. Several slaverunner guards stand before it, and I realize they might not know I'm not one of theirs. After all, the Times Square entrance is an entire avenue away. If I drive right for it, confidently, maybe they'll assume I'm one of theirs, and keep it open.

I aim right for it, going faster and faster, closing the distance. A hundred yards…fifty…thirty…. I race right for the opening, and so far, it's still open. There's no stopping now. And if they bring it down, we're dead.

I brace myself, and so does Ben. I'm almost expecting us to crash.

But a moment later, we are through it. We made it. I exhale with relief.

We're in. I'm doing 100 now as I race down Eighth Avenue, against the one way. I am about to make a left, to try to catch them on Broadway, when suddenly, Ben leans forward and points.

"THERE!" he screams.

I squint, trying to see what he's pointing at. The windshield is still covered in blood and pine needles.

"THERE!" he screams again.

I look again, and this time I see it: there, ten blocks ahead. A group of Humvees, parked outside Penn Station. I see the slaverunner car I've been chasing, the vehicle parked out front, sitting there, exhaust still smoking. The driver is out of the car, hurrying down the steps to Penn Station, dragging Bree and Ben's brother, both of them handcuffed, chained together. My heart leaps at the sight of her.

The empty fuel gauge is beeping louder than ever, and I gun it. All I need is a few more blocks. *Come on. Come on!*

Somehow, we make it. I screech up to the entrance, and am about to pull to a stop and jump out, when I realize we have lost too much time. There is only one way we're going to catch them: I have to keep driving, right into Penn Station. It's a steep decline, down narrow, stone steps, to the entrance. It's not a staircase meant for cars, and I wonder if our car can handle it. It's going to be painful. I brace myself.

"HOLD ON!" I scream.

I make a sharp left and floor it, gaining speed. I'm up past 140. Ben clutches the dash, as he realizes what I'm doing. "SLOW DOWN!" he screams.

But it's too late now. We are airborne, flying over the ledge, then driving straight down the stone steps. My body is so jolted, the tires bouncing with every step, that I am unable to control the car. We fly faster and faster, carried by our own momentum, and I brace myself as we crash right through the doors of Penn Station. The door goes flying off its hinges, and the next thing I know, we are inside.

We gain traction and I finally get control back of the car, as we drive on dry ground for the first time. We drive down another flight of steps, screeching through. There is a tremendous slam, as we hit the ground floor.

We are in the huge Amtrak console, and I'm driving across the cavernous room, tires screeching as I try to even out the car. Up ahead are dozens of slaverunners, milling about. They turn and look at me with shock, clearly unable to comprehend how a car got down here. I don't want to give them time to gather themselves. I aim right for them, like bowling pins.

They try to run out of the way, but I speed up and smash into several of them. They hit our car with a thud, bodies twisting, and go flying over the hood.

I keep driving, and in the distance, I see the slaverunner who kidnapped my sister. I spot Ben's brother, being loaded onto a train. I assume Bree is already on it.

"That's my brother!" Ben screams.

The train door closes and I gun our car one last time, for all it's worth, aiming right for the slaverunner who stole her. He stands there like a deer in the headlights, having just shoved Ben's brother onto the train. He stares right at me as I close in.

I smash into him, sandwiching him against the train and cutting him in half. We hit the train doing 80, and my head slams into the dash. I feel the whiplash, as we grind to a halt.

My head is spinning, my ears ringing. Faintly, I can hear the sound of other slaverunners rallying, chasing after me. The train is still moving—our car didn't even slow it. Ben is sitting there, unconscious. I wonder if he's dead.

It takes a superhuman effort, but somehow I peel myself out of the car.

The train is gaining speed now, and I have to run to catch up to it. I run alongside the train and finally leap, gaining a foothold on the ledge and grabbing onto a metal bar. I stick my head in a window, looking for any sign of Bree. I scramble along its outside, looking window to window, making my way towards a train door to let myself in.

The train is going so fast, I can feel the wind in my hair, as I desperately try to reach the door. I look over and my heart drops to see that we are about to enter a tunnel. There is no room. If I don't get in soon, I will smash into the wall.

Finally, I reach over and grab the door handle. Just as I'm about to open it, suddenly, I feel a tremendous pain smashing into the side of my head.

I go flying through the air, and a moment later land hard on my back, on the cement floor. It is a ten foot drop, and the wind is knocked out of me as I lay there, on my back, watching the train speed away. I realize that someone must have punched me, knocked me off the train.

I look up and see the face of a vicious slaverunner standing over me, scowling down. Several more slaverunners hurry over, too. They're closing in around me. I realize I'm finished.

But it doesn't matter: the train is speeding away, and my sister is on it.

My life is already over.

PART III

THIRTEEN

I wake to blackness. I am so disoriented, so achy, at first I wonder if I am dead or alive. I lie on a cold, metal floor, twisted in an unnatural position, my face against the floor. I turn, slowly reach out, place my palms against the floor, and try to push myself up.

Every movement hurts. There doesn't seem to be any part of me that is spared from pain. As I slowly sit upright, my head is splitting. I feel dizzy, nauseous, weak, and hungry all at the same time. I realize I haven't eaten in at least a day. My throat is parched, and I'm dying of thirst. I feel like I've been put through a blender.

I sit there, my head spinning, and finally I realize that I'm not dead. Somehow, I am still alive.

I look around the room, trying to get my bearings, wondering where I am. It is black in here, and the only light filters in through a narrow slit underneath a door, somewhere on the far side of the room. It is not enough to show me anything.

Gradually, I rise to one knee, holding my head, trying to alleviate the pain. Just this small gesture makes my world spin. I wonder if I've been drugged, or if I'm just this dizzy from the endless string of injuries I sustained in the last 24 hours.

With a supreme effort, I force myself to my feet. Big mistake. All at once, I feel pain from at least a dozen different areas: the wound in my arm; my cracked ribs; my forehead, from where it smashed against the dash; and from the side of my face. I reach up and feel a big welt; that must be where the slaverunner punched me when I was clinging to the train.

I try to remember…. Penn Station…running over slaverunners…smashing into the train…running for the train…jumping onto it…and then being hit…. I think back, and realize that Ben didn't accompany me. I remember seeing him sitting in the car, unconscious. Suddenly, I wonder if he survived the crash at all.

"Ben?" I call out tentatively, into the darkness.

I wait, hoping for a response, hoping maybe he is in here with me. I squint into the blackness, but am unable to see anything. There is nothing but silence. My sense of dread deepens.

I wonder again if Bree was on that train, and where it was going. I recall seeing Ben's brother on it, but I can't remember actually seeing Bree. I am surprised that any train still works these days. Could they be transporting them to Arena One?

None of that matters now. Who knows how many hours I've been out, how much time I've lost. Who knows where the train was heading, or how many hundreds of miles it has already gained. There is no way I can catch up to them—assuming I can even escape from here. Which I doubt. I feel a sense of anguish and despair as I realize that it was all for nothing. Now, it is just a matter of awaiting my punishment, my certain death, my retribution from the slaverunners. They will probably torture me, then kill me. I just pray it's over quick.

I wonder if there is any possible way I can escape from here. I begin to take a few tentative steps in the blackness, holding my hands out in front of me. Each step is agony, my body so weary, heavy with aches and pains. It is cold in here, too, and I am trembling; I haven't been able to get warm for days, and I feel like I'm running a fever. Even if by some chance I can find a way to escape, I doubt I'm in shape to get very far.

I feel a wall and run my hands along it as I move about the room, making my way towards the door. Suddenly, I hear a noise from outside. This is followed by the sound of footsteps, several pair of combat boots marching along steel floors. They echo ominously in the darkness as they get closer.

There is a rattling of keys, and the door to my cell is pushed open. Light floods the interior, and I raise my hands to my eyes, blinded.

My eyes haven't adjusted yet, but I see enough to make out silhouettes of several figures in the entrance. They are tall and muscular, and looked to be dressed in slaverunner uniforms, with their black face masks.

I slowly lower my hands as my eyes adjust. There are five of them. The one standing in the center silently holds out a pair of open handcuffs. He doesn't speak or move, and from his gesture, it seems clear I'm supposed to walk over and allow him to cuff me. It seems they are waiting to take me somewhere.

I quickly survey my cell, now that it is flooded with light, and see it is a simple room, ten by ten feet, with steel floors and walls, and nothing in it to speak of. And no way to escape. I slowly run my hands along my waist and feel that my weapon belt has been stripped and taken away. I'm defenseless. It would be no use in trying to fight these soldiers, who are well-armed.

I don't see what I have to lose by allowing them to cuff me. It's not like I have a choice. Either way, this will be my ticket out of here. And if it's a ticket to my death, at least I'll get it over with.

I walk slowly to them and turn around. I feel the cold, metal cuffs clamp down on my wrists, way too tightly. Then I am grabbed from behind, by my shirt, and given a shove out into the corridor.

I stumble down the corridor, the slaverunners right behind me, their boots echoing like a group of Gestapos. The halls are sporadically lit by dim emergency lights, every twenty feet or so, and each offers just enough light to see by. It is a long, sterile, hallway, with metal floors and walls. I am shoved again, and increase my pace. Each step is agony, as my body protests, but the more I walk, the more the stiffness begins to loosen.

The hall ends and I've no choice but to turn right, and as I do, I can see it opens in the distance. I'm shoved again as I am marched down this new hall, and next thing I know, I am standing in a vast and open room.

I am surprised to see that the room is filled with hundreds of slaverunners. They are lined up in neat rows along the walls, forming a semi-circle, dressed in their black uniforms and facemasks. We must still be underground somewhere, as I spot no windows or natural light, the gloomy room lit only by torches placed along the walls. They crackle in the silence.

In the center of the room, on the far side, is what I can only describe as a throne—an enormous chair built atop a makeshift wooden platform. On this chair sits a single man, clearly their leader. He looks young, maybe in his 30s, yet has an odd shock of white hair, sticking straight up and extending out in every direction, like a mad scientist. He wears an elaborate uniform made of green velvet, with military buttons all along it, and high collars framing his neck. He has large, grey, lifeless eyes, which bulge open and stare back at me. He looks like a maniac.

The rows of slaverunners part ways, and I'm shoved from behind. I stumble forward, towards the center of the room, and am guided to stand before their leader.

I stand about ten yards away, looking up at him, the slaverunners standing guard behind me. I can't help wondering if they're going to execute me on the spot. After all, I've killed many of theirs. I scan the room for any sign of

Bree, or Ben, or his brother. There is no one. I am alone.

I wait patiently in the tense silence, as the leader looks me up and down. There is nothing I can do but wait. Apparently, my fate is now in the hands of this man.

He looks at me as if I were a thing of prey, and then, after what feels like forever, he surprises me by slowly breaking into a smile. It is more of a sneer, marred by the huge scar running along his cheek. He begins to laugh, deeper and deeper. It is the coldest sound I've ever heard, and echoes in the dim room. He stares down at me with glistening eyes.

"So, you are the one," he says finally. He voice is unnaturally gravelly and deep, as if it belongs to a hundred-year-old man.

I stare back, not knowing how to respond.

"*You* are the one that has wreaked such havoc among my men. You are the one that managed to chase us all the way into the city. Into MY city. New York is mine now. Did you know that?" he asks, his voice suddenly becoming sharp with fury, as his eyes bulge. He clutches the arms of the chair and I can see his arms trembling. He looks like he's just escaped from a mental hospital.

Again, I don't know how to respond, so I remain silent.

He slowly shakes his head.

"A few others once tried—but no one has ever managed to cross into my city before. Or come all the way down to my home. You knew it would mean certain death. And yet still, you came." He looks me up and down.

"I like you," he concludes.

As he stares at me, summing me up, I feel more and more uncomfortable, bracing myself for whatever is to come.

"And look at you," he continues. "Just a girl. A stupid, young girl. Not even big, or strong. With hardly any weapons to speak of. How can it be that you killed so many of my men?"

He shakes his head.

"It is because you have heart. That is what is valuable in this world. Yes, that is what is valuable." He suddenly laughs. "Of course, you did not succeed, though. How could you? This is MY city!" he suddenly shrieks, his body shaking.

He sits there, trembling, for what feels like forever. My sense of apprehension deepens; clearly, my fate is the hands of a maniac.

Finally, he clears his throat.

"Your spirit is strong. Almost like mine. I admire it. It is enough to make me want to kill you quickly, instead of slowly."

I swallow hard, not liking the sound of this.

"Yes," he continues, staring. "I can see it in your eyes. A warrior's spirit. Yes, you are just like me."

I don't know what he sees in me, but I pray that I am nothing like this man.

"It is rare to find someone like you. Few have managed to survive out there, all these years. Few have such spirit…. So, instead of executing you now, as you deserve, I am going to reward you. I am going to offer you a great gift. The gift of free will. A choice.

"You can join us. Become one of us. A slaverunner. You will have every luxury you can imagine—more food than you can dream of. You will lead a division of slaverunners. You know your territory well. Those mountains. I can use you, yes. You will lead expeditions, capture all remaining survivors. You will help grow our army. And in return, you will live. And live in luxury."

He stops, staring me down, as if waiting for a response.

Of course, the thought of this makes me sick. A slaverunner. I can't think of anything I'd despise more. I open my mouth to respond, but at first my throat is so parched, nothing comes out. I clear my throat.

"And if I refuse?" I ask, the words coming out more softly than I want.

His eyes open wide in surprise.

191

"Refuse?" he echoes. "Then you will be put to death in the arena. You will die a vicious death, to all of our amusement. That is your other option."

I think hard, wracking my brain, trying to buy more time. There is no way I will ever accept his proposition—but I need to try to think of a way out.

"And what about my sister?" I ask.

He leans back and smiles.

"If you join us, I will free her. She will be free to return to the wilderness. If you refuse, of course, she will be put to death, too."

My heart pounds at the thought of it. So, that means that Bree is still alive. Assuming he is telling the truth.

I think hard. If my becoming a slaverunner would save Bree's life, is that something she'd want me to do? She wouldn't. Bree would never want to be the one responsible for my kidnapping other young girls and boys, taking their lives away. I would do anything to save her. But I have to draw the line here.

"You will have to put me to death," I finally respond. "There is no way I would ever be a slaverunner."

There is a murmur among the crowd, and the leader reaches up and slams his palm on the chair of his arm. The room immediately quiets.

He stands, scowling down at me.

"You *will* be put to death," he snarls. "And I will I have a front row seat to watch it."

FOURTEEN

I am marched back down the corridor, still handcuffed. As I go, I can't help but wonder if I made the wrong decision. Not about giving up my life—but about giving up Bree's. Should I have said yes for her sake?

By refusing, I have effectively given her a death sentence. I feel torn by remorse. But ultimately, I still can't help but think that Bree would rather die, too, than see innocent people get hurt.

I feel numb as they shove me from behind, back down the corridor from which I came, and wonder what will become of me now. Are they marching me to the arena? What will it be like? And what will become of Bree? Will they really kill her? Have they already killed her? Will they put her into slavery? Or, worst of all, will she be forced to fight in the arena, too?

And then an even worse thought come to mind: might she be forced to fight against me?

We turn the corner and I suddenly see a group of slaverunners marching towards me, leading someone. I can't believe it. It is Ben. My heart floods with relief. He is alive.

His broken nose is swollen, there are bruises under his eyes, blood drips from his lip, and he looks as if he's been roughed up. He looks as weak and exhausted as I do. In fact, I hope I don't look as bad as he. He, too, stumbles down the hall, and I assume they are taking him to see their leader. I assume they will make him the same offer. I wonder what he will decide.

As we walk towards each other, only a few feet away, his head hangs low and he doesn't even see me coming. He's either too weak, or too demoralized, to even look up. It appears he has already accepted his fate.

"Ben!" I call out.

He lifts his head, just as our paths cross, and his eyes open wide with hope and excitement. He is clearly shocked to see me. Maybe he's surprised I'm alive, too.

"Brooke!" he says. "Where are they taking you? Have you seen my brother?"

But before I can respond I am shoved hard from behind, and Ben is shoved, too. A slaverunner reaches over and clamps my mouth with his disgusting, smelly palm, and as I try to call out, my words are muffled.

A door is opened, and I am shoved back into my cell. I go stumbling in, and the door is slammed behind me, the metal reverberating. I spin around and bang on the door, but it's no use.

"LET ME OUT!" I scream, banging. "LET ME OUT!"

I realize it is no use, but somehow, I can't stop myself from screaming. I scream at the world, at these slaverunners, at Bree's absence, at my life—and I don't stop screaming until I don't know how much later.

At some point I lose my voice, tire myself out. Finally, I find myself slumped on the floor, against the wall, curled up.

My screams turn to sobs, and eventually, I cry myself to sleep.

*

Time passes, I don't know how much, and I drift in and out of sleep. I lie curled up on the metal floor, resting my head in my hands, but it is so uncomfortable, I twist and turn. I have fast, troubled dreams, and force myself to stay awake. My dreams are so disturbing—of Bree being whipped as a slave, of myself being tortured in an arena—that, as exhausted as I am, I'd rather be awake.

I force myself to sit up, and I sit there, staring into the darkness, holding my head in my hands. I will myself to focus of anything that might take me away from this place.

I find myself thinking about life before the war. I am still trying to piece together exactly why Dad left, when he did, and why he never came back for us. Why Bree and I left. Why Mom wouldn't come with us. Why things changed so much overnight. If there is anything I could have done differently. It is like a puzzle I turn over and over again.

I find myself thinking back, to one day before the war began. The day when everything changed—for the second time.

It was a warm September day, and I was still living in Manhattan with Mom and Bree. Dad had been gone for over a year, and every day we waited for some sign of him. But there was nothing.

And while we all waited, day after day, the war grew worse. One day a blockade was declared; weeks later, they declared a conservation of water; then, food rations. Food lines became the norm. And from there things became even worse, as people grew desperate.

It became more and more dangerous to walk the streets of Manhattan. People started doing anything they could to survive, to find food and water, to hoard medicine. Looting became the norm, and order broke down more each day. I didn't feel safe anymore. And more importantly, I didn't feel Bree was safe, either.

My Mom clung to her denial; like most people, she kept insisting things would come back to normal soon.

But things only got worse. Battles came closer to home. One day I heard distant explosions, and I ran to the roof and saw, on the horizon, battles on the cliffs of New Jersey. Tank against tank. Fighter jets. Helicopters. There were explosions, entire neighborhoods on fire.

And then, one horrible day, on the far horizon, I saw a tremendous explosion, one that was different than the others, one that shook our whole building. Miles away, on the horizon, I saw a mushroom cloud rise. That was the day I knew that things would never get better. That the war would never end. A line had been crossed. We would slowly and certainly die here, trapped on the blockaded island of Manhattan. My Dad would be in battles forever. And he would never return.

I realized the time for waiting was over. I knew that, for the first time in his life, he would *not* be good to his word, and I knew then what I had to do: it was time to make a bold move for the survival of what was left of our family. To do what he would want his daughter to do: to get us off this island, far from here, and into the safety of the mountains.

I had been pleading with Mom for months to accept the fact that Dad would not come home. But she refused to accept it. She kept insisting that we couldn't leave, that this was our home, that life would be even more dangerous outside the city. And most of all, that we couldn't abandon Dad. What if he came home and we were gone?

She and I would argue about it every day until we were both red in the face, screaming at each other. We reached a stalemate. We ended up hating each other, barely talking to one another.

Then came the mushroom cloud. My Mom, unbelievingly, still refused to leave. But I had made up my mind. We were leaving—with or without her.

I went downstairs to get Bree. She had snuck out, to scavenge for food; I allowed her this, since she never went far, and always came back within the hour. But this time, she was late; she was gone for hours now, and it was unlike her. I had a sinking feeling in my chest as I ran down flight after flight, determined to find her and get the hell out of here. In my hand I held a homemade Molotov cocktail. It was the only real weapon I had, and I was prepared to use it if need be.

I ran into the streets screaming her name, looking for her everywhere. I checked down every alley she liked to play in—but she was nowhere to be found. My dread deepened.

And then I heard a faint screaming in the distance. I recognized her voice, and I sprinted towards it.

After blocks, the screaming grew louder. Finally, I turned down a narrow alleyway, and I saw her.

Bree was standing at the end of an alley, surrounded by a group of attackers. There were six of them, teenage boys. One of them reached out and tore her shirt while another pulled her ponytail. She swung her backpack to try to fend them off, but it did little good. I could tell that in a matter of moments, they would rape her. So I did the only thing I could do: I lit the Molotov cocktail and threw it at the foot of the largest boy I could find….

I am jolted out of my reverie by the sudden sound of creaking metal, a door slowly opening, of light flooding the room, then the door slamming. I hear chains, then footsteps, and sense another body near me in the blackness. I look up.

I'm relieved to see that it is Ben. I don't know how much time has passed, or how long I've been sitting here. I sit up slowly.

Our cell is lit by dim, emergency bulbs, red, encased in metal, high up along the wall. It is just enough to see by. I see Ben stumbling into the cell, looking disoriented; he doesn't even realize I'm here, on the floor.

"Ben!" I whisper, my voice hoarse.

He wheels and sees me, and his eyes open wide in surprise.

"Brooke?" he asks tentatively.

I struggle to get to my feet, feeling aches and pains tear through every part of my body as I take a knee. As I begin to stand, he runs over and grabs my arm and pulls me up. I know I should be grateful for his help, but instead, I find myself resenting it: it is the first time he has touched me, and it was uninvited, and that makes me feel funny. Plus, I don't like being helped by people in general—and especially by a boy.

So I shake off his arm off and stand on my own.

"I can handle myself," I snap at him, and my words come out too harsh. I regret it, wishing that, instead, I told him how I really felt. I wish I'd said: *I'm happy you're alive. I'm relieved that you're here, with me.*

As I think about it, I realize that I don't quite understand why I am so happy to see him. Maybe I'm just happy to see another regular person, like me, a survivor, in the midst of all these mercenaries. Maybe it's because we've both suffered through the same ordeal in the last 24 hours, or maybe because we've both lost our siblings.

Or maybe, I hesitate to wonder, it's something else.

Ben stares back at me with his large blue eyes, and for a brief moment, I find myself losing sense of time. His are eyes are so sensitive, so out of place here. They are the eyes of a poet, or painter—an artist, a tortured soul.

I force myself to look away. There's something about those eyes that makes me unable to think clearly when I look back at them. I don't know what it is, and that bothers me. I've never felt this way about a boy before. I can't help wondering if I just feel connected to Ben because of our shared circumstance, or if it's something else.

To be sure, there are many moments when I am annoyed and angry with him—and I still find myself blaming him for everything that happened. For example, if I hadn't stopped and saved him on the highway, maybe I'd have rescued Bree and be back home by now. Or if he hadn't dropped my gun out the window, maybe I could have saved her in Central Park. And I wish he was stronger, more of a fighter. But at the same time, there is something about him which makes me feel close to him.

"I'm sorry," he says, flustered, and his voice is already that of a broken man. "I didn't mean to offend you."

Slowly, I soften. I realize it's not his fault. He's not the bad guy.

"Where did they take you?" I ask.

"To their leader. He asked me to join them."

"Did you accept?" I ask. My heart flutters as I wait for the answer. If he says yes, I would think so much less of him; in fact, I wouldn't even be able to look at him again.

"Of course not," he says.

My heart swells with relief, and admiration. I know what a sacrifice that is. Like me, he has just written his own death sentence.

"Did you?" he asks.

"What do you think?" I say.

"No," he says. "I suspect not."

I look over and see that he cradles one of his fingers, which is bent out of shape. He looks like he's in pain.

"What happened?" I ask.

He looks down at his finger. "It's from the car accident."

"Which one?" I ask, and can't help but break into a small, wry smile, thinking of all the accidents we had in the last 24 hours.

He smiles back, even as he winces in pain. "The last one. When you decided to crash into a train. Nice move," he says, and I can't tell whether he means it or is being sarcastic.

"My brother was on the train," he adds. "Did you see him?"

"I saw him board," I say. "Then I lost him."

"Do you know where the train was going?"

I shake my head. "Did you see my sister on it?"

He shakes his head. "I couldn't really tell. It all happened so fast."

He stands there and lowers his head, looking distraught. A heavy silence follows. He looks so lost. The sight of his crooked finger bothers me, and my heart goes out to him. I decide to stop being so edgy, and to show him some compassion.

I reach out and take his injured hand in both of mine. He looks up at me, surprised.

His skin is smoother than I'd expected; it feels as if he's never worked a day in his life. I hold his fingertips gently in mine, and I am surprised to feel slight butterflies in my stomach.

"Let me help you," I say, softly. "This is going to hurt. But it needs to be done. We have to straighten it before it sets," I add, lifting his broken finger and examining it. I think back to when I was young, when I'd fallen in the street and came in with a broken pinky finger and Mom had insisted on taking me to a hospital.

Dad had refused, and had taken my finger in his hands and snapped it back into place in one quick motion, before my Mom could react. I had screamed in pain, and I remember even now how much it hurt. But it worked.

Ben looks back at me with fear in his eyes.

"I hope you know what you're doing—"

Before he can finish, I have already snapped his crooked finger back into place.

He screams out, and backs away from me, holding his hand.

"Damn it!" he screams, pacing around, holding his hand. Soon he calms, breathing hard. "You should have warned me!"

I tear a thin strip of cloth off of my sleeve, take his hand again, and tie his finger to the one next to it. It is a lame stint, but it will have to do. Ben stands inches away, and I can feel him looking down at me.

"Thanks," he whispers, and there is something in his voice, something intimate, that I haven't sensed before.

I feel the butterflies again, and suddenly feel I am too close to him. I need to stay clear-headed, strong, detached. I back away quickly, walking over to my side of the cell.

I glance over and see that Ben looks disappointed. He also looks exhausted, dejected. He leans back to the wall, and slowly slumps down to a sitting position, resting his head on his knees.

It's a good idea. I do the same, suddenly feeling the exhaustion in my legs.

I take a seat opposite him in the cell, and lower my head into my hands. I'm so hungry. So tired. Everything aches. I would do anything for food, water, pain killers, a bed. A hot shower. I just want to sleep—and sleep forever. I just want this whole thing behind me. If I'm going to die, I just want it to happen quickly.

We sit there for I don't know how long, both in silence. Maybe an hour passes, maybe two. I can't keep track of time anymore.

I hear the sound of his belabored breathing, through his broken nose. It must be so hard for him to breathe, and my heart goes out to him. I wonder if he's fallen asleep. I wonder when they will come for us, when I will hear those boots again, marching us to our deaths.

Ben's voice fills the air, a soft, sad, broken voice: "I just want to know where they took my brother," he says, softly. I can hear the pain in his voice, how much he cares for him. It makes me think of Bree.

I feel the need to force myself to be tough, to force myself to stop all of this self-pitying.

"Why?" I snap back. "What good would it do? There's nothing we can do about it anyway." But in truth, I want to know the same thing—where they've taken her.

Ben shakes his head sadly, looking crushed.

"I just want to know," he says softly. "For my own sake. Just to know."

I sigh, trying not to think of it, not to think about what's happening to her right now. I try not to think about whether she thinks I've let her down. Abandoned her.

"Did they tell you they're putting you in the arena?" he asks. I can hear the fear in his voice.

My heart flutters at the thought. Slowly, I nod.

"You?" I ask, already guessing the answer.

Grimly, he nods back.

"They say no one survives," he says.

"I know," I snap back. I don't need reminding of this. In fact, I don't want to think of it at all.

"So, what are you gonna do?" he asks.

I look back at him.

"What do you mean? It's not like I have any options."

"You seem to have a way out of everything," he says. "Some last minute way of dodging things. What's your way out of this one?"

I shake my head. I've been wondering the same thing, but to no avail.

"I'm out of ways," I say. "I've got nothing."

"So that's it?" he snaps back, annoyed. "You're just going to give up? Let them bring you to the arena? Kill you?"

"What else is there?" I snap back, annoyed myself.

He squirms. "I don't know," he says. "You must have a plan. We can't just sit here. We can't just let them march us off to our deaths. *Something.*"

I shake my head. I'm tired. I'm exhausted. I'm hurt. I'm starving. This room is solid metal. There are hundreds of armed guards out there. We're underground somewhere. I don't even know where. We have no weapons. There's nothing we can do. *Nothing.*

Except *one* thing, I realize. I can go down fighting.

"I'm not letting them march me to my death," I suddenly say, in the darkness.

He looks up at me. "What do you mean?"

"I'm going to fight," I say. "In the arena."

Ben laughs, more like a derisive snort.

"You're kidding. Arena One is filled with professional killers. And even these killers get killed. No one survives. Ever. It's just a prolonged death sentence. For their amusement."

"That doesn't mean I can't try," I snap back, my voice rising, furious at his pessimism.

But Ben just looks back down, head in his hands, and shakes his head.

"Well, *I* won't stand a chance," he says.

"If you think that way, then you won't," I snap back. It is a phrase that Dad often used with me, and I am surprised to hear those same words now coming out of my mouth. It disturbs me a bit, as I wonder how much of him, exactly, I've absorbed. I can hear the toughness in my own voice, a toughness I never recognized until this day, and I almost feel as if he's speaking through me. It's an eerie feeling.

"Ben," I say. "If you think you can survive, if you can *see* yourself surviving, then you will. It's about what you force yourself to imagine in your head. About what you *tell* yourself."

"That's just lying to yourself," Ben says.

"No it's not," I answer. "It's training yourself. There's a difference. It's seeing your own future, the way *you* want it to be, and creating it in your head, and then making it happen. If you can't see it, then you can't create it."

"You sound like you actually believe you can survive," Ben says, sounding amazed.

"I don't believe it," I snap. "I *know* it. I *am* going to survive. I *will* survive," I hear myself saying, with growing confidence. I have always had an ability to psych myself up, to get myself so into a head that there's no turning back.

Despite everything, I find myself swelling with a newfound confidence, a new optimism.

And suddenly, at that moment, I make a decision: I am determined to survive. Not for me. But for Bree. After all, I don't know that she is dead yet. She might be alive. And the only chance I have of saving her is if I can stay alive. If I survive this arena. And if that's what it takes, then that is what I will do.

I will survive.

I don't see why I wouldn't stand a chance. If there's one thing I can do, it's fight. That's what I've been raised to be good at. I've been in a ring before. I've gotten my butt kicked. And I've gotten stronger for it. I'm not afraid.

"So then how are you going to win?" Ben asks. This time his question sounds genuine, sounds as if he really believes I might. Maybe something in my voice has convinced him.

"I don't need to win," I say back, calmly. "That's the thing. I only need to survive."

Barely do I finish uttering the words when I hear the sound of combat boots marching down the hall. A moment later, there comes the sound of our door opening.

They have come for me.

FIFTEEN

Our cell door groans open and light floods in from the hallway. I raise my hands to my eyes, shielding them, and see the silhouette of a slaverunner. I expect him to march over and take me away, but instead he leans down, drops something hard and plastic on the floor, and kicks it. It scrapes across the floor and stops abruptly as it slams against my foot.

"Your last meal," he announces in a dark voice.

Then he marches out and slams the door, locking it.

I can already smell the food from here, and my stomach reacts with a sharp hunger pang. I lean over and pick up the plastic container carefully, barely able to make it out in the dim light. it is long and flat, sealed with a foil top I pull back the foil and immediately the smell of food—real, cooked food, which I haven't had in years—comes rushing up at me, even more powerful. It smells like steak. And chicken. And

211

potatoes. I lean over and examine it: there is a large, juicy steak, two chicken legs, mashed potatoes, and vegetables. It is the best smell of my life. I feel guilty that Bree is not here to share it.

I wonder why they've given me such an extravagant meal, and then I realize it's not an act of kindness, but a self-serving act: they want me strong for the arena. Perhaps they are also tempting me one last time, offering me a preview of what life would be like if I accept their offer. Real meals. Hot food. A life of luxury.

As the smell infiltrates every pore of my body, their offer becomes more tempting. I haven't smelled real food in years. I suddenly realized how hungry I am, how malnourished, and I seriously wonder if, without this meal, I would even have strength to fight.

Ben sits up and leans forward, looking over. Of course. I suddenly feel selfish for not thinking of him. He must be as starving as I am, and I am sure the smell, which fills the room, is driving him crazy.

"Share it with me," I say in the darkness. It takes all my willpower to make this offer—but it is the right thing to do.

He shakes his head.

"No," he says. "They said it was for you. Have it. When they come for me, they'll give me a meal, too. You need this now. You're the one that's about to fight."

He's right. I do need it now. Especially because I don't just plan on fighting—I plan on winning.

It doesn't take much convincing. The smell of the food overwhelms me, and I reach out and grab the chicken leg and devour it in seconds. I take bite after bite, barely slowing to swallow. It is the most delicious thing I've ever had. But I force myself to set one of the chicken legs aside, saving it for Ben. Ben might get his own meal, like he said—or he might not. Either way, after all we've been through, I feel it's only right to share.

I turn to the mashed potatoes, using my fingers to shovel them into my mouth. My stomach growls in pain, and I realize I *need* this meal, more than any meal I've ever had. My body screams out for me to take another bite, and another. I eat way too fast, and within moments, I've devoured more than half of them. I force myself to save the rest for Ben.

I turn to the steak, lifting it with my fingers, and take big bites, chewing slowly, trying to savor each bite. It is the best thing I've had in my life. If this turns out to be my last meal, I'd be content with this. I save half, then move on to the vegetables, eating only half of these. Within moments, I'm done—and I still don't feel satisfied. I look down at what I set aside for Ben and want to devour every last bite. But I summon my willpower, and slowly rise to my feet, cross the room, and hold the tray out before him.

He sits there, head resting on his knees, not looking up. He's the most defeated-looking person I've ever seen. If it were me sitting there, I would have watched him eat every bite, would have imagined what it tasted like. But it seems that he just has no will left to live.

He must smell the food, so close, because finally, he raises his head. He looks up at me, eyes open in surprise. I smile.

"You didn't really think I'd eat it all, did you?" I ask.

He smiles, but shakes his head and lowers it. "I can't," he says. "It's yours."

"It's yours now," I say, and shove it into his hands, and let go. He has no choice but to take it.

"But it's not fair—" he begins.

"I've had enough," I lie. "Plus, I need to stay light for the fight. I can't maneuver on a full stomach, can I?"

My lie isn't very convincing, and I can tell he doesn't really buy it. But I can also see the effect that the smell of the food has on him, can see his primal urge taking over. It is the same impulse I felt just a few minutes ago.

He reaches down and devours it. He closes his eyes and leans back and breathes deeply as he chews, savoring each bite. I watch him finish, and can see how much he needs it.

Instead of crossing back to my side of the room, I decide to take a seat on the wall beside him. I don't know how much longer I have until they come for me, and for some reason I feel like being closer to him in the last minutes we have together.

We sit there, beside each other, in silence for I don't know how long. I feel on edge, listening for any sound, constantly wondering if they are coming. As I think about it my heart begins to beat faster, and I try to put it out of my mind.

I had assumed they would take us both to the arena together, and am surprised they are separating us. It makes me wonder what other surprises they have in store. I try not to think about.

I can't help wondering if this is the last time I will see Ben. I realize I haven't known him long, and that I really shouldn't care either way. I know I should keep my head clear, my emotions calm, and focus just on the fight before me.

But for some reason I can't stop thinking about him. I'm not sure why, but somehow I am beginning to feel attached to him. I realize I will miss him. It doesn't make any sense, and I am mad at myself for even thinking this way. I barely know him. It annoys me that I will be upset, more upset than I should be, about saying goodbye.

We sit there in a relaxed silence, a silence between friends. It is no longer awkward. We don't speak, but I feel that in the silence he is hearing me, hearing me say goodbye. And that he's saying goodbye, too.

I wait for him to say something, anything, back to me. After minutes pass, a part of me starts to wonder if maybe he's not speaking for a reason, if maybe he doesn't feel the same way about me. Maybe he doesn't even care for me at all; maybe he even resents me for getting him into this mess. Suddenly, I doubt myself. I need to know.

"Ben?" I whisper, in the silence.

I wait, but all that I hear is the labored sound of his breathing, through his broken nose. I look over, and see that he is fast asleep. That explains the silence.

I study his face, and even as bruised up as it is, it is beautiful. I hate the idea of our being separated. And of his dying. He's too young to die. I guess I am, too.

The meal makes me sleepy, and in the darkness, despite myself, I find my eyes closing. Before I know it, I am slumped against the wall, sliding my head over until it rests on Ben's shoulder. I know I should wake, stay on edge, prepare myself for the arena.

But in moments, despite my efforts, I am fast asleep.

*

I am awakened by the echo of boots marching down the corridor. At first I think it's just a nightmare—but then I realize it's not. I don't know how many hours have passed. My body feels rested, though, and that tells me I must have been asleep for a long time.

The boots grow louder and soon stop before the door. There is a dangling of keys, and I sit up straighter, my heart pounding out of my chest. They have come for me.

I don't know how to say goodbye to Ben, and I don't know if he even wants me to. So instead, I just stand, every muscle in my body aching, and prepare to leave.

Suddenly, I feel a hand on my wrist. It is surprisingly strong, and the intensity of his grip ripples through me.

I'm afraid to look down at him, to look into those eyes—but I have no choice. He's staring right at me. His eyes radiate concern, and in that moment, I can see how much cares for me. The intensity of it scares me.

"You did good," he says, "getting us this far. We never should have lived this long."

I stare back, not knowing how to respond. I want to tell him that I'm sorry for all this. I also want to tell him that I care for him. That I hope he survives. That I survive. That I see him again. That we find our siblings. That we make it home.

But I feel that he knows all this already. And so I end up not saying a word.

The door swings open, and in march the slaverunners. I turn to go, but Ben yanks on my wrist, forcing me to turn back to him.

"Survive," he says, with the intensity of a dying man.

I stare back.

"Survive. For me. For your sister. For my brother. *Survive.*"

The words ring in the air, like a mandate, and I can't help but feel as if they come from Dad, channeled through Ben. It sends a shiver up my spine. Before, I was determined to survive. Now, I feel as if I have no choice.

The slaverunners march over and stand behind me.

Ben lets go and I turn and stand proudly, facing them. I feel a surge of strength from the meal and the sleep, and I stare back at them defiantly.

One of them holds out a key. At first, I don't understand why—but then I remember: my handcuffs. They have been on so long, I've forgotten they were there.

I reach out, and he unlocks them. There is a huge relief of tension, as the metal unclasps and is taken away. I rub my wrists where the circular marks are.

I march out the room before they can shove me, wanting the advantage. I know that Ben is watching me, but I can't bear to turn around and look at him. I have to be strong.

I have to survive.

SIXTEEN

I am marched down the corridor by the slaverunners, and as I walk down the endless, narrow halls, I begin to hear a faint rumbling. At first, it is hard to make out. But as I get closer, it begins to sound like the noise of a crowd. A cheering crowd, with shouts coming in fits.

We turn down yet another hallway, and the noise becomes more distinct. There is a huge roar, followed by a rumbling, like an earthquake. The corridor actually trembles as I walk down it. It feels like the vibration of a hundred thousand people stomping their feet.

I am pushed to the right, down yet another hallway. I resent being poked and prodded by these slaverunners, especially as I am being marched to my death, and I would like nothing more than to turn around and deck one of them. But I'm unarmed, and they are bigger and stronger, and it would be a no-win situation. Besides, I need to conserve my strength.

I am prodded one last time, and the hallway opens up. In the distance there appears a harsh light, like a floodlight, and the noise of the crowd grows inconceivably loud, like a living thing. The hallway opens into a broad and high tunnel. The light gets brighter and brighter, and for a moment I wonder if I am walking out to daylight.

But the temperature hasn't changed and I realize I am still underground and being walked down an entrance tunnel. To the arena. I think of the time Dad took me to a baseball game, when we were heading to our seats, walking inside the stadium—when we walked down a tunnel and suddenly the stadium opened up before us. As I walk out, down the ramp, it feels like that. Except this time, I am the star of the show. I stop and stare, in awe.

Spread out before me is an enormous stadium, packed with thousands and thousands of people. In its center is a ring, shaped in an octagon; it resembles a boxing ring, except instead of ropes around its perimeter, there is a metal cage. The cage rises high in the air, about fifteen feet, completely enclosing the ring except for its open roof. It reminds me of the cage ring once used by the Ultimate Fighting Championship, but bigger. And this cage, covered in blood stains, with spikes on the inside, protruding from it every ten feet or so, clearly is not meant for sport—but for death.

There is the sound of clanging metal, and I look up and see two people fighting inside the ring, one of them just thrown against the cage. His body slams into the metal, narrowly missing a spike, and the crowd erupts into a cheer.

The smaller opponent, covered in blood, bounces off the cage and looks disoriented. The bigger one, enormous, looks like a sumo wrestler. He is Asian, and must be at least five hundred pounds. After throwing the small, wiry man, the sumo wrestler charges, grabs him with two hands and lifts him easily over his head, as if he were a doll. He walks him in slow circles, and the crowd cheers wildly.

He throws the man completely across the ring. He goes flying and smashes sideways into the cage, again narrowly missing a spike. He lands on the hard floor of the ring, not moving.

The entire crowd erupts in a roar and jumps to its feet, screaming.

"FINISH HIM!" a crowd member screams, above the din.

"KILL HIM!" screams another.

"CRUSH HIM!"

Thousands of people start screaming, stomping their boots on the metal bleachers, and the noise becomes deafening. Sumo holds out his arms, taking it all in, slowly circling, savoring the moment. The cheers grow louder.

Sumo slowly, ominously, crosses the ring, heading towards the unconscious man, who is lying face first on the floor. As he gets close, he suddenly drops heavily to one knee, landing right on the small of the man's back. There is a sickening cracking noise as his 500 pounds make impact on the small man's spine, shattering it. The crowd groans, as it becomes clear that he's broken the small man's back.

I turn away, not wanting to look, feeling horrible for the little, defenseless man. I wonder why they don't end this. Clearly, the wrestler has won.

But apparently, they don't plan on ending it—and sumo is not finished. He grabs the man's limp body with two hands, picks him up, and throws him face first across the ring. The man smashes into the metal cage face-first, and collapses to the floor again. The crowd roars. His body lands in an unnatural position, and I can't tell if he's dead or not.

The wrestler is still not satisfied. He raises his arms, slowly circling, as the crowd chants.

"SU-MO! SU-MO! SU-MO!"

The roar reaches a deafening pitch, until sumo crosses the ring one last time, raises a foot, and lowers it on the defenseless man's throat. He stands with both feet on the man's throat, crushing it. The man's eyes open wide as he reaches up with both hands, trying to get the feet off his neck. But it is futile, and after a few seconds of struggle, finally, he stops. His hands fall to his side, limp. He is dead.

The crowd jumps to its feet, roaring.

Sumo picks up the dead body, hoists it high above his head, then hurls it across the ring. This time he aims for one of the protruding spikes, and impales the body into it. The body clings to the side of the cage, a spike sticking through the stomach, blood dripping down.

The crowd roars even louder.

I'm shoved hard from behind, and I stumble out into the bright light, heading down the ramp, into the open stadium. As I enter, I finally realize where exactly I am: it is the former Madison Square Garden. Except now the place is dilapidated, the roof caving in, with sunlight and water getting in in places, and the bleachers rusted and corroded.

The crowd must spot me, because they turn to me, and let out a cheer of anticipation. I look closely at the faces, screaming and cheering, and see they are all Biovictims. Their faces are deformed, melted away. Most are as thin as racks, emaciated. They comprise some of the most sadistic-looking types I've ever seen, and there are an endless array of them.

I am led down the ramp, towards the ring, and as I reach it, I can feel the thousands of eyes fixate on me. There are jeers and boos. Apparently, they don't like newcomers. Or maybe they just don't like me.

I am marched ringside and prodded to a small metal ladder on one side of the cage. I look up at Sumo, who scowls down at me from inside the ring. I look over at the dead body, still impaled on the cage. I hesitate: I'm not eager to enter this ring.

I am prodded roughly by a gunpoint in the small of my back, and I have no choice but to take my first step on the ladder. Then another, and another. The crowd cheers, and I feel weak in the knees.

A slaverunner opens the cage door, and I take my first step in. He slams it behind me, and I can't help but flinch. The crowd cheers again.

I turn and survey the stadium, looking for any sign of Bree, of Ben, of his brother—of any friendly face. But there are none. I force myself to look across the ring, at my opponent. Sumo stands there, looking down at me. He smiles, then erupts into laughter at the sight of me. I'm sure he thinks I will be an easy kill. I don't blame him.

Sumo turns his back on me and raises his arms out wide, facing the crowd, craving adulation. Clearly, he is not troubled by me, and thinks this match is already over. He is already reveling in his victory to come.

Dad's voice suddenly fills my head:

Always be the one to start a fight. Never hesitate. Surprise is your best weapon. A fight starts when YOU start it. If you wait for your opponent to start it, you've already lost. The first three seconds of a fight always determine its outcome. Go. GO!

Dad's voice screams in my head, and I let it take over me. I don't stop to think how crazy this is, how outmatched I am. All I know is that, if I do nothing, I will die.

I let Dad's voice carry me away, and it is as if my body is being controlled by someone else. I find myself charging across the ring, focusing on Sumo. His back is still to me, his arms are still out, he is still enjoying the spectacle. And now, at least for this moment, he is exposed.

I race across the ring, every second feeling like an eternity. I focus on the fact that I am still wearing these combat boots, with their steel-tipped toes. I take three huge steps, and before Sumo can react, I leap into the air. I fly through the air, letting my momentum carry me, and aim carefully, right for the back of his left knee.

The bigger they are, the harder they fall, I hear Dad say.

I pray he's right.

I wind up, knowing I only have one shot at this.

I kick him in the back of his knee with all that I have. I feel the impact of my steel-tipped toe in his soft flesh, and I pray that it works.

To my amazement, his knee buckles out from under him, and he lands on one knee on the floor of the ring, his weight shaking it.

The crowd suddenly roars in delight and surprise, clearly not expecting this.

The biggest mistake you can make in a fight is to hit someone and walk away. You don't win a fight with a single punch, or a single kick You win it with combinations. After you kick him, kick him again. And again. And again. Don't stop until he can't get up.

Sumo begins to turn towards me, and I can see the shock on his face. I don't wait.

I swing around and plant a roundhouse kick perfectly on the back of his neck. He goes down, face first, hitting the floor hard, shaking it with his weight. The crowd roars.

Again, I don't wait. I jump up high and do a dropkick, digging the heel of my boot, right into the small of his back. Then, without pausing, I wind up and kick him hard in the side of the face my steel tip, aiming for his temple. The soft spot. I kick it again and again and again. Soon, he's covered in blood, and he's reaching up to protect his head.

The crowd goes insane. They jump to their feet, screaming.

"KILL HIM!" they scream. "FINISH HIM!"

But I hesitate. The sight of him lying there, limp like that, makes me feel bad. I know that I shouldn't, that he's a merciless killer, but still, I can't quite bring myself to finish him off.

And that is my big mistake.

Sumo takes advantage of my hesitation. Before I know it, he reaches out and grabs my ankle. His hand is huge, impossibly huge, wrapping around my leg as if it were a twig. With one easy motion, he pulls me by the leg, spins me, and sends me flying across the ring.

I slam into the metal cage, missing one of the sharp spikes by an inch, and fall to the floor.

The crowd cheers. I look up, stunned, my head spinning. Sumo is already getting to his feet and charging. Blood trickles down his face. I can't believe I did that. I can't believe he's even vulnerable. And now, he must be really pissed.

I'm shocked by how fast he is. In the flash of an eye he's almost on top of me, leaping into the air, preparing to land on top of me. If I don't get out of the way fast, I'll be crushed.

At the last second I roll and just barely manage to evade him as he lands hard beside me, shaking the floor so hard that it actually bounces and sends me up into the air.

I roll away, and keep rolling until I'm on the far side of the ring. I hurry to my feet, and he gets up, too. We stand there on opposite sides of the ring, facing each other, each breathing hard. The crowd is going crazy. I can't believe I've managed to live this long.

He's gearing up to charge, and I realize I'm out of options. There aren't many places to go in this ring, especially with a man this size. One wrong move, and I'm finished. I got lucky with the element of surprise. But now I actually have to fight.

Suddenly, something falls through the air. I look up and see that something is being dropped down through the open roof of the cage. It lands with a crash on the floor between us. It is a weapon. A huge battle axe. I never expected this. I guess this is their way of keeping the games even, prolonging their entertainment. The axe lands in the center, equidistant between us, about ten feet away.

I don't hesitate. I race for it, and am relieved to see I am faster than he is: I get there and grab it first.

But he is quicker than I'd imagined, and just as I bend over and pick it up, I feel his huge hands around my rib cage, and he is picking me up, hoisting me from behind in a huge bear hug. He hoists me higher, effortlessly, as if I were an insect. The crowd roars.

He squeezes harder and harder, and I feel all the air crushed out of me, feel as if each one of my ribs is going to crack. I manage to hold onto the axe—but that does little good. I can't even maneuver my shoulders.

He spins me before the crowd, having fun with me. The crowd reacts, screaming in delight. If I can just get my arms free, I can use the axe.

But I can't. I feel all the air leaving my body, and realize that in another moment or two, I'll be suffocated.

Finally, I realize, my luck has run out.

SEVENTEEN

Sumo doesn't seem to want to kill me yet. Instead, it seems as if he's enjoying our fight— and that he wants to toy with me.

So instead of crushing me to death, he spins me around fast, several times, then throws me. The axe goes flying from my hands and the world goes rushing by as I fly through the air. I smash, head first, into the metal wall of the cage.

I bounce off it, and land hard on the ground. The crowd roars. Again I manage to miss one of the cage's protruding spikes, but barely. I look up and see the body of his last victim, still impaled on the cage wall, and realize I am lucky. The axe hits the ground with a clang several feet away from me.

My head is ringing, and I'm disoriented as I lay there, face first on the ground. Out of the corner my eye, I see him charging. But I'm too beat to move.

Move, soldier! MOVE!

Somehow, I force myself into motion. I scramble to my knees, crawl over to the axe as fast as I can, grab it with both hands, and spin around with it.

My timing is perfect. As Sumo is gearing up to stomp me, the axe comes flying around and connects with his calf. I feel the blade entering his flesh. Blood squirts all over me.

There is a tremendous roar from the crowd. I realize I must've done some serious damage.

He falls over, like a log, and lands with a crash. He is screaming and reaching up for where his foot once was, and I am shocked to see that my axe has chopped it off. Blood gushes everywhere, and he lies there, screaming, grabbing at his stump.

"KILL HIM! KILL HIM!" the crowd chants.

I know that this is my chance, that I should finish him off. But still, as I stand over him, holding the axe, I just can't bring myself to.

Instead, I just want to get far away from him. But I am stuck in one corner, and his body is blocking my path. So I run and jump over him, trying to get to the opposite side.

Another mistake. Once again, I have underestimated him. He reaches up and grabs my ankle in mid-air and I fall to the ground, face first, hitting it hard. The crowd screams.

He grabs my ankle and drags me towards him, one hand at a time. I feel like I'm being pulled into a conveyor belt, as I slide on my stomach, inevitably towards him. I realize that in another second I'll be on top of him, and he'll crush me to death with his upper body.

I am still clutching the axe handle, and with my final bit of energy, I manage to lift my upper body, spin around, and with both hands, bring the blade down hard, aiming right for his head. There is a sickening noise as the blade lodges into his forehead.

For a moment, I freeze, as does the crowd. I can still feel his hand gripping my ankle, and wonder if the blade went deep enough. Then, finally, his hand releases and his eyes open wide. I am stunned to realize that he is dead. I have killed him.

The crowd is completely silent. I scramble away from him, not trusting that anyone his size could actually be dead, that I could have actually killed him. I stand at the far end of the ring, breathing hard, warily looking down, waiting for him to resurrect. But he does not. He is dead. Really dead.

Suddenly, the crowd roars, jumps to its feet, erupts in a huge cheer. They whistle and clap and stomp, and it never ends.

And that is when I realize: I have won. I can really do it. I can survive.

*

I sense motion, and look up.

The leader sits up there, high on his own pedestal, watching over all of us. Slowly, he stands, and as he does, the crowd begins to quiet. Even from here, I can see the look of surprise on his face. Clearly, he had not expected this.

He nods, and the cage door opens. In march a half dozen slaverunners, holding guns. Two of them march right for me, holding out their guns, and for a moment, I wonder if they're going to kill me. But then I see the other four going to drag out the bodies of the last two victims. I realize these two are just standing guard, in case I make any rash moves. They aren't taking any chances.

The other four each grab hold of Sumo, and with a supreme effort they drag his immense weight across the ring. It must be a real struggle for them, because they go slowly, and I can hear them straining. After about a minute, they finally managed to drag him off, trailing blood. One of them comes back and grabs the small man's impaled body off the cage, as if an afterthought. The other two slaverunners march out and slam the cage door behind them.

I now stand alone, wondering what might come next. I wait for a few moments, wondering if maybe they will release me now, although I know, even as I think it, that it's a silly idea. I know that there are no survivors in Arena One. Ever.

Sure enough, moments later, the crowd erupts into an enormous cheer, and I look down and see another contestant being marched towards the ring. I'm surprised to see that this one is a woman. She marches right to the metal ladder, looking confident and defiant, and as they open the door she ascends the ladder in three quick steps and jumps in.

"SHI-RA! SHI-RA! SHI-RA!" the crowd roars.

With long black hair and black eyes, Shira looks to be in her 30s; she is incredibly well-built, her muscles bulging, with large breasts. She wears just a tight elastic top and tight black shorts, and her toned, muscular legs and arms ripple. She looks like a curvy, female action model. Curiously, she wears a small backpack on her back, and I wonder if it's part of her outfit, or if she wears it for a reason.

She stares at me coolly from the opposite side of the ring. Unlike Sumo, she doesn't seem to take me for granted, studies me as if I'm a serious contender. And that worries me. She seems much craftier. Oddly, I feel more on-edge facing her than I did him. I sense she has tricks up her sleeve.

She slowly begins to circle the perimeter of the ring, and I circle, too, keeping my distance. We circle each other, two wary opponents, each waiting for the other to make the first move. After a few seconds of this, she suddenly shrieks and charges, her hands held out before her like claws, aimed right for my face.

I wait until the last second, then sidestep her, holding out my foot as I do. It works: she charges right past me, trips, and falls on her face. The crowd screams in approval.

But she spins around in the same motion and with one hand grabs the back of my leg and with the other, grabs my hair from behind. It is a dirty trick, and she pulls me down, backwards, and I fall flat on my back, hitting the floor with a painful thud. In the same motion, she rolls over, on top of me, and grabs me tight in a bear hug, like a wrestler. She holds me tight and won't let go, rolling over with me again and again.

She has my arms in a vice, and I can't wiggle free. I feel her slowly squeezing the life out of me, and my breathing becomes more shallow.

"BITE HER! BITE HER! BITE HER!" the crowd chants.

I don't understand why they're chanting this, until suddenly, Shira leans back ahead and opens her mouth wide. She's sharpened her teeth with a file, and they are pointy, like fangs. She lowers her head, aiming right for my shoulder.

I struggle to get free, but she's deceptively strong, and she has me in a lock I just can't get out of. She lowers her head, and next thing I know I'm in horrific pain, as her two teeth sink into my shoulder blade. I feel them puncturing my skin, feel hot blood pouring out of it, and I scream out in pain.

The intense pain gives me a newfound rush of adrenaline, though, and in a sudden burst of strength I manage to get my hands down into her solo plexus and push for all I can. This time, it works. She goes flying off of me.

I roll over quickly, my face red with exertion, my shoulder burning from the pain; I reach over and feel it, and my hand comes back red, covered in blood. Now I'm pissed.

I charge her, and before she can gain her knees I wind up and kick her hard, connecting in her ribs. There is a sound of cracking ribs, and the crowd ooohs. Without waiting, I wind up again and kick her again, hard in the face.

She collapses, blood pouring from her face. She is confused, squarely on the ground, and now I have the advantage.

I know that I should kick her in the head repeatedly, finish her off. But still, somehow, I can't bring myself to. I still feel bad killing this woman, lying there, defenseless. I stand there, hesitating, as the crowd erupts into a chant.

"KILL HER! KILL HER! KILL HER!"

Still, I can't bring myself to. I hesitate. And it is another stupid mistake.

I don't see her hand reaching slowly behind her back, unlatching her backpack. And by the time I realize what she's doing, it's too late.

Her pack opens and suddenly, out comes a bright, multi-colored snake.

It slithers right for me.

EIGHTEEN

The snake hits the ground and darts at me in a flash. I'm so shocked, I don't even know how to react. The snake doesn't hesitate, though. It retracts its fangs and sinks them into my calf.

The pain is excruciating. I drop to one knee as the three-inch fangs sink into my flesh. It feels like my skin is on fire, as if it is going to burn off in pain.

My reflexes take over, and without thinking, I reach over, grab the snake by its head, yank it off, and hold it out in front of me. It hisses back as I hold it, and I pull back my arm and throw it across the ring. It slams into the metal cage and drops to the ground. The crowd cheers.

The snake immediately darts across the floor, coming right back at me. Now my calf is on fire, hurting so bad that it makes me forget the pain in my shoulder. Making matters worse, Shira is beginning to get up again.

Suddenly, something falls through the air. I hear a clang, and look down to see another weapon has been dropped: this time, it's a spear.

I run over and grab it. And as the snake slithers back towards me, I hurl the spear down at it. I miss.

The snake lunges at me, and I sidestep just in time. But the snake slithers around, coming back. I raise the spear again, spin around, and bring it down. This time, it's a perfect strike.

The spear lodges right into the snake's head, pinning it into the ground. It goes limp.

The crowd roars.

Just when I think I can relax, suddenly, I feel myself slammed from behind, feel an elbow hit me hard, right on my spine. I go flying forward, head smashing into the metal railing, barely missing a protruding spike. My head spins from the pain.

I turn around and see Shira charging, her face contorted with fury. She jumps high in the air, feet flying forward, to kick me in the chest. I notice that her toes have sharpened metal blades protruding from them: if she kicks me, it will be fatal.

I spin away at the last second, and she kicks the gate instead, bouncing off it and falling hard on her back. The crowd roars.

I try to run across the ring, to go for the spear, but as I run past her, she reaches out and grabs my foot with her hand, tripping me. I land hard, face first, on the ground. A second later, I feel her on top of me, bear hugging me from behind, wrapping her arms and legs around my body. The crowd roars.

I roll over, and now she is on her back on the floor, grabbing me from behind. She wraps her muscular legs around mine, and then reaches up with her forearm, which is solid muscle, and wraps it over my throat. She is going to choke me to death. I have no leverage to maneuver. Once again, I'm losing.

With my free hand, I try to reach back over my shoulder. Just a foot behind me, out of reach, is the spear, still lodged in the snake. I stretch as much as I can, reaching with my fingertips, and they just graze the spear shaft. I am so close. But I am losing air.

I bend my leg, still in excruciating pain from the snake bite, dig my heel into the floor and push, sliding us both back. I manage to move us an inch. Just enough to grab hold of the spear.

Finally, I have it. But the world is getting dizzy, and I am seeing stars as I am losing oxygen fast. I know I only have a few seconds left to live.

With one last, supreme effort, I lift the spear and bring it down towards me, and at the last second dodge my head out of the way. I bring it down hard, with both hands.

The spear barely misses my face and instead lodges into Shira's throat. I pull down harder and harder, hearing the awful sound of metal penetrating flesh, until finally, her grip around my throat loosens.

I feel her go limp beneath me, feel her hands and legs slowly letting go. I feel her hot blood pouring out of her neck, onto my own. Finally, I am able to break free, and I roll away and jump to my feet.

I stand over her and look down, rubbing my throat, gasping for breath. Her eyes are open wide, staring off to the side.

After a moment of stunned silence, the crowd again jumps to its feet, roaring with approval, even more thunderous than before. Now, they love me.

*

As I stand there, looking down at Shira's corpse, I don't feel a sense of pride; rather, I think only of the snakebite, the burning pain in my calf, and I wonder if it's poisonous. I look down and see that my calf is already red and swollen. Each step I take brings a fresh stab of pain. I am guessing that if it was poisonous I'd already be dead, or at least paralyzed. Still, the pain is incredible, and walking is difficult. I don't know how I'll be able to continue fighting like this.

Not to mention the rest of me: my cracked ribs, the wound on my arm from the shrapnel, the new bite wound on my shoulder, my swollen face…. I stand there, clinging to the fence and catching my breath. I really don't know how I'll be able to fight one more person. Now I understand why Arena One has no survivors.

I sense motion and look way up high, and see the leader scowling down at me. He does not look pleased. The crowd continues to cheer, and I can't help wondering if maybe I've embarrassed the leader in some way. Clearly, the arena bouts are designed to be quick, meant to be basically a glorified execution. They don't seem to be meant to last more than one round. Clearly, he had expected me to die sooner.

Making matters worse, I see people trading money furiously in the crowd. I wonder if the leader and his people had placed bets against me—and if my winning has cost the house money. I wonder what the odds were. If I were betting, I'd guess it would be 500 to 1 against me.

His advisors huddle around him, looking flustered, whispering in his ear, as if devising a plan. Slowly, he nods in response.

As he does, the door to the cage opens, and in march two slaverunners. They hurry to

Shira's corpse and drag her dead body across the ring. One of them reaches down and grabs the spear and the limp carcass of the snake, and carries it, too. More blood stains the floor, which is now red and slick. I stand there, taking it all in, still catching my breath, when suddenly I hear a faint rumbling. This is followed by something more distinct, and I feel the ground beneath me tremor, then shake. Soon, it becomes a deafening roar.

The entire crowd jumps to its feet, stomping like crazy as it turns its back on me and faces one of the entrance tunnels. In march a dozen men, holding torches. They clear a path for one obviously very special person. The crowd roars louder and louder, the stomping growing deafening. I don't like the sound of this. They must know who it is.

After several more seconds, I catch a glimpse of what they're screaming about. Behind an entourage of a dozen torchbearers, I spot what can only be my new opponent. I gulp at the sight.

He is quite possibly the largest and most muscular man I have ever seen. He towers over the torchbearers by at least a foot, and every square inch of his body is bulging with muscles. He's easily three times the size of any man I've ever seen. He wears a black face mask, ominous and threatening, so I can't see his face. Maybe I'm better off.

His hands and forearms are each covered in black gauntlets, made of a hard material and covered in spikes. He is naked save for his tight, black shorts and black combat boots. The muscles in his thighs ripple with every step.

As he gets closer to the ring, the crowd goes crazy. Finally, they break into a chant:

"MAL-COLM! MAL-COM! MAL-COLM!"

He seems impervious to the chanting; he just doesn't seem to care. Surrounded by an entourage of two dozen people, he looks like a caged beast, ready to tear apart anything in his path. I can't even conceive that this person is coming to fight me. It is a joke. I don't stand a chance.

I got lucky with Sumo because he was overconfident and careless; I got lucky with Shira, too, but it nearly went the other way. But this man: it is obvious he can overpower me with a single hand. I'm not a pessimist. But as he climbs the ladder, enters the ring, and stands there, twice my size, it is enough to make my knees weak. He's not a man. He is a monster, something out of a fairytale. I wonder if they save him for special occasions, to sic on people who have defied the games, who have embarrassed the leader. Or if perhaps they save him as a last resort, to make sure that they put someone to death quickly and easily, without taking any more chances.

He holds his arms out wide and throws back his head, and the crowd goes crazy. The roar is so loud, it actually hurts my ears. The brute never takes his eyes off of me, which I can see through the mask. I can feel them piercing me—soulless, black eyes. He slowly lowers his arms, still staring at me. I let go of the cage and stand on my own two feet, facing him. I do my best to stand upright, to appear fearless. I doubt it works.

I don't know what to do next. In this arena there is no official noise or signal to mark the start of a match. And if there was, I have a feeling that no one would pay attention to it anyway. Matches seem to begin whenever the contestants decide they do. And I'm in no mood to start this match. He is taking his time, too, savoring each moment, trying to intimidate me. It's working.

My only hope, I realize, is if the leaders decide to throw me down another weapon. And as I look up at their scowling faces, I see no sign of that.

Suddenly, he moves. He saunters slowly towards me, as if he has all the time in the world. As if he wants to savor this. I study his physique, looking for any possible weakness. But I find none: he is a wall of solid muscle.

As he gets close I slowly back away, circling along the wall of the cage. I realize this will make me seem weak, and probably embolden him. But I can't see how he could be more emboldened than he already is, and I still don't know how to fight this guy. Maybe, if I evade him long enough, I'll get an idea. Or they'll throw me a weapon. Or I'll tire him out. Although these all seem doubtful.

He slowly approaches, and I keep backing away. The crowd gets antsy, hissing and booing, heckling me. They want blood. And I am no longer their favorite.

He walks a bit faster towards me, and I back away just as fast. He sidesteps left and I sidestep right. I can't keep this up forever: he's getting closer, and the distance is shortening.

Suddenly, he gets impatient and lunges at me, racing to grab me; at the last second, I sidestep, and run to the side. He grabs the thin air, and I'm already on the other side of him.

The crowd laughs at him. He turns around, and I can see his neck turn a shade of crimson. Now he's really pissed. He charges me, sprinting with all he has. I have nowhere left to go.

At the last second, I try to sidestep to my right, but this time he sees it coming, and reaches out and grabs hold of my shirt. Without pausing, he turns and with one hand, spins and throws me. I go flying like a ragdoll across the ring, slamming into the metal cage. Luckily, I just miss a protruding spike.

The crowd roars in approval. I lie there, feeling the wind knocked out of me, feeling the throbbing in my calf and shoulder. With a supreme effort, I manage to get to my hands and knees, but as soon as I do, I feel his hands on my back, grabbing my shirt. He throws me again, head first.

I go flying like a cannonball across the other side of the ring. I feel myself airborne, and then smash headfirst into the metal cage. The pain is deafening. I bounce off it, and land on my back, on the floor, and am winded again.

The crowd roars, stomping its feet.

I look up just in time to see a huge foot stomping down, right for my face. At the last second I manage to roll out of the way. I feel the air rush by my ear as his foot slams into the floor just inches away. The crowd ooohs. It was a close call. A split second more, and his foot would have crushed my face to bits.

I roll over and without thinking, sink my teeth into his foot. I feel them pierce his flesh, and taste his salty blood as it trickles down my lips. I hear him grunt in pain and it makes me realize he's human. I'm surprised by that. It's a dirty move, but it's all I can think of.

He snaps his leg away and kicks me hard across the face. I go flying, turning over several times, and slam into the corner of the cage.

He touches his bloody foot and examines his hand and sneers down at me with a newfound hatred. I wonder if he has just decided to kill me slowly instead of quickly.

I scramble to my feet and face him, and this time, I feel that I need the element of surprise. As crazy as it is, I charge him.

I leap into the air and do a flying front kick, aiming for his groin. I'm hoping that if I can kick him hard, in just the right spot, with my steel-tipped toes, maybe I can make an impact.

But he is too good of a fighter for that. He must spot my telegraphed action a mile away, because without even making an effort, he reaches down and blocks my leg. His metal gauntlet smashes into my calf, right into my wound, before I can make an impact. The pain is numbing. It stops me cold, and I drop to the ground, grabbing my calf in agony.

I try to get up, but he backhands me with his other gauntlet, hard across the face, and the force of it knocks me back, face-down, to the ground. I can feel the taste of blood in my mouth, and look down to see the floor covered in my dark-red blood. The crowd cheers.

I try to get up again, but before I can, I feel his hands on my back, feel him pick me up in the air, wind back, and throw me. He aims high, towards the top of the cage, and I go flying across the ring, right into it. This time, I think quick.

I reach out as I'm flying towards the wall, and as I hit it, I grab hold of the chain-link, clutching it. The wall sways a few times, but I manage to hang on. I'm up high on the metal cage, nearly fifteen feet off the ground, clinging for my life.

The brute looks annoyed. He charges towards me, reaching up to grab me and pull me down. But I scramble up, even higher. He reaches up to grab my leg, but I pull it up in the nick of time. I'm just out of his reach.

He looks perplexed, and I can see the skin on his neck redden with frustration. He hadn't expected this.

The crowd jumps to its feet, roaring its approval. Clearly, they haven't seen this tactic before.

But I don't know how long I can hang on. My muscles are already weak, and as I cling to the cage, suddenly, I feel it swaying. I look down and see that the brute has grabbed the cage wall with both hands, and is shaking it violently. I cling to it like a buoy in a storm-tossed sea. I sway violently, but no matter how much he shakes it, I refuse to let go.

The crowd screams its approval, and laughs at him. I glance down and see his skin turn a darkening shade of red. He looks humiliated.

He reaches out, grabs the metal, and begins to pull himself up. But he is slow, awkward. He is far too heavy to be agile, and this cage is not meant to hold someone of his bulk. He climbs towards me, but now I have the advantage. He uses both hands to pull himself up, and as he gets close, I swing back one leg and kick him hard in the face, connecting on the corner of his temple, right at the corner of his facemask, with my steel-tipped toe.

It is a solid kick, one he does not expect—and to my surprise, it works. He falls back off the fence, a good ten feet, and lands hard, flat on his back, on the ground. He lands with such force, the entire ring shakes. It sounds as if a tree trunk has been dropped from the sky. The crowd roars, screaming its approval.

As I look down, I see that my kick has dislodged his facemask, which goes flying across the floor. He gets to his feet and scowls up at me, and for the first time, I can see his face.

I wish that I hadn't.

It is a hideous, grotesque face, and barely even looks human. Now I understand why he wears the mask. His face is entirely burnt and charred, with huge lumps all over it. He is a Biovictim, and the worst I've ever seen. He's missing a nose, and has slits for eyes. He looks more like a beast than a man.

He snarls and roars up at me, and if I wasn't afraid before, my heart pounds with fear now. I feel as if I'm fighting something out of a nightmare.

But for now, at least, I am safe. I have outsmarted him. There is nothing he can do except stand down there and look up at me. We are at a stalemate.

That is, until suddenly, everything changes.

Stupidly, I am looking down, over my shoulder, at the ring below me. I never bother to look in front of me, never imagined there could be any danger from that direction. But one of the slaverunners, outside the ring, has managed to sneak up on me, with a huge pole, and shock me with it, right in the chest. I feel an electric jolt run through my entire body. It must be some sort of cattle prod; they probably reserve it for situations like this.

The electric shock sends me flying back, off the cage, falling through the air, and landing flat on my back on the floor. The force of it knocks the wind out of me again, and my body is still shaking from being electrified. The crowd roars in delight as I'm back down on the floor of the ring, helpless.

I can barely breathe, or feel my fingertips. But I have no time to reflect. The brute charges right for me, and looks madder than ever. He leaps into the air and raises his knees high, preparing to bring both feet down on my face, to stomp me to oblivion.

Somehow, at the last second, I manage to roll out of the way. I feel the wind of his kick rush past my ear, and then the thunderous stomp. It is enough to shake the floor, and I go bouncing off it like a plaything. I roll away, get to my hands and knees, then run to the far side of the ring.

Something suddenly drops from the sky, lands on the floor in the center of the ring. I look down and am surprised to see it is a medieval mace, with a short wooden handle and a foot-long chain, at the end of which is a spiked, metal ball. I've seen these before, in pictures of knights in armor: it was a deadly weapon used in the Middle Ages.

I run for, reach down and grab it before he can. Not that he even shows any interest in grabbing it. He doesn't even go for it, clearly feeling he doesn't need it. I don't blame him.

I grab hold of the shaft and swing it, filled with a newfound confidence. If I can just connect, with just one blow, maybe I can actually win. It is a weapon of beauty, and the spiked metal ball swings around and around at the end of the chain, establishing a perimeter before me, keeping him at bay. I swing it again and again, like a helicopter, and it manages to keep him off guard, wary.

But he still slowly approaches, and as he does, I back up. As I take another step back, though, I suddenly slip on a pool of blood: my feet go out from under me, and I fall flat on my back. As I do, I lose my grip on the mace, and it goes flying across the cage. It actually by chance flies right at his head; but he is more agile than I suspect and ducks it easily. It goes over his head and smashes into the wall of the cage. The crowd ooohs at the close call.

I'm flat on my back, and before I can get up, he's standing over me and reaches down, grabs my shirt and picks me up by my chest with both hands. He lifts me up high, way over his head, like a wrestler, then parades me across the ring, before the thousands of revelers. They eat it up, going wild.

"MAL-COLM! MAL-COLM! MAL-COLM!"

Maybe this is his trademark move, before he finishes people off for good. As I dangle there in the air, so high above his head, helpless, I squirm, but it is futile. I know that there is nothing I can do. I am at his disposal. And I feel that any second will be my last.

He slowly walks me around the ring, again and again, savoring the adulation, the victory. The noise of the crowd grows to a deafening pitch. He lifts me, even higher, preparing to hurl me, and the last thing I think, before I go flying, is that I'm glad that Bree isn't here to see my death.

NINETEEN

He throws me and I go flying through the air at full speed, not knowing I could move that fast, and land hard on the floor on the opposite side of the ring. I feel another rib crack, and as my head rolls and smashes into the metal, I feel another welt form on my forehead. I wonder how much more abuse my body can take.

I sense him coming at me again, and this time, I am just too beat up to move. I lay there, on the floor, face down, struggling to catch my breath. He takes his time. It is clear that he will kill me when he reaches me. It is a death walk.

I'm too tired and weak and delirious to do anything more than accept my fate. I feel I am destined to die. Here, in this place. At this moment. I feel as if I've failed, let Bree down.

As I lay there, breathing hard, blood coming from my mouth, slowly, over the sound of the ringing in my ears, over the din of the crowd, there gradually comes another sound. It is a voice. The voice of my Dad. It is a stern voice.

The voice he always used to chastise me. To force me to push myself. To be more than I could be.

Be tough, Marine! Stop feeling sorry for yourself! If you think you're a failure, then you are! Be strong! BE STRONG!

His voice becomes deafening, drowning out everything. I look up, my vision blurry, and for a moment I could swear I actually see Dad standing there, hands on his hips, scowling down. There is disapproval—even disgust—on his face. And that is what motivates me. That is what makes something snap inside.

I could never stand to see my father disapproving of me. I would always do whatever it took just to silence him, just to prove him wrong. This time is no different. I feel a rush of adrenaline as I feel myself surge with anger, with the need to prove him wrong. I'm filled with a new fury, and it forces me to my hands and knees.

BE STRONG!

The brute takes three big steps, winding up to deliver a knockout kick to my face. I can already tell that if the kick connects, it will break every bone in my face.

But now, I am ready. I surprise him by rolling out of the way at the last second, a split second before the kick reaches me. He misses and instead kicks the metal fence. He kicks it with such force that his foot lodges into one of the metal chain links.

I jump to my feet and in the same motion run across the ring and grab the mace. The brute yanks at his foot, trying to get it out of the cage—but he is stuck.

This time, I don't wait. This time, I don't hesitate. Finally, I have learned my lesson.

I charge across the ring, and with all I have, I swing the mace, wind up the ball. I realize I only have one shot at this, and I take aim for his huge, bald, muscular head.

I get closer to him. Ten feet…five.… I swing and let the ball go.

Suddenly, he yanks his foot out of the cage and turns and faces me.

I've already set the chain in motion and the ball is already spinning, flying over my head, through the air. And just as he turns to face me, the ball comes swinging around and lodges right into the side of his head. It lodges into his temple, and as it does, blood squirts out. I let go of the shaft.

The crowd is stunned into silence.

The brute takes a step back, stumbles, then reaches up in shock, grabs the shaft, and yanks it out of his own head. As he does, brains and blood come out.

I stand there, horrified, frozen. I can't fathom how someone could continue to function after a blow like that.

But then, after a moment, he drops the shaft, and buckles to his knees. He falls forward on his face. His hands lay limp at his side, and a second later, to my shock, I realize he is dead. I have killed him.

After a second of stunned silence, the crowd suddenly leaps to its feet. It roars and screams louder than I've ever heard. And this time, they chant my name.

"BROOKE! BROOKE! BROOKE!"

I barely even hear it. Whatever strength was left in me suddenly disappears, and a moment later, I feel the world spinning, feel my knees go weak, feel myself collapsing. The last thing I see is the floor racing up towards me, striking me in the face.

And then my world is blackness.

TWENTY

I'm not sure if I'm dead or alive. My body aches more than I could imagine, and I wonder if this is what it's like to be on the other side. Somehow, I feel as if I'm still alive: if I were dead, I am hoping it would not be this painful.

I peel open one eye and see I am lying, face down, on a metal floor, in a darkened room, lit by red emergency lights. I look up, and struggle to make out the shape before me.

"Brooke?" a voice asks. It is a male voice, and I know I recognize it from somewhere, but can't remember where.

"Brooke?" he asks again, softly.

I feel a hand on my shoulder, gently prodding me.

I manage to open my eye a bit more, and finally recognize the face: Ben. He leans over me, gently prodding me, trying to see if I'm alive.

"This is for you," he says.

There is the sound of plastic scraping against the metal floor, and I am struck by the smell of food. But I'm too groggy to look at it, and I don't really register what's happening.

"I have to go now," he says. "Please. I want you to have this."

A second later there comes the sound of a door opening, and light floods the room. There is the sound of marching boots, chains, handcuffs being released. Then footsteps recede and the door closes, and as it does, suddenly, I realize: they have just taken Ben away.

I want to raise my head, to open my eyes, to call out to him. To thank him. To warn him. To say goodbye.

But my head, too heavy, won't lift, and my eyes begin to shut of their own accord. Moments later, I fall back into a heavy sleep.

*

I don't know how much time has passed when I wake again. I feel the cold metal of the floor on the side of my face, and this time I am able to gradually lift my head, peel myself off. My head is splitting, and every ounce of my body is killing me.

As I sit up, I feel a sharp pain in my ribs, now on both sides. My face is swollen, welts and bruises all over it, and my shoulder is killing me.

Worst of all, there's an intense throbbing in my calf, an unbearable pain as I attempt to straighten my leg. At first, I don't know what it's from, and then I remember: the snakebite.

Propping myself with one hand, I manage to sit halfway up. I look around the darkened room for any sign of Ben. But he is gone. I am alone.

I look down and see a tray of food before me, untouched. His food. I reach out and touch it: it is cold. I feel bad that he has left it; I'm sure he needed it at least as much as me. I realize what it took to sacrifice this meal. If this was his last meal, that means they've taken him away, to fight. My heart leaps at the realization. Surely, that means he is already dead.

I look down again at his food, and it feels like the food of a dead man. I can't bring myself to touch it.

There is a sound of boots, and the metal door slams open. In march four slaverunners, who drag me to my feet and prod me out the room. The pain is indescribable as I stand, walk. My head is so heavy, and the room spins, and I don't know if I'm going to make it without collapsing.

I am pushed and prodded down the corridor, and as I go, the sound of a distant crowd grows louder. My heart drops as I realize I'm being led back to the arena.

If they think I can fight again, it is a joke. I can barely walk. Anyone who squares off with me will have easy pickings. I don't have any will left to fight—or any strength, even if I did. I have already given this arena everything I have.

I am shoved one last time as the tunnel to the arena opens up. The roar becomes deafening. I squint at the harsh light as I am lead down the ramp, as I realize that I'm counting my final minutes.

The crowd jumps to its feet as they see me. They stomp violently. This time, instead of hisses and jeers, they seem to love me.

"BROOKE! BROOKE! BROOKE!"

It is a surreal feeling. I feel like I've achieved fame, but for actions that I detest, and in the last place on earth I'd ever want it.

I'm prodded again, all the way to ringside, back to the metal ladder. I look up and see the cage open, and climb and walk in helplessly.

As I enter, the crowd goes wild.

I am still half-asleep, and this is all so surreal, I can't help wondering if I did this before, or if it was all a dream. I look down and see the huge welt on my calf, and know that it was real. I can't believe it. I am back here again. This time, for a certain death.

They weren't kidding when they said no survivors. Now I know there will be no exceptions.

I stand in the empty ring and survey the stadium, wondering who my next opponent will be, where he will enter from. As I do, suddenly, there comes a cheer from the far side of the stadium. The tunnel opens up, and in marches another contestant. I can't see who it is, as he's blocked by an entourage of slaverunners. The crowd goes crazy as he gets closer. But my view is so obscured, it's not until he reaches the very edge of the ring, until he is climbing the ladder, until the cage opens and he's actually pushed inside, that I see who it is.

As I do, any ounce of fight that is left in me falls away.

I am horrified.

It can't be.

Standing before me, staring back with equal shock, is Ben.

TWENTY ONE

I stand there in shock, staring back at Ben, who looks like a deer in the headlights. I don't know how they could be so cruel. Of all the people they could pit me against, why did it have to be him?

The crowd seems to sense our connection— and they love it: they scream and holler as the cage slams shut with a bang. They place bets furiously, eager to see which one of us is willing to kill the other first.

Ben stands there looking so lost, so out of place. Our eyes lock, and we share a moment. His large blue eyes, so gentle, are tearing up. He looks like a lost little boy. I can already see that he would never lift a finger to harm me.

Before this moment, I was resigned to just go quietly to my grave. But now, seeing Ben here, caught in this same predicament, so helpless, my will to live returns. I have to find a way to get us out of here. I have to save us. If not for me, than for him.

I think quick, my heart racing a million miles an hour, as I try to concentrate, to drown out the deafening crowd.

The crowd bursts into boohs and jeers, furious that neither of us are making a move to fight. Eventually their disappointment grows into a rage, and they start throwing things at the cage. Rotten tomatoes and all sorts of objects slam against the metal as the crowd hails things down on us.

I suddenly feel a sharp electric shock in my kidneys, and I wheel and see I was just shocked by the cattle prod, the long pole inserted through the chain-link. A slaverunner quickly retracts it as I try to snatch it away from him. I look over and see that they jab Ben at the same time. It is a dirty trick: they're trying to force us into action, to stir us into a rage, to prod us closer to each other. The crowd roars its approval.

But we still stand there, staring at each other, neither of us willing to fight.

"You gave me your last meal," I say to him, over the din of the crowd.

He nods back, slowly, too frozen with fear to speak.

Suddenly, something falls from the sky, lands before us. It is a weapon. A knife. I look down closely at it, and am horrified to see that it is my Dad's knife, the Marine Corps logo emblazoned on its side.

The crowd cheers as the object lands, assuming this will cause us to fight.

I see Dad's knife, and I think of Bree. And I realize, once again, that I have to survive. To save her. If she's still alive.

Suddenly, the crowd quiets. I look around, trying to understand what's happening. I haven't heard it quiet before. I look up and see the leader is standing, high up on his podium. Everyone has gone silent with rapt attention.

"I am declaring a change to the rules of the arena!" he announces, his deep voice booming. He speaks slowly, deliberately, and the crowd hangs on his every word. This is clearly a man who is used to being listened to.

"For the first time ever, we will allow a survivor. Just one!" he announces. "The winner of this match will be granted clemency. As will their siblings. After this match, they will be free to go."

The leader slowly sits back down, and as he does, the crowd bursts into an excited murmur. More bets are placed.

I look back down at the knife, and now I see that Ben glances at it, too.

A chance to survive. To be free. Not just for me—but for Bree. If I kill Ben, it will save her. It is my chance. It is my ticket out.

As I see Ben looking at the knife, I can see the same thoughts racing through his mind, too. It is a chance for him to save his little brother.

I lunge for it, and in a single motion, I reach down and pick it up.

Getting it was easy. Ben never even makes a move for it.

But I'm cut from a different cloth than him. I need to do what I have to to survive. For Bree to survive.

So I lean back, take aim, and prepare to throw my Dad's knife.

Do it, Brooke! Save your sister! You have a responsibility! DO IT!

I lean forward and with all my might, throw the knife.

And that is the moment that changes everything.

PART IV

TWENTY TWO

I throw my Dad's knife with everything I have, and in that moment, the crowd holds its breath, completely silent. The blade glimmers in the light as it goes flying end over end, through the air, racing. It is the strongest and most accurate throw I've ever done. I already know it will find its target. And that it will mean certain death.

In moments, I will be free.

A second later, the sound of metal meeting flesh punctures the air, and I see that it was, indeed, a perfect strike.

The entire crowd gasps, horrified.

For once in my life, I have ignored my father's advice. I have not killed Ben.

I have killed their leader.

*

The knife lodges in the center of the leader's forehead; I'd managed to throw it perfectly, just high enough to clear the fence, by a millimeter, and yet still maintain the perfect angle to hit him, thirty yards away. It hits him so hard, it pins his head to the chair. He sits there, eyes wide open, frozen in shock, dead.

There is stunned silence in the arena. For several seconds, the crowd is too shocked to even react. I can hear a pin drop.

And then, pandemonium. Thousands of people jump up from their seats and run in every direction. Some, terrified, flee for their lives; others see this as their chance to be set free, and run for the exits; others start fighting with each other, while others start fighting with the slaverunners. It is as if a violent energy, long contained, has been set loose.

Slaverunners scurry in every direction, trying to maintain order.

I look to the cage door, wondering if we can escape that way, but already guards are fiddling with its lock, trying to unchain it so that they can come and get us.

I run to Ben, who still stands there, shocked, and grab him by the arm.

"FOLLOW ME!" I scream.

I take his hand as I run across the ring, jump up onto the cage and scale its wall. I climb straight up, relieved to see Ben beside me.

Just in time. The slaverunners burst open the metal gate and rush right for us.

But we are already at the top of the cage, fifteen feet high. I look over the edge and hesitate for a moment: it is a steep drop, and a hard landing. Ben hesitates, too.

But we have no choice. It's now or never.

I jump.

I land hard on my feet, fifteen feet below on the concrete. My calf explodes in pain as I tumble to the ground. As I hit, rolling, my cracked ribs hurt just as much. The pain is excruciating, but at least I don't feel as if I've broken anything else. I've made it.

I look over, hoping to see Ben beside me in the chaos, as the crowd scurries in every direction around me. But my heart drops to see he's not there. I turn and look up and see he is still up there, high on the cage wall. He's hesitating at the top. He's afraid to jump.

The slaverunners are reaching up, beginning to climb, about to get him. He is terrified, frozen in inaction.

I scramble to my feet and yell up at him.

"BEN!" I scream. "JUMP! DO IT!"

I can hear the panic in my voice. There is no time. If he doesn't jump now, I'll have to leave without him.

Suddenly, thankfully, Ben plunges into the crowd. He hits the ground hard, tumbling. And then, after a moment, he gets up. He looks dazed, but as far as I can tell, unhurt. I grab his arm and we run.

It is such pandemonium, no one even notices us. People are brawling with each other, fighting to get out. I manage to weave through the masses, hiding in anonymity. I check back and see the group of slaverunners behind us, on our trail.

I head towards one of the exit tunnels where hundreds are fleeing, and we blend in with the stampede, ducking and weaving through the people. Behind us, I sense the slaverunners parting ways through the crowd, coming after us. I don't know how far we can make it. The thick crowd is barely moving.

I enter the blackness of one of the tunnels, and as I do, I suddenly feel a hand grab me hard around my mouth and yank me backwards. Another hand clasps Ben by the mouth and drags him back, too.

We've been caught, yanked back into the blackness. I am being held tight in a recess in the wall, and my captor holds me in a strong, deadly grip. I'm unable to resist. As I stand there, I wonder if I'm about to die.

Suddenly, right in front of me, the group of slaverunners runs past. They keep running down the tunnel, thinking they are following us. I can't believe it: we've lost them.

Now I'm thankful for being pulled aside. And as the grip around my mouth loosens, I wonder why my captor just did us a favor. He releases his grip completely, and I look back over my shoulder and see a large soldier, dressed in black but not wearing a mask. He looks different than the others. He looks to be about 22, and his chiseled features are perfect, with a strong jawline and short, cropped brown hair. He towers over us, and stares down with green eyes that are a surprising contrast to his demeanor: they exude softness, and are starkly out of place here.

"Come with me," he says urgently.

He turns and disappears into a side door, hidden in the wall. Ben and I exchange a glance, then instantly follow, ducking under the door and into the side chamber.

This man has just saved our lives. And I have no idea who he is.

*

The soldier closes and locks the door behind us. It is a small room, like a cell, with a tiny window way up at its top. No sunlight comes through, so I assume it's still night. The room is lit by only a small red emergency light. He turns to us and we all stand there, facing each other.

"Why did you save us?" I ask.

"You're not saved yet," he answers, coldly. "There are still thousands of those things out there, looking for you. You'll have to sit tight, wait it out, until daylight. Then we can make a break for it. Our chances are slim. But we have no choice."

"But why?" I press. "Why are you doing this?"

He walks away, checking the lock on the door again. Then, his back to us, he murmurs, "Because I want out of here, too."

I stand as quietly as I can in the small room, Ben on one side of me and the soldier on the other. I listen to the stampede of footsteps just outside the door, racing down the hall. The screaming and hollering seems to go on forever, as the angry mob sounds as if it's alternately looking for us and beating each other up. It's like I've opened Pandora's box: it's total mayhem outside that door. I pray that no one else thinks to check in the recess of the wall—or if they do, that the lock holds.

My fear springs to life, as I hear a jiggling on the doorknob. The soldier slowly reaches out his gun, aims it at the door, and leans back. He hold it steady, leveling it at the door.

I stand there, trembling, sweat pouring down my back even though it's cold in here. Whoever is out there keeps fiddling with the knob. If it opens, we're finished. We might kill the first one, but the gunshot would alert the others, and the entire mob would find us. I hold my breath for what seems like forever, and finally, whoever is fiddling, stops. I hear him turn and run away.

I breathe a sigh of relief. It was probably just a passerby, looking for shelter.

Slowly, the soldier relaxes, too. He lowers and holsters his gun.

"Who are you?" I ask, speaking in hushed tones for fear of being heard.

"Name's Logan," he says, not offering his hand.

"I'm Brooke and this is—" I begin, but he cuts me off.

"I know," he says, curtly. "All contestants are announced."

Of course.

"You still haven't answered my question," I press. "I didn't ask your name. I asked *who* you are."

He looks back at me coldly, defiant.

"I'm one of them," he says reluctantly. "Or, at least, I used to be."

"A slaverunner?" Ben asks, his voice rising in surprise and disgust.

Logan shakes his head.

"No. A gamekeeper. I stood guard in the arena. I never went on slaverunning missions."

"But that still puts you on their side," I snap, and can hear the judgment in my voice. I know

I should give him a break—after all, he just saved our lives. But still, I think of those people who took Bree, and it's hard to feel any sympathy.

He shrugs. "Like I said, not anymore."

I glare back at him.

"You don't understand," he says, by way of explanation. "Here, there are no options. Either you join them, or you die. It's that simple. I had no choice."

"I would have chosen to die," I say, defiantly.

He looks at me and in the dim light I see the intensity in his green eyes. I can't help noticing, despite myself, how gorgeous they are. There is a nobility to him, a chivalrous quality, that I've never seen.

"Would you?" he asks. He looks me over. "Maybe you would," he says finally. "Maybe you're a better person than I. But I did what I had to to survive."

He paces, crossing to the far side of the room.

"But like I said, none of that matters now," he continues. "The past is the past. I'm getting out."

I realize how judgmental I'm being, and I feel bad. Maybe he's right. Maybe if I was still living here, in the city, I would have joined them, too. I don't know what pressures he was under.

"So what now?" I say. "You're leaving them? Defecting?"

"I'm escaping," he says. "I've had enough. Watching you fight—it did something to me. You had such spirit. I knew that this was my moment, that I had to leave, even if I die trying."

I hear the sincerity in his voice and know that he speaks the truth. I'm surprised to hear that I've inspired him. I wasn't trying to inspire anyone—just to stay alive. And I am grateful for his help.

But based on the number of feet I hear charging outside the door, it sounds like it's a lost cause anyway. I don't see how we can ever get out of here.

"I know where there's a boat," he continues, as if reading my mind. "It's docked on the west side, at 42nd. It's a small motor boat. They use it to patrol the Hudson. But the first patrol doesn't leave until after dawn. If I get there at dawn, before them, I can steal it. Take it upriver."

"To where?" I ask.

He looks back at me blankly.

"Where would you go?" I press.

He shrugs. "I don't know. I don't care. Anywhere but here. As far as the river will take me, I guess."

"You think you can survive the mountains?" Ben suddenly asks. I can hear an edge to his voice, something unfamiliar, something I haven't heard before. If I didn't know better, it sounds to me like possessiveness. Like jealousy.

Suddenly, my face flushes as I realize: Ben has feelings for me. He's jealous of Logan.

Logan turns and stares Ben down coldly. "*You* managed to," he says. "Why couldn't I?"

"I'd hardly call what I did surviving," Ben says. "It was more like a slow death."

"It beats being here," Logan says. "Besides, I'm not a defeatist. I will find a way to survive. I got weapons and ammo, and a few days food. That's all I need. I'll do whatever I have to."

"I'm not a defeatist," Ben retorts, annoyed.

Logan just shrugs.

"The boat's meant for two," he says, looking away from Ben, to me. It is clear from his gaze that he only wants me to come. I wonder if he likes me, or if it's just a guy thing, just plain old competition and jealousy, for the sake of it. Logan must see the determination in my stare, because he adds, "But I guess, if it has to, it can hold three."

He paces.

"I'll help you guys escape. At dawn, you'll follow me. We'll take the boat up the Hudson. I'll drop you back at your homes, wherever they are, then I'll continue on my way."

"I'm not going anywhere without Bree," I say, firmly.

Logan turns and looks at me.

"Who's Bree?" he asks.

"My sister."

"And I'm not going without my brother," Ben adds.

"We came down here for a reason," I explain. "To rescue our siblings. And to bring them back. I'm not leaving without her."

Logan shakes head, as if annoyed.

"You don't know what you're saying," he says. "I'm giving you a way out. A free ticket. Don't you realize there's no other way out of here? That they'll hunt you down before you go ten feet? Even if you find your sister—then what?"

I stand there and cross my arms, fuming. There's no way I'll let him talk me out of it.

"Besides, I hate to say this but…" he trails off, and I realize he is checking himself.

"But what?" I press.

He hesitates, as if debating whether to say anything. He takes a deep breath.

"There's no way you'll ever find them."

I feel my heart drop at his words. I stare at him, wondering what he's holding back.

"What aren't you telling us?" I ask.

He shifts his eyes from mine to Ben's to the floor, avoiding my gaze.

"What do you know?" I press. My heart is pounding—I am afraid he is going to tell me that Bree is dead.

He hesitates, toeing the ground, looking down. Finally, he begins to talk.

"They were separated," he begins. "They were too young. They always separate the older from the younger. The stronger from the weaker. The boys from the girls. The stronger, older ones are set aside for the arena. But the younger, weaker ones..." He trails off.

My heart pounds, as I wonder what he's going to say.

"Well?" Ben prods.

"The young boys, they send to the mines."

"The mines?" Ben asks, stepping forward in indignation.

"The coal mines. Crosstown. Beneath Grand Central. They put them on a train crosstown. Put them down in the shafts, far beneath the earth. They use the coal for fire. That's where your brother is. That's where that train was going. I'm sorry," he says, and sounds genuine.

Ben suddenly marches for the door, his face red.

"Where are you going?" I ask, alarmed.

"To get my brother," Ben snaps back, not even slowing.

Logan steps up and holds out an arm, blocking Ben's way. Now that I look at them side by side, I see that Logan towers over Ben, a half a foot taller and twice as broad, with his huge, muscular shoulders. Beside him, Ben seems tiny. They are starkly different looking people, polar opposites: Logan is the all-American jock type, while Ben, thin, unshaven, with his longish hair and soulful eyes, is the sensitive-artist type. They couldn't be more different. But they each share a strong will, a streak of defiance.

"You're not going anywhere," Logan says in his deep, authoritative voice.

Ben looks up at him, scowling.

"You walk out that door," Logan continues, "and you give us away. Then we'll all be dead."

Ben's shoulders relax, and I can see him relent.

"You want to find your brother," Logan continues, "you can. But you need to wait till dawn, when we all bust out of here together. Just a few more hours. Then you can go to your death if you want."

Ben slowly relents, then turns his back and resentfully crosses to our side of the room.

"What about Bree?" I say, my voice steely cold. I am afraid to ask it. But I need to know. "Where did they take her?"

Logan slowly shakes his head, avoiding my gaze.

"WHERE?" I press, stepping forward, my voice venomous. My heart is pounding with terror.

He clears his throat.

"The young girls," he begins, "the ones who are too young for the arena…they ship them off to slavery," he says. He looks up at me. "The sex trade."

My heart rips in two. I want to run out the door, screaming, looking for her anywhere. But I know that would be futile. I need to know more. I feel my face redden, my entire body rise with heat, my fists clench with indignation.

"Where did they take her?" I press, my voice steely cold.

"They ship the sex slaves to Governors Island. They load them on buses and bus them downtown. Then they put them on a boat. The next bus leaves at dawn. Your sister will be on it."

"Where are these buses?" I demand.

"Across the street," he says. "34th and 8th. They leave from the old post office."

Without thinking I march for the door, feeling the horrific pain in my leg as I go. Again,

Logan holds out his arm and stops me. It is strong and muscular, like a wall.

"You have to wait, too," he says. "Until daybreak. It would do you no good to look for her now. She's not on the bus yet. They keep them underground until loading time, in a cell somewhere. I don't even know where. I promise you. At dawn, they'll bring them up and load them. If you want to go after her, that's when you can do it."

I stare into his eyes, scrutinizing them, and see the sincerity. Slowly, I relent, breathing deep to control myself.

"But you need to know it's a lost cause," he says. "You'll never bust her out. She'll be chained to a group of slaves, and these will be chained to an armored bus, and the bus will be flanked by dozens of soldiers and vehicles. You won't be able to get anywhere near it. You'll just end up killing yourself. "Not to mention," he adds, "most of the buses don't even make it through the wasteland."

"The wasteland?" I press.

He clears his throat, reluctant.

"To reach the Seaport, the pier for Governors Island, the buses have to go downtown, have to leave the walled area. The wall starts at 23rd Street. South of that, it's the wasteland. That's where the crazies live. Thousands of them. They attack every bus that goes through there. Most don't even make it. That's why they send lots of buses at once."

My heart drops at his words.

"That's why I'm telling you: leave with me in the morning. At least you'll be safe. Your siblings are already a lost cause. At least *you* can survive."

"I don't care what the odds are," I retort, my voice steely and determined. "I don't care if I die trying. I'm going after my sister."

"And I'm going after my brother," Ben adds. I'm surprised by his determination, too.

Logan shakes his head.

"Suit yourself. You guys are on your own. I'm taking that boat at dawn and I'll be long gone."

"You'll do what you have to do," I say, with disgust. "Just like you always have."

He sneers back at me, and I can see I've really hurt him. He turns away abruptly, crosses to the far side of the room, and leans against the wall and sits, sulking. He checks and cleans his pistol, not looking at me again, as if I no longer exist.

His sitting reminds me of the pain in my calf, of how exhausted I am. I go to the far wall, as far away from him as I can get, and lean back against it and sit, too. Ben comes over and sits beside me, his knees almost touching mine, but not quite. It feels good to have him there. I feel as if he understands.

I can't believe we are both sitting here right now, alive. I never would have imagined this. I was sure we were being marched off to our deaths earlier, and now I feel as if I'm being given a second chance at life.

I think of my sister, and his brother—and suddenly it strikes me that Ben and I will have to part ways, go to different parts of the city. The thought of it disturbs me. I look over and study him, as he sits there with his head down, and I see that he's just not cut out to be a fighter. He won't survive on his own. And somehow, I feel responsible.

"Come with me," I suddenly say. "It will be safer that way. We'll go downtown together, find my sister, and then find a way out of here."

He shakes his head.

"I can't leave my brother," he says.

"Stop and think about it," I say. "How will you ever find him? He's crosstown somewhere, hundreds of feet below ground, in a mine. And if you do find him, how will you get out of there? At least we know where my sister is. At least we have a chance."

"How will you get out after you find her?" he asks.

It is a good question, one for which I have no response.

I simply shake my head. "I'll find a way," I say.

"So will I," he answers. But I can detect the uncertainty in this voice, as if he already knows that he won't.

"Please, Ben," I plead. "Come with me. We'll get Bree and make it out of this. We'll survive together."

"I can say the same thing," he says. "I can ask you to come with me. Why is your sister more important than my brother?"

It is a good point, one for which I have no response. He's right. He loves his brother as much as I love my sister. And I understand. There's nothing I can say to that. The reality hits me that we will part ways at dawn. And I will probably never see him again.

"OK," I say. "But promise me one thing, will you?"

He looks at me.

"When you're done, head to the East River, make your way down to the pier at the South Street Seaport. Be there at dawn. I'll be there. I'll find a way. Meet me there, and we'll find a way to make it out together." I look at him. "Promise me," I command.

He studies me, and I can see him thinking.

"What makes you so sure you'll even make it downtown, to the Seaport?" he asks. "Past all the crazies?"

"If I don't," I say, "that means I'm dead. And I don't plan on dying. Not after everything I've been through. Not while Bree's alive."

I can hear the determination in my own voice, and I barely recognize it—it sounds as if a stranger is speaking through me.

"That's our meeting place," I insist. "Be there. Promise me."

Finally, he nods.

"OK," he says. "Fine. If I'm alive, I'll be there. At dawn. But if I'm not, that means I'm dead. And don't wait for me. Do you promise? I don't want you waiting for me," he insists. "Promise me."

Finally, I say, "I promise."

He reaches out his frail hand towards me. I slowly take it in mine.

We sit there, holding hands, our fingers clasped within each other's, and I realize it is the first time I've held his hand—really held his hand. The skin is so soft, and it feels good to hold it. Despite myself, I feel small butterflies.

We sit there, our backs to the wall, beside each other in the dim room, holding hands for I don't know how long. We both look away, neither of us saying a word, each lost in our own world. But our hands never part, and as I sit there, falling asleep, I can't help but wonder if this is the last time I'll see him alive again.

TWENTY THREE

I open my eyes as a rough hand shoves my shoulder.

"LET'S GO!" comes an urgent whisper.

I open my eyes with a jolt, disoriented, unsure if I'm awake or asleep. I look all around, trying to get my bearings, and see grey, pre-dawn daylight filtering in through a window high up. Daybreak. I've fallen asleep sitting on the floor, my head resting on Ben's shoulder, who still sits beside me, sleeping. Logan shoves him roughly, too.

I jump into action, scurrying to my feet. As I do, the pain in my calf is excruciating, exploding in my leg.

"We're losing time!" Logan snaps. "Move! Both of you! I'm leaving. If you want to follow me out, now's your chance!"

Logan hurries to the door and leans his ear against it. I feel a rush of adrenaline as I cross the room, Ben now awake and beside me, and take a position behind Logan. We listen. All seems quiet outside. There are no more footsteps, no shouts, jeers…nothing. I wonder how many hours have passed. It sounds like everyone has disappeared.

Logan seems satisfied, too. Holding his gun in one hand, he slowly reaches out with his free hand, unlocks the door, and checks to see if we're ready. He then slowly pulls open the door.

Logan cautiously steps outside, rounds the corner sharply, ready to shoot.

He gestures for us to follow, and I come out and I see the corridors are empty.

"Move!" he whispers frantically.

He runs down the corridor and I run behind him for all I'm worth. Every step is a small explosion of pain in my calf. I can't help looking down at it, and as I do, I wish I hadn't: it's now swelled up to the size of a baseball. It's also bright red, and I worry it's infected. All my other muscles ache, too, from my ribs to my shoulder to my face—but it's my calf that concerns me most. The others are just injuries; but if my calf is infected, I'll need medicine. And fast.

But I can't focus on this now. I continue to run, hobbling down the corridor, Ben beside me and Logan about ten feet in front. The steel corridors are dimly lit by sporadic emergency lights, and I follow Logan in the darkness, relying on his knowledge of this place. Luckily, there is still no one in site: I assume they are all out looking for us.

Logan makes a right down another corridor, then a left. We follow, trusting he knows his way out of here. I realize my fate is in his hands. He is our lifeline now, and I'll just have to put my trust in him. I have no choice.

After several more twists and turns, Logan finally comes to a stop before a door. I stop beside him, out of breath. He pushes it open, peeks out, then opens it all the way. He reaches back, grabs Ben by the shoulder and pulls him forward.

"There," he says, pointing. "See it?"

I lean forward. In the distance, across the vast, open terminal, are train tracks.

"That train, the one beginning to move. It goes to the mines. It leaves once a day. If you want to go, now's your chance. Catch it!"

Ben turns and looks at me one last time, eyes open wide with adrenaline. He surprises me by reaching out, grabbing my hand, and kissing the back of it. He holds it for another second and looks at me meaningfully, as if this might be the last time he sees me.

He then turns and sprints across the terminal, heading for the train.

Logan glances at me derisively, and I can feel his jealousy.

I don't know what to think of the kiss myself. As I watch him run for the train, I can't help but wonder if it will be the last time I see him.

"This way!" Logan snaps, as he starts running down a different corridor.

But I sit there, frozen, watching Ben run.

Logan turns back to me, annoyed, impatient. "MOVE!" he whispers.

I realize I'm frozen in place, watching Ben run. He runs across the entire open expanse of Penn Station, runs along the tracks, then jumps up onto the back of the slowly moving train. He holds tight onto the metal bars as it goes. He holds on tight as the train disappears, into a black tunnel. He's made it.

"I'm leaving!" Logan says, then turns and sprints down another corridor.

I snap out of it, sprinting after him. I go as fast as my legs will take me, but Logan is already far ahead and he turns again, out of sight. My heart pounds as I wonder if I've lost him.

I turn down another corridor and run up a ramp, and finally, I spot him again. He stands along a wall, beside a glass door, waiting for me. Through it, I can see outside. Eighth Avenue. It is a world of white. I am shocked to see that there is a raging blizzard out there.

I run up to Logan and stand beside him, my back against the wall, struggling to catch my breath.

"See there?" he asks, pointing.

I follow his gaze, trying to see between the sheets of snow.

"Across the street," he says, "in front of the old post office. Those buses parked out front."

I strain to look, and spot three large buses, covered in snow. They look like school buses, but are modified, with thick bars built on every side, like armored vehicles. Two of them are painted yellow, and one is black. As I watch, I see dozens of young girls, chained to each other, being loaded onto them. My heart leaps, as I spot Bree. She's a couple hundred yards away, in the chain gang, being loaded onto one of the two yellow buses.

"There she is!" I scream. "That's Bree!"

"Give it up," he says. "Come with me. You'll survive, at least."

But I am filled with a new resolve, and I look at him with dead seriousness.

"It's not about surviving," I reply. "Don't you realize that?"

Logan looks back into my eyes and I can see that, for the first time, he gets it. He really gets it. He sees that I'm determined, that nothing on earth is going to change my mind.

"OK, then," he says. "This is it. Once we burst out those doors, I'm heading uptown, for the boat. You're on your own."

He suddenly reaches down and places something heavy in palm. I look down and see it's a gun. I am surprised, and grateful.

I am about to say goodbye, but suddenly hear an engine, and look out and see clouds of black exhaust exiting the buses' tailpipes. Before I know it, all three buses start to pull out in the thick snow.

"NO!" I scream, and suddenly burst forward. Before I even think it through, I kick open the door and burst outside. A wave of icy snow and wind hits me in the face, so cold and wet that it takes my breath away.

I run out into the blinding blizzard, snow hitting my face, snow up to my knees. I run and run, heading across the white, open expanse towards the buses. Towards Bree.

I am too late. They have a good hundred yards on me, and are gaining speed in the snow. I sprint after them, my leg killing me, barely able to catch my breath, until I realize that Logan was right. It is useless. I watch the buses turn a corner, and they are soon out of sight. I can't believe it. I just missed her.

I check back over my shoulder, and Logan is gone. My heart drops. He must have taken off already. Now I'm completely alone.

Desperate, I try to think quick, to come up with an idea. I scan my surroundings, and see, in front of Penn Station, a row of Humvees. Slaverunners sit on the roofs and hoods. They are all huddled in their coats against the snow, their backs to me. None of them look in my direction. They are all fixated on watching the buses leave.

I realize I need a vehicle. It is my only chance to catch those buses.

I sprint, hobbling, towards the Humvee in the rear, the only one with no slaverunner sitting on its roof. The Humvee is running, exhaust coming from its tailpipe, and I see a slaverunner sitting in the driver's seat, warming his hands.

I creep up to the driver's side door and yank it open, holding out my gun.

This slaverunner wears no facemask, and I can see the shock in his face. He holds up his hands in fear, not wanting to be shot. I don't give him time to react, to alert the others. Pointing my gun to his face, I reach in, grab him by the shirt, and yank him out. He falls hard to the snow.

I'm about to jump into the driver's seat, when suddenly I feel a tremendous pain in the side of my head, the impact of something metal. Knocked over by the blow, I fall down to the snow.

I look up and see that another slaverunner has snuck up on me, has cracked me in the side of the head with his gun. I reach up and feel my head, and feel blood trickling onto my hand. It hurts like hell.

The slaverunner stands over me, and lowers his gun towards my face. He grins, an evil grin, cocks the pin, and I know he's about to fire. Suddenly, I realize I'm about to die.

A gunshot rings, and I brace myself.

TWENTY FOUR

I feel my face splatter in blood, the warmth of it sticking to my skin, and I wonder if I'm dead.

I slowly open my eyes, and then realize what has happened. I am not dead; I was not even fired upon. The slaverunner was shot from behind, in the back of the head, and his brains splattered all over me. Someone shot him. Someone saved me.

I look up to see Logan standing behind him, his gun outstretched, still smoking. I can't believe it. He's come back for me.

Logan reaches down and holds out a hand. I take it. It's huge and rough, and he pulls me to my feet in one swift motion.

"GET IN!" he screams.

I run to the passenger side and jump in. Logan jumps into the driver's side, slams the door, and while I am barely in, he pulls out, gunning the Humvee. It slips and slides in the snow as we peel out.

The other slaverunners notice; they scramble, jump off their hoods and take off after us. One of them charges on foot. Logan reaches out his window, aims, and shoots him in the head, killing him before he can fire. Another charges us, hand outstretched with his gun, aiming right at us. I reach out my window and fire. It is a direct hit in the head, and he goes down.

I aim for another one, but suddenly I go flying back, as the torque of the car sends me backwards. Logan is flooring it, and we are all over the place in the snow. We turn the corner and gain speed quickly on the three bulky buses. They are only a few hundred yards ahead of us.

Behind us, though, a half dozen Humvees are on our tail. They are gaining speed and I realize that they will soon overtake us. We are outmanned.

Logan shakes his head. "You couldn't just come with me, could you?" he says in exasperation, as he puts it into fifth gear and floors it again. "You're more stubborn than I am."

We gain more speed as we follow the buses crosstown on 34th Street, heading east. We cross Seventh Avenue…then Sixth…then the buses make a sharp right on Fifth and we follow, only a hundred yards behind.

I check the rearview and see the Humvees right on us. One of the slaverunners reaches out his window and aims his gun, and next thing I know, bullets ricochet off our vehicle, echoing off the metal. I flinch, and am grateful it's bulletproof.

Logan steps on it, and I watch the streets fly by: 32nd street…31st…30th…. I look up and am shocked to see an enormous wall right before us, blocking off Fifth Avenue. There is a narrow arched opening in the middle of it, the only way in or out.

Several guards open its huge metal bars, allowing the three buses to pass through, single file.

"We have to stop!" Logan screams. "Beyond those gates is the wasteland! It's too dangerous!"

"NO!" I scream back. "You can't stop! Go! GO!"

Logan shakes his head, sweating. But to his credit, he sticks to the course.

The gate closes. Logan doesn't slow, though.

"Hold on!" he screams.

I brace myself for impact, and a moment later, there's a tremendous crash of metal.

Our Humvee smashes into the iron gate, and the impact is tremendous. I brace myself, not thinking we're going to make it.

But luckily, this Humvee is built like a tank: I can't believe it, but as we make impact, the iron gate comes off and flying into the air. Our windshield is cracked and our hood is badly dented, but luckily, we are unhurt. We are gaining on the buses, now only fifty yards ahead.

I check the rearview, expecting to see the other Humvees behind us—and am shocked to see them all slam on their brakes before the open gate. None of them dares follow us. I can't understand—it's as if they're afraid to pass through to this side of the wall.

"What are they doing?" I ask. "They're stopping! They stopped following us!"

Logan doesn't seem surprised—which I don't understand either.

"Of course they stopped."

"Why?"

"We crossed the wall. It's the wasteland. They're not that stupid."

I look at him, still not understanding.

"They're scared," he says.

I don't understand: how can a large group of armed warriors, in machinegun-mounted Humvees, be scared?

I look around us, take in our surroundings, and am suddenly more wary than I've ever been. A chill runs up my spine. What can be so dangerous about this place that a squadron of soldiers in Humvees are afraid to enter it?

As I lean forward and look closely, I suddenly spot movement. I look up high, and see faces of Biovictims, faces terribly scarred, sticking out of all the abandoned buildings. There are hundreds of them.

Suddenly, the manholes all around us begin to rise. Heads stick up out of the ground, and I am shocked to see dozens more Biovictims rise up from the ground. We pass an abandoned subway station, and dozens more come running up the stairs. They run right for us.

My heart starts to pound at the sight of these people. There are hundreds of them, charging from every direction. I feel like I've entered their territory, crossed a line into a place I'm not supposed to be. I realize I have to get to Bree as soon as possible, and get us the hell out of here.

A crazy jumps up and grabs onto my open window. He reaches a hand in and grabs at me. I lean back, then wind up and hit him in the face with the butt of the pistol. He falls, his body sliding in the snow.

The buses swerve erratically in front of us, and Logan swerves, following their path. The motion is making me nauseous.

"Why are you swerving like that?" I ask.

"Mined!" Logan yells back. "This entire goddamn wasteland is mined!"

As if to hammer home his point, suddenly there is a small explosion in the road before us, and one of the buses manages to swerve out of the way at the last second. My heart drops. How much worse can this place get?

"Catch up to her bus!" I scream over the roaring of the engine.

He floors it, and we close the gap. We're maybe 30 yards away now, and I'm trying to formulate a plan. As we're closing in, suddenly, a crazy rises from a manhole, raises an RPG to his shoulder, and fires.

The missile races across the air and hits one of the buses—the black one. It is a direct hit. The bus explodes right in front of us, bursting into flames, forcing us to swerve at the last second.

The bus skids and lands on its side, then bursts into a huge ball of flames. I think of all the girls I saw board it, and my heart sinks at the sight. Now there are only two buses left. I thank God Bree was on one of the yellow ones. Now time is even more of the essence.

"HURRY!" I yell. "DRIVE UP TO HER BUS!"

We are heading right for the Flatiron building. Fifth Avenue forks, and one of the yellow buses bears left, heading down Broadway, while the other bears right, staying on Fifth. I have no idea which one carries Bree. My heart pounds with anxiety. I have to choose.

"Which bus?" Logan screams, frantic.

I hesitate.

"WHICH BUS?" he screams again.

We are coming up on the intersection and I have to choose. I think hard, desperately trying to remember which one she boarded. But it is no use. My mind is a blur, and the two buses look identical to me. I just have to guess.

"Go right!" I scream.

As the last second, he swerves right. He guns it after one of the buses. I pray I have chosen the right one.

Logan floors it, and manages to speed up to the bus. We are now just yards behind it, sucking in its exhaust. The back windows are grimy and I can't really make out the faces inside, but I do see shapes, the bodies of all those young, chained girls. I pray that one of them is Bree.

"Now what?" Logan screams.

I am wondering the exact same thing.

"I can't run them off the road!" Logan adds. "I might kill her!"

I think fast, trying to formulate a plan.

"Get closer," I say. "Pull up beside it!"

He pulls up to the back, our bumpers nearly touching, and as he does, I lift myself out of the seat and begin to crawl out the open window, sitting on the ledge of the door. The wind is so strong, it nearly knocks me off.

"What are you doing!?" Logan screams, and I can hear his concern. But I ignore it. There's no time for second-guessing now.

Snow and wind whip my face as Logan pulls up right beside the bus. I steady myself, waiting for the perfect moment. The back of the bus is now only a foot away, and there is a wide, flat ledge by its bumper. I brace myself, my heart pounding.

And then I leap.

My shoulder slams into the side of the bus as I land on the ledge. I reach out and grab the thick, metal bars, and I make it. The metal is freezing on my bare hands, but I hold on tight. The ground flies by beneath me in a blur. I can barely believe it. I made it.

The bus must be doing 80 in the snow, and it swerves erratically. I wrap one arm thoroughly around the bar, hugging it with all that I have, and just barely manage to hang on.

We hit a pothole and I slip, nearly losing my grip. One of my feet dips down and drags on the snow—it is my wounded leg, and I scream out in pain as it bumps along the ground. With a supreme effort, I slowly pull myself back up.

I try to open the back door, but my heart drops to discover that it is locked, with a padlock and chain. My hand shaking, I manage to remove my gun from my belt. I lean back and brace myself, and fire.

Sparks fly. The padlock breaks, and the chain clatters and falls to the ground.

I open one of the doors, and it pops open with tremendous force, flying against the wind, and nearly knocking me off. I pull myself through the open door and into the back of the bus.

I now stand inside, in the aisle of the school bus. I quickly hurry down it, looking back and forth frantically as I go. There are dozens of young girls in here, chained to each other, and chained to their seats. As I go, they all look up at me, terrified. I scan each row quickly, from left to right, looking for any sign of my sister.

"BREE!" I yell out, desperate.

As the girls catch on to my presence and realize I might be a key to their salvation, they start crying, hysterical.

"HELP ME!" one of them screams.

"PLEASE, GET ME OUT OF HERE!" another screams.

The driver catches on to my presence; I look up and catch him starting at me in the rearview. He suddenly swerves the bus hard. As he does, I go flying across the aisle and bang my head on the metal casing of the ceiling.

I regain my balance, but then he swerves in the other direction, and I go flying across the other side of the bus.

My head is pounding, but I steady myself, this time clutching the seats as I pull myself carefully forward, going row to row. I look each way for Bree, and there are only a few rows left.

"BREE!" I scream out, wondering why she's not raising her head.

I check the next two rows, then the next two, then the next two…. Finally, I reach the last row, and my heart drops.

There's no sign of her.

The realization hits me like a hammer: I chose the wrong bus.

Suddenly, I glimpse motion out the window and hear an explosion. I turn to see our Humvee, Logan inside, go flying up in the air as it hits a land mine. It lands on its side, skidding through the snow. Then it stops.

My heart drops. Logan must be dead.

TWENTY FIVE

I take my eyes off the driver for too long, and it is a stupid mistake.

He pulls out a handgun, and now aims it right at me. He smiles a cruel smile. He has me.

He cocks back the trigger and is about to fire. I brace myself. There is nowhere to go, and I realize I'm dead.

Suddenly, over the driver's shoulder, I see a crazy jump out of a manhole, aim his RPG right at us, and fire. I watch as the missile sails through the air, coming right for us.

A tremendous explosion rocks our world. The noise is deafening, and I am thrown up into the air, smashing my head, as I feel the tremendous impact of the heat. Then my world turns sideways, as the bus smashes onto its side, skidding.

Because I'm the only one standing, the only one not buckled or chained down, I'm the only one who goes flying across the bus. I go flying through an open window, propelled out of the bus, and as I do, the bus explodes—and the shockwave sends me flying even further. I continue flying through the air and land twenty yards away, face-first in a mound of snow.

Flames rip through the air, just searing my back, and I roll in the snow and luckily put them out. I feel the tremendous heat of the waves of fire behind me.

I turn to see the entire bus is up in flames, on its side, in the snow. The flames must rise twenty feet high. It is an inferno. My heart drops as I realize that no one could possibly survive that. I think of all those innocent little girls, and I feel sick.

I lay there in the snow bank, trying to catch my breath from the smoke. My head spins, and I hurt more than ever. It is an effort to sit up. I turn and set my sights on our Humvee. It sits there in the distance, at the base of the Flatiron building, on its side, like a dead beast, two of its tires blown off.

Logan. I wonder if he is alive.

I claw myself to my feet with my last ounce of strength, and manage to hobble his way. He is a good fifty yards away, and it feels like I am crossing a desert to reach him.

As I get close, another manhole opens up, and a crazy suddenly sprints right to me, holding out a knife. I reach down and raise my gun, take aim, and shoot him in the head. He lands on his back, dead. I reach down and take his knife, and put it in my belt.

I check over my shoulder as I run, and several hundred yards back I spot a group of crazies charging right towards me. There must be at least fifty of them. And all around them I see more manholes open up, more crazies crawl up from the ground, and come running out of the subway stations, scurrying up from the steps. I wonder if they live in the subway tunnels. I wonder if any subways are even still running.

But there is no time to think about that now. I race for the Humvee and as I reach it, I realize it's destroyed, useless. I climb up on it and open the driver side door. I brace myself as I look in, praying I don't see Logan dead.

Luckily, I don't. He is still sitting in the driver's seat, buckled, unconscious. There's blood splattered on the windshield and he's bleeding from his forehead, but at least he's breathing. He's alive. Thank God he's alive.

I hear a distant noise, and turn to see the crazies getting closer. I need to get Logan out of here—and fast.

I reach in, grab his shirt, and begin to yank him up. But he is heavier than I can manage.

"LOGAN!" I scream.

I pull harder, shaking him, afraid the Humvee will blow any minute. Slowly, he begins to wake. He blinks and looks around. He realizes.

"You OK?" I ask.

He nods back. He looked stunned, frightened, but not seriously injured.

"I can't get out," he says back in a weak voice. I see him struggling, and look over and see the twisted metal of his seatbelt buckle.

I climb in, reach over him, and jab at the buckle. It's jammed. I check back over my shoulder and see the crazies are even closer. Fifty yards, and closing in. I use both hands, pushing it for all I have, sweating from the exertion. *Come on. Come on!*

Suddenly I get it. The buckle snaps and the seatbelt goes flying back. Logan, free, rolls over, banging his head. He then begins to pull himself out.

Just as Logan sits up, his eyes suddenly open wide, and he reaches out with one hand and roughly pushes me aside. He raises a gun with the other and takes aim just past my head and fires. The fire is deafening in my ear, which rings badly from it.

I turn and see he's just killed a crazy, a few feet away. And the others are only thirty yards behind him.

The crazies are closing in fast. And there's no way out.

TWENTY SIX

I think quick. I see an RPG lying in the snow, a few feet away from the dead body of a crazy. It looks intact, never fired. I run to it, my heart pounding as I run right towards the mob. I only hope that it works—and that I can figure out how to use it in the next few seconds.

I kneel down in the snow and scoop it up, my hands freezing, and hold it up against my shoulder. I find the trigger and take aim at the mob, now barely twenty yards away. I close my eyes, praying that it works, as I squeeze the trigger.

I hear a loud whooshing noise, and a moment later I'm knocked backwards off my feet. The force of it sends me flying about ten feet, landing flat on my back in the snow. I hear an explosion.

I look up and am shocked at the damage I've done: I managed a direct hit on the mob, at close range. Where there were dozens of bodies a second ago, there is now nothing but body parts spread over the snow.

But there is no time to revel in my small victory. In the distance, dozens more crazies crawl up from the subway stations. I don't have any more RPGs to fire, and don't know what else to do.

Behind me I hear a noise of smashing metal and turn to see Logan standing on the hood of the Humvee. He lifts his leg and kicks at the machine gun mounted to its hood. Finally, it comes flying off. He picks it up, and a chain of ammo dangles from it, which he wraps over his shoulder. The gun is massive, made to be mounted on a car—not carried—and looks like it weighs over fifty pounds. He holds it with both hands, and even as big as he is, I can see it weighing him down. He runs past me and takes aim at the new group of crazies. He fires.

The noise is deafening, as the machine gunfire rips through the snow. The impact is tremendous: the huge bullets tear the incoming crowd in half. Bodies drop like flies wherever Logan aims the gun. Slowly, finally, the gunfire stops, and the world returns to its still, snowy silence. We have killed them all. For now, at least, there are no more crazies in sight.

I look around, survey this canvas of destruction: there is the destroyed black school bus, taken out by the RPG, the destroyed yellow one, lying on its side, in flames, bodies are everywhere, and our Humvee is a shell beside us. It looks like the scene of an intense military battle.

I look down and follow the tracks where the other bus went, the one with Bree on it. They forked left at the Flatiron.

I chose the wrong bus. It's not fair. It's just not fair.

As I study the scene, catching my breath, all I can think of is Bree, those tracks. They lead to her. I have to follow them.

"Bree's on the other bus," I say, pointing at the tracks. "I have to find her."

"How?" he asks. "On foot?"

I examine our Humvee and see that it is useless. I have no other choice.

"I guess so," I say.

"The Seaport's at least fifty blocks south," Logan says. "That's a long walk—and in dangerous territory."

"You have any other ideas?"

He shrugs.

"There's no turning back," I say. "Not for me, anyway."

He examines me, debating.

"You with me?" I ask.

Finally, he nods.

"Let's move," he says.

*

We follow the tracks, walking side by side in the snow. Each step is a fresh burst of hell, as my calf, so swollen, is beginning to feel like a separate entity from my body. I hobble, doing my best to keep pace with Logan. Luckily, he is weighed down by the heavy machine gun, and is not walking too fast himself. The snow is still coming down in sheets, the wind whipping it right into our faces. If anything, the storm feels like it's getting stronger.

Every few feet another crazy pops out from behind a building, charges us. Logan fires at them as they come, mowing them down one at a time. They all hit the snow, staining it read.

"Logan!" I scream.

He turns just in time to see the small group of crazies charging us from behind. He mows them down at the last second. I pray that he has enough ammo to get us wherever it is we need to go. My gun only has a single bullet left, and I feel I need to save it for a desperate moment. I feel so helpless, and wish I had rounds of ammo myself.

As we pass another block, several crazies jump out from behind a building and charge us at once. Logan fires, but doesn't see the other crazy, charging us from the other side. He's charging too fast, and Logan won't make it in time.

I pull out the knife from my belt, take aim, and throw it. It lodges in the crazy's forehead, and he drops to the snow at Logan's feet.

We continue down Broadway, gaining speed, moving as fast as we can. As we go, the crowd of crazies seems to thin out. Maybe they see the damage we are doing and become wary of approaching. Or maybe they are just waiting, biding their time. They must know we will run out of ammo, and will eventually have nowhere to go.

We pass 19th street, then 18th, then 17th...and suddenly, the sky opens up. Union Square. The square, once so pristine, is now one big, untended park, filled with trees and waist-high weeds, sprouting up through the snow. The buildings are all in ruin, the glass storefronts shattered and the facades blackened from flames. Several of the buildings have collapsed, are nothing but piles of rubble in the snow.

I look over, checking to see if the Barnes & Noble that I once loved is still standing. I remember the days when I would go there with Bree, when we would go up the escalator and get lost in there for hours. Now, I am horrified to see that there is nothing left. Its old, rusted sign lies face-down on the ground, half covered in snow. There's not a single book left in the shell of its windows. In fact, there's no way of knowing what the store even was.

We hurry across the square, sidestepping rubble as we follow the bus tracks. All has become eerily quiet. I don't like it.

We reach the southern side of the square, and I'm saddened to see the huge statue of George Washington mounted on a horse toppled, lying in pieces on its side, half-covered in snow. There is really nothing left. Anything and everything that was good in the city seems to have been ruined. It is astonishing.

I stop, grabbing onto Logan's shoulder, trying to catch my breath. My leg hurts so bad, I need to rest it.

Logan stops and is about to say something—when suddenly we both hear a commotion and turn. Across the square, dozens of crazies suddenly rise up from the subway entrance, heading right for us. I can't believe how many there are: there seems to be a never-ending stream of them.

Worse, Logan takes aim and pulls the trigger, and this time we hear nothing but an empty, horrifying click. His eyes open wide in surprise and fear. Now we have nowhere to turn, nowhere to run. This huge group of crazies, at least a hundred and growing, are closing in. I turn in every direction, looking frantically for any source of escape, any vehicles, any weapons. Any source of shelter. But I find none.

It seems we have reached the end of our luck.

TWENTY SEVEN

I frantically scan our surroundings, and I spot the façade of what was once a Whole Foods. It is abandoned, like everything else, completely gutted. But unlike the other stores, it appears the doors are still intact. I wonder if maybe we can get in and lock them behind us.

"This way!" I scream to Logan, who stands there, frozen in indecision.

We run to the entrance of the Whole Foods, the crazies just 30 yards behind us. I expect them to be yelling, but they are dead silent. With all the snow, they don't even make a sound, and that somehow is even more eerie than if they were screaming.

We reach the doors and I try the handle and am relieved it's open. I run in, Logan behind me, then turn and slam it behind us. Logan removes the heavy machinegun from his shoulder and shoves it between the door handles, barring the doors. He wedges it in there, and it is a perfect fit. I test the doors, and they don't budge.

We turn and run deeper into the store. It is cold in here, empty, gutted. There aren't any remnants of food, just torn and empty packaging, all over the floor. There are no weapons, no supplies. No hiding places. Nothing. Whatever was once here was looted long ago. I scan for exits, but see none.

"Now what?" Logan asks.

There's a sudden crash against the metal door, and I see dozens of crazies slam into it. I can already tell our lock won't last long. I search the store again, frantic for an idea. And then, in the distance, I spot something: a stairwell.

"There!" I yell, pointing.

We both run across the store, burst open the door, and find ourselves in a stairwell. Logan looks at me.

"Up or down?" he asks.

It's a good question. If we go down, maybe there's a basement. Maybe there are some sort of supplies, and maybe we can barricade ourselves in down there. Then again, it could be a death trap. And judging from the look of this place, I doubt there are any supplies. If we go up, maybe there's something on a higher floor. Maybe an exit through the roof.

My claustrophobic side gets the better of me.

"UP!" I say, despite the pain in my leg.

We start ascending the metal steps. Logan climbs so fast, it is a struggle for me to catch up. He stops and turns, realizing, then runs back, wraps an arm around me, holds me tight, and pulls me up the steps faster than I can manage on my own. Each step is torture, feels like a knife entering my calf. I curse the day that snake was born.

We run up flight after flight. When we cross the fourth flight I have to stop, gasping for breath. My breath is raspy, and sounds scary even to me: I sound like a 90 year old woman. I think my body has endured too much in the last 48 hours.

Suddenly, there is a horrific crash. We both look at each other, then look down the stairwell. We realize at the same time that the crazies have broken in.

"COME ON!" he screams.

He grabs me, and I feel a surge of adrenaline as we run twice as fast up the steps. We clear the sixth flight, then the seventh. I hear the sound of the crazies barging into the stairwell, and look down and see them starting to sprint up the steps. They know exactly where we are.

I look up and see there is only one more flight to go. I force myself, gasping for breath, up the last flight of steps. We reach the landing and race for the metal door to the roof. Logan puts a shoulder into it, but it won't open. It's locked. Apparently, from the outside. I can't believe it.

The mob of crazies is getting closer, the sound of them on the metal stairwell deafening. In moments, we will be torn to bits.

"STAND BACK!" I scream to Logan, getting an idea.

This is as good a place as any to use my last round. I pull out my gun, take aim, and with the last round I have left, I fire at the knob. I know it's risky to fire in such close quarters—but I don't see what choice we have.

The bullet ricochets off the metal, missing us by an inch, and the lock opens.

We run through the door, out into daylight. I survey the roof, wondering where we can go, if there's any possible escape. But I see nothing. Absolutely nothing.

Logan suddenly takes my hand and runs with me to the far corner of the roof. As we reach the edge I look over and see, below us, a huge stone wall. It spans University Place, running across 14th Street and blocking off everything south of it.

"The 14th Street wall!" Logan screams. "It separates the wasteland from the desert."

"The desert?" I ask.

"It's where the bomb went off. It's all radiated—everything south of 14th street. No one goes there. Not even the Crazies. It's too dangerous."

There's a sudden crash of metal, and the door to the roof slams open. The mob pours out, running right for us.

Far below I see a snow bank, about eight feet high. The snow is thick, and if we land just right, maybe, just maybe, it can cushion our fall. But it is a far jump, about fifty feet. And it would put us on the Desert side of the wall.

But I don't see what choice we have.

"That snow bank!" I yell, pointing. "We can jump for it!"

Logan looks down and shakes his head, looking scared.

I check over our shoulder: the crazies are 30 yards away.

"We have no choice!" I yell.

"I'm scared of heights," he finally admits, looking very pale.

I reach over and take his hand, and step up on the ledge. He pauses for a second, fear his eyes, but then comes.

"Close your eyes!" I yell. "Trust me!"

And then, with the crazies only a few feet away, we jump.

TWENTY EIGHT

As we plummet through the air, screaming, I hope my aim is accurate. We rush towards the ground so fast, I know that if we miss, we will surely die.

A moment later I am immersed in a cloud of snow, as I land dead center in the eight-foot snow bank, Logan right beside me, still holding my hand. I hit it with tremendous speed and sink down into it, all the way to the bottom, until my feet hit hard on the cement. Luckily, the snow is thick, and it cushions most of the impact of the fall. When I hit bottom, it only feels as if I've jumped from a few feet high.

I sit at the bottom, snow piled high above my head, in complete shock. I look up and several feet above me see sunlight poking through the snow. I sit there, frozen, afraid to move, to begin to claw my way out of the mountain of snow, to find out if anything is broken. I feel like I'm on the beach, buried under a pile of sand.

Slowly, I move a hand, then an arm, then a shoulder…. I begin to gradually pull myself out, free myself from the hole that I'm in. It is awkward, but I manage to claw my way up and out of the pile of snow. I stick my head out, like a gopher coming up from a hole in a lawn. I turn and see Logan doing the same.

I crane my neck and look up: all the way up there, still standing on the roof, looking down, is the mob of crazies. They are arguing amongst themselves, and it appears they aren't willing to do the jump we just did. I don't blame them: I look up at the height and marvel that I had the guts to take such a leap myself. I probably wouldn't do it again if I stopped to think about it.

I stand, breaking free of the snow bank, and Logan does, too. I am completely covered in snow and reach up and brush it off. I take a few steps, testing myself, checking to see if anything is broken. My calf still hurts—worse than ever—but otherwise, remarkably, I think I survived relatively intact, with only a few more aches and bruises to show for it.

I look over at Logan, who's walking, and am relieved to see he didn't break anything, either. Just as importantly, I'm relieved to see we are now on this side of the wall. The desert. It might mean a slow death—but at least we're safe for now.

I look down the desolate, abandoned University Place: all the stores are burnt out, some of them crumbled to the ground. There is no one and nothing here. As chaotic and violent as the wasteland was, the desert is quiet. Peaceful. Finally, for the first time in a while, I let my guard down.

But I know that I shouldn't. If this part of the city really is radiated, then it holds more danger than all the other places combined. Every second here could contaminate us. And who knows who—or what—still survives in the zone. I'd hate to run into it.

"Let's move," Logan says, following the bus tracks, which go straight through the arch in the wall, and continue down University.

We walk at a quick pace down University, checking over our shoulders as we go. Now more than ever I wish I had a weapon. I see Logan checking his body habitually and can tell he wishes he had one, too. Our only hope now is just to follow these tracks, find Bree, and get out of here as soon as possible.

We pass 10th Street, then 9th, then 8th, and suddenly the sky opens up on our right. I look over and am shocked to see what was once Washington Square Park. I remember so many nights here, before the war, hanging out with friends, sitting around and watching the skateboarders do their tricks on the cement plaza. Now, as I look at it, I'm aghast: there is nothing left. The huge arch that marked its entrance is toppled, lies on the ground, crumbled, covered in snow. Even worse, where the park once was, there is now nothing but a vast crater, sinking hundreds of feet deep into the earth. It stretches as far as the eye can see. It is as if a whole section of the city has been scooped out.

Logan must see me staring.

"That's where the bomb hit," he explains. "The first to hit the city."

I can't believe it. It looks like the Grand Canyon. I can see the bomb's rippling effect, radiating out, building façades melted away in every direction. Everything that I once knew is gone. It now looks more like the surface of Mars.

"Let's go," Logan says impatiently, and I realize that the sight disturbs him, too.

The bus tracks continue down University until it ends, then go left on West 4th. We follow them as they cut through the Village and turn right on Bowery. This avenue is wider, and it is desolate here, too. There is not a soul in sight.

I should feel more relaxed, yet oddly enough, I feel more on edge than ever. It is too ominous, too quiet. All I hear is the howling of the wind, the snow whipping into my face. I can't help feeling that at any moment something might jump out at me.

But nothing does. Instead, we walk and walk, down block after block, always heading further downtown. I feel like we are crossing a vast desert, with no end in sight. And this, it turns out, is the real danger of this zone. The distance. The cold. The bus tracks never seem to end, and with each step, my leg gets worse, and I grow weaker.

Slowly, the late afternoon sky, heavy with storm clouds, grows darker. As we cross the huge street that I once knew as Houston, I wonder how much further I can go.

If Logan is right, if they are really taking her to the South Street Seaport, I know we still have a ways to go. I'm already feeling dizzy, delirious with hunger. My leg feels five times the size, and, ironically, this walking might be the worst trial of all.

Somehow I continue on, trekking further down Bowery. We hike in silence, hardly saying a word to each other. There is so much I want to say to him. I want to thank him for saving my life; he's already saved me three times in a single day, and I'm starting to wonder if it's a debt I can repay. I also want to thank him for giving up his boat, for coming with me. I think of how much he's sacrificed for me, and it overwhelms me. I want to ask him why he did it.

I'm impressed by his fighting skills. Logan reminds me of what my Dad must have been like in battle—or, at least, my vision of him. I begin to wonder where Logan is from. If he is from here. If he has family here. Or family alive anywhere. I also want to ask him how he feels about me. Does he like me? Of course, I could never actually ask him. But still, I wonder. Does he have any feelings for me? Why didn't he escape when he had the chance? Why did he risk his life to follow me? Thinking about it, I feel guilty. I have endangered him. He could be safe somewhere right now.

And most of all, despite myself, I want to know if he has a girlfriend. Or ever did. I immediately chide myself, feeling disloyal to Ben, who, after all, I just left. But these two guys—Logan and Ben—are so different from each other. They are like two different species. I reflect on the feelings I have for Ben, and I realize they are still there, and still genuine: there is something about him, a sensitivity, a vulnerability, that I really like. When I look into Ben's large, suffering eyes, there is something I can relate to.

But when I look at Logan, I feel attracted to him in an entirely different way. Logan is big and strong and silent. He's noble, a man of action, and he can clearly handle himself. He's a bit of a mystery to me, and I wish I knew more. But I like that.

I find myself really liking certain things about Ben, and certain, different, things about Logan. Somehow my feelings for both seem to be able to co-exist inside, perhaps because they are so different that I don't feel like they are competing with each other.

I allow myself to get lost in these thoughts as we trek on, directly into the blizzard. It takes my mind away from the pain, the hunger, the cold.

The streets narrow again as we pass through a neighborhood I once knew was as Little Italy. I remember coming here with Dad, having an Italian dinner in one of the small, crowded restaurants packed with tourists. Now, nothing remains. All the storefronts are destroyed. There is nothing but waste. Emptiness.

We trudge on, and walking gets harder as the snow reaches our knees. I am counting the steps now, praying for our arrival. We reach another broad street, and the crooked sign reads "Delancey." I look to my left, expecting to see the Williamsburg Bridge.

Incredibly, it is gone.

The enormous bridge is demolished, clearly destroyed in some battle, its metal entrance twisting up into the sky like some sort of modern sculpture. All that labor, all the design, all the manpower—all destroyed, and probably at a moment's notice. For what? For nothing.

I look away in disgust.

We continue further downtown, crossing Delancey. After several more blocks we hit the main artery of Canal Street, and I'm almost afraid to look to my left, to look for the Manhattan Bridge. I force myself to. I wish I hadn't. Like the Williamsburg, this bridge is destroyed, too, nothing but shards of metal left, twisted and torn, leaving a gaping opening over the river.

We push on, my feet and hands so frozen that I wonder if I have frostbite. We pass through what was once Chinatown, with its taller buildings and narrow streets, now unrecognizable. Like every other neighborhood, it is just an abandoned pile of rubble.

Bowery forks to the right, onto Park Row, and I'm breathing hard as we make it a few more blocks and finally reach a huge intersection. I stop and stare, in awe.

To my right lies the structure that was one City Hall, now lying in ruins, a mere pile of rubble. It is awful. This incredible building, once so grand, is now nothing but a memory.

I'm afraid to turn around, to look at the Brooklyn Bridge behind me—that beautiful work of art that I used to walk across with Bree on warm summer days. I pray that it is still there, that at least one beautiful thing remains. I close my eyes and turn slowly.

I am horrified. Like the other two bridges, it is destroyed. Nothing remains, not even the base, leaving a gaping hole over the river. In its place, where it once stood, there are huge piles of twisted metal sticking up out of the river.

Even more startling, lying there, in the midst of the river, sticking up on a crooked angle, are the remnants of a huge military plane, half submerged, its tail sticking up. It looks like it took a nosedive and never came up. It is shocking see such a huge plane sticking up out of the river, as if a child threw his toy into a bath and never bothered to clean it up.

It is darker, almost twilight, and I can't go any further. Amazingly, the winds and snow only continue to pick up. The snow is past my knees, and I feel as if I'm being slowly swallowed alive. I know the Seaport isn't far, but it is too painful to take another step.

I reach up and lay a hand on Logan's shoulder. He looks over at me, surprised.

"My leg," I say, through clenched teeth. "I can't walk."

"Put your arm over my shoulder," he says.

I do, and he leans over, places a hand behind my back and holds me tight, propping me up.

We walk together, and the pain lessens. I feel embarrassed, self-conscious: I never want to be dependent on a guy. On anyone. But now, I really need it.

We make a left, walking under the structure that once lead to the bridge, and then make a right onto what was once Pearl Street. It is uncanny. After all this journeying, somehow we have ended up back in the neighborhood I grew up in. It is so weird to be back here. On the day I left, I swore I'd never come back. Never. I was sure that Manhattan would be destroyed, and never even imagined I would see it again.

Walking back through here, down these narrow cobblestone streets, this old historic district, once teeming with tourists, with everything I knew, is the most painful of all. Memories come flooding back, places where, in every corner, Bree and I would play. I am flooded with memories of spending time here with Mom and Dad. Memories of when they were actually happy with each other.

Our apartment was in the shopping district, above one of the stores, in a small, historic building. I remember resenting it growing up, all those annoying Saturday nights when the nightlife never seemed to end, when people would talk and smoke under my bedroom window until five in the morning. Now I would do anything for that noise, that activity. I would give anything to be able to walk across the street to a café and order breakfast. I get a sharp hunger pang just thinking of it.

As fate would have it, we turn down Water Street—the very block I used to live on. My heart flutters, as I realize we're going to walk past my very apartment. I can't help wondering if Dad is looking down, guiding me. Or maybe it's Mom, if she's dead. Maybe she's the one looking down. Maybe, though, she's taunting me. Reprimanding me. After all, this is the place where I abandoned her, all those years ago. She could have come with me. But she wouldn't leave. And I knew that. Still, I feel I did what I had to do at the time—for me, and most importantly, for Bree. What else was I supposed to do? Just sit here with her and wait for our deaths?

I can't help seeing the irony in all of it, though, in all the twists and turns that life has taken. I took Bree and fled to safety, but now she is captured, and right back here, where we started from, and I'll probably never get her back. And the way I feel now, I can't imagine surviving more than a few more hours myself. So what good did our leaving do us, after all? If I had just stayed put, with Mom, at least we would have all died together, in peace. Not a long slow, torturous death of starvation. Maybe Mom had it right all along.

We pass my apartment building and I brace myself, wondering what it will look like. And I know it's ridiculous, but a part of me wonders if Mom is still there, sitting up in a window. Waiting.

I look up, and am shocked: my former building is now just a pile of rubble, covered in snow. High weeds grow up from between the rocks, and it looks like it collapsed long ago. I feel as if someone punched me in the gut. My home is gone. Mom is really gone.

"What's wrong?" Logan asks.

I realize that I've stopped, that I'm standing there, staring. I lower my head, grab his shoulder, and continue on.

"Nothing," I respond.

We continue into the heart of the shopping district of the South Street Seaport. I remember sitting here, looking at the shining cobblestone, at all the expensive shops, feeling as if I were in the most pristine place in the world. A place impervious to change. Now I look around and see nothing but devastation. There aren't even any signs, any markers to indicate what it once was.

We turn left on Fulton and in the distance I spot the waterfront. It is twilight now, thick gray clouds gathering on the horizon, and I finally feel a surge of hope as I see the water, just blocks away. I see the bus tracks, turning down this road, coming to an end at the pier. We have made it.

We walk faster and I feel a surge of adrenaline as I wonder if Bree could be there, on the pier. I unconsciously check my belt for weapons, and remember I have none left. No matter. If she's there, I will find a way to get her back.

We walk out onto the wooden pier of the Seaport, once teeming with tourists, now desolate. The tall, historic sailing ships are still there, bobbing in the water—but now they're just rotting hulls. At the end of the pier I see the bus, parked. I hurry towards it, my heart pounding, hoping that Bree is somehow still on it.

But of course the bus has been unloaded long ago. I reach the side of the bus and look in to find it empty. I check the snow and see the tracks where the girls were unloaded, led down a ramp to a boat. I look out at the water, and in the distance, I spot a large, rusted barge, maybe half a mile off, docked on Governor's Island. I see a line of girls being unloaded. Bree is among them. I can feel it.

I feel a surge of determination. But also of hopelessness. We have missed the boat. We're too late.

"There's another boat in the morning," Logan says. "At dawn. There always is, once a

335

day. We just need to wait it out. Find shelter for the night."

"If you make it through the night," comes a voice.

I am shocked to hear a strange voice behind us, and I spin around.

Standing there, about ten feet away, I am amazed to see, is a group of about a dozen people, dressed in yellow military fatigues. In their center stands a person who looks like their leader. His face is melted, distorted, as are the faces of the others. He looks even worse than the Biovictims, if that's possible. Maybe it's from living in this radiated zone.

Somehow, they have managed to creep on us. We are outnumbered, and I see all the weapons in their belts, the guns in their hands. We have no chance.

"You're in our territory now," he continues. "Why shouldn't we kill you ourselves?"

"Please," I plead. "The slaverunners took my sister. I have to get her back."

"We don't like slaverunners any more than you do. They ride their buses through here like it's their territory. IT'S MY TERRITORY!" he shrieks, his face distorted, his eyes bulging. "DO YOU HEAR ME? IT'S MINE!"

I flinch at the sound of his voice, so distorted with rage. I am delirious with exhaustion, with pain, and can hardly even stand.

I see him take a step towards us, and brace myself for an attack. But before I can even finish the thought, suddenly my world starts to spin. It spins, again and again, and before I know it, I am falling towards the ground.

And then, everything is black.

TWENTY NINE

I open my eyes with an effort. I'm not sure if I'm dead or alive, but if I'm alive, I didn't know life could feel this way: every muscle in my body is on fire. I am shaking and shivering and have never been so cold my life—yet at the same time I am also burning up, a cold sweat running down the back of my neck. My hair clings to the side of my face, and every joint in my body hurts more than I can describe. It is like the worst fever I've ever had—times a hundred.

The epicenter of pain is my calf: it throbs, and feels like the size of a softball. The pain is so intense that I squint my eyes, clench my jaw, and pray silently that someone would just cut it off.

I look around and see I'm lying on a cement floor, on the upper story of an abandoned warehouse. The wall is lined with large factory windows, most of the glass panes shattered. Intermittent breezes of cold air rush in, along with gusts of snow, the flakes landing right in the room. Through the windows I can see the midnight sky, a full moon hanging low, amidst the clouds. It is the most beautiful moon I've ever seen. It fills the warehouse with ambient light.

I feel a gentle hand on my shoulder.

I lift my chin and manage to turn it just a bit. There, kneeling by my side, is Logan. He smiles down. I can't imagine how bad I must look, and I'm embarrassed for him to see me like this.

"You're alive," he says, and I can hear the relief in his voice.

I think back, trying hard to remember where I last was. I remember the Seaport…the pier…. I feel another wave of pain run up my leg, and a part of me wishes that Logan would just let me die. He holds up a needle, prepping it.

"They gave us medicine," he says. "They want you to live. They don't like the slaverunners any more than we do."

I try to register what he's saying, but my mind is not working clearly, and I shiver so much, my teeth are chattering.

"It's Penicillin. I don't know if it will work— or if it's even the real thing. But we have to try."

He doesn't have to tell me. I can feel the pain spreading and know there is no alternative. We have to try.

He reaches down and holds my hand, and I squeeze his. He then leans over and lowers the needle right to my calf. A second later, I feel the sharp sting of the needle entering my flesh. I breathe sharply and squeeze his hand harder.

As Logan pushes the needle in deeper, I suddenly feel the burning liquid enter. The pain is beyond what I can take, and despite myself, I hear myself shriek, echoing in the warehouse.

As Logan takes it out, I feel another cold gust of wind and snow, cooling the sweat on my forehead. I try to breathe again. I want to look up at him, to thank him. But I can't help it: my eyes, so heavy, close on themselves.

And a moment later, I am out again.

*

It is Summer. I am thirteen years old, and Bree is six, and we skip hand in hand through the lively streets of the Seaport. They are jam-packed with life, everyone out and about, and Bree and I run down the cobblestone streets, laughing at all the funny people.

Bree plays a sort of hopscotch game on the cracks, half hopping and half-skipping every few steps, and I try to follow in her path. She laughs hysterically at this, and then laughs even harder as I chase her around and around a statue.

Behind us, smiling, hand-in-hand, are my parents. It is one the few times I can remember their being happy together. It is also one of the few times I can remember my father actually being around. They trail behind us, watching over us, and I've never felt so safe in my life. I feel that the world is perfect, that we will always be as happy as this moment.

Bree finds a seesaw and she's ecstatic, beelining for it and jumping on. She doesn't hesitate, knowing that I will jump on the other side and even her out. Of course I do. She is lighter than me, and I make sure not to jump too hard, so that she can balance with me.

I blink. Time has passed, I'm not sure how much. We're now at a waterfront park somewhere. Our parents are gone, and we are alone. It is sunset.

"Push me harder, Brooke!" Bree screams.

I look over and see that Bree is seated on a swing. I reach over and push her. She goes higher and higher, laughing hysterically.

Finally, she jumps off. She comes around and hugs me, wrapping her little hands tight around my thighs. I kneel down and give her a proper hug.

She leans back and looks at me, smiling.

"I love you, Brooke," she says, smiling.

"I love you too," I answer.

"Will you always be my big sister?" she asks.

"I will," I say.

"Do you promise?" she asks.

"I promise," I say.

*

I open my eyes, and for the first time in as long as I can remember, I am out of pain. It is amazing: I feel healthy again. The pain in my leg is mostly gone, and as I reach down and feel it, the swelling has shrunk to the size of a golf ball. The medicine really worked.

My aches and pains have also reduced dramatically, and I sense that my fever has, too. I don't feel nearly as cold, and I'm not sweating as much. I feel as if I've been given a second chance at life.

It is still dark in here. I look up and can no longer see the moon, and wonder how much time has passed. Logan is still sitting there, by my side. He sees me and reacts immediately, reaching over and brushing my forehead with a damp cloth. I see he's not wearing a coat, and look down and see he has draped his over me. I feel terrible; he must be freezing.

I feel a fresh wave of appreciation for him, feel closer to him than ever. He must really care for me. I wish I could tell him how much I appreciate it. But right now, my mind is still moving slow, and just doesn't seem to form the words.

He reaches down and puts a hand behind my head and lifts it.

"Open your mouth," he says softly.

He places three pills on my tongue, then pours bottled water into my mouth. My throat is so dry that it takes a few tries to swallow—but finally, I feel it go down. I lift my head a bit more and take another long sip.

"Fever reducers," he says.

"I feel much better," I say, with new energy. I reach over and grab his hand and squeeze it tight in appreciation. I know that he has saved my life. Again. I look up at him. "Thank you," I say earnestly.

He smiles, then suddenly pulls his hand away. I'm not sure how to interpret this. Does he not care for me as much as I think? Did he only do this out of obligation? Does he care for someone else? Did I overstep my boundaries in some way? Or is he just shy? Embarrassed?

I wonder why it bothers me so much, and suddenly it dawns on me: I have feelings for him.

He reaches down and removes something from a backpack.

"They gave us this," he says.

He pulls out a piece of dried fruit and hands it to me. I take it in awe, feeling a hunger pang already.

"What about you?" I ask.

He shakes his head, as if deferring. But I won't eat it otherwise. I break mine in half and shove it into his hand. He grudgingly accepts it. I then devour mine, and it is quite possibly the best thing I've ever eaten. It tastes like cherries.

He smiles as he eats, then reaches into the pack and pulls out two pistols. He hands me one. I study it in awe.

"Fully loaded," he says.

"They must really hate those slaverunners," I say.

"They want us to get your sister. And they want us to inflict damage," he says.

The gun is heavy in my hand; it feels so good to have a weapon again. Finally, I don't feel defenseless, and I feel as if I have a fighting chance to get her back.

"Next boat leaves at dawn," he says. "A few hours to go. You up for it?"

"I'll be on that boat even if I'm a corpse," I say, and he smiles.

He examines his own gun, and I am suddenly overcome with a desire to know more about him. I don't want to pry, but he is so silent, so enigmatic. And I am feeling more and more attached to him. I want to know more.

"Where were you going to go?" I ask him. My voice is hoarse, my throat dry, and it comes out more scratchy than I would like.

He looks at me, puzzled.

"If you'd escaped, in the beginning. If you'd taken that boat?"

He looks away and sighs. A long silence follows, and after a while, I wonder if he is going to answer.

"Anywhere," he finally says, "far away from here."

I think about that, and I feel that he's holding something back. I'm not sure why. But I just feel that he's the type to have a more concrete plan.

"There must be somewhere," I say. "*Some* place you had in mind."

He looks away. Then, after a long silence, reluctantly, he says, "Yes, there was."

It is clear from his tone that he doesn't expect to be able to reach it now. After a long pause, I realize he's not going to volunteer it. I don't want to pry, but I have to know.

"Where?" I ask.

He looks away, and I can see he doesn't want to tell me for some reason. I wonder if maybe he still doesn't trust me. Then, finally, he speaks.

"There's supposed to be one town left. A safe place, untouched, where everything is perfect. Unlimited food and water. People live there as if there was never a war. Everyone's healthy. And it's safe from the world."

He looks at me.

"That's where I was going."

For a moment I wonder if he's pulling my leg. He must realize that it sounds incredulous—infantile, even. I can't believe that someone as mature and responsible as him would believe in such a place—or would make a plan to find it, no less.

"Sounds like a place of fairytales," I say, smiling, half-expecting him to tell me he was just kidding.

But to my surprise, he suddenly scowls down at me.

"I knew I shouldn't have said anything," he says, sounding hurt.

I am shocked by his reaction. He really *does* believe it.

"I'm sorry," I say. "I thought you were joking."

He looks away, embarrassed. It's hard for me to even comprehend it: I gave up thinking of anything good still existing in the world long ago. I can't believe he still clings to this belief. Him, of all people.

"Where is it?" I finally ask. "This town?"

He pauses for a long time, as if debating whether to tell me.

Finally, he says: "It's in Canada."

I am speechless.

"I was going to take the boat all the way up the Hudson. Find out for myself."

I shake my head. "Well, I guess we all have to believe in something," I say.

The second I say it, I regret it. It comes out too harshly. That's always been my problem—I never seem able to say the right things. I can be too tough, too critical—just like Dad. When I get nervous, or embarrassed, or afraid to say what I really mean—especially around boys— sometimes it just comes out wrong. What I meant to say was: *I think it's great that you still believe in something. I wish I did, too.*

His eyes darken, and his cheeks flush with embarrassment. I want to retract it, but it's too late. The damage is done. I've screwed things up already.

I try to quickly think of something, anything, to change the subject. I'm not good at conversation. I never have been. And it might be too late to salvage it anyway.

"Did you lose anyone?" I ask. "In the war?"

I am such an idiot. What a stupid question. I've just gone from bad to worse.

He breathes deeply, slowly, and I feel as if now I've really hurt him. He bites his lower lip, and for a moment, it looks like he's holding back tears.

After an interminable silence, he finally says: "Everyone."

If I wake up in the morning and he's gone, I won't blame him. In fact, I'd be surprised if he sticks around. Clearly, I should just shut up and wait for dawn.

But there's one more thing I need to know, one thing that's burning inside. And I just can't stop myself from mouthing the words:

"Why did you save me?" I ask.

He looks at me with intensity, through red eyes, then slowly looks away. He turns, and I wonder if he's going to respond at all.

A long silence follows. I hear the wind whistling through the empty windows, the snowflakes landing on the floor. My eyes grow heavy and I'm beginning to fall back asleep, drifting in and out of consciousness. And the last thing I hear, before my eyes close for good, are his words. They are so faint and soft that I'm not even sure if he really says it, or if I just dream it:

"Because you remind me of someone."

*

I fall in and out of sleep for the next few hours, partly dreaming and partly flashing back. During one of my episodes, I finally remember what happened on that day we left the city. As much as I'd like to forget, it all comes flooding back to me.

When I found Bree in that alley, surrounded by those boys, and threw the Molotov cocktail—there was a small explosion, and then shrieks filled the air. I managed to hit their ringleader, and the boy lit up in a ball of fire. He ran about, frantic, as the others tried to put him out.

I didn't wait. In the chaos, I ran right past the flaming boy, and right for Bree. I grabbed her hand and we ran away from them, through the back alleys. They chased us, but we knew those back streets better than anyone. We cut through buildings, in and out of hidden doors, over dumpsters, through fences. Within a few blocks, we'd thoroughly lost them, and made it back to the safety of our apartment building.

It was the last straw. I was determined to leave the city right then and there. It was no longer safe—and if Mom wouldn't see that, then we'd have to leave without her.

We burst into our apartment, and I ran straight to Mom's room. She was sitting there, in her favorite chair, staring out the window, as she always did, waiting for Dad to return.

"We're leaving," I said, determined. "It's too dangerous here now. Bree was almost killed. Look at her. She's hysterical."

Mom looked at Bree, then back to me, not saying a word.

"He's not coming back," I said. "Face it. He's dead."

Mom reached back and smacked me. I was stunned. I still remember the sting of it.

"Don't you *ever* say that," she snapped.

I narrowed my eyes, furious that she'd dare hit me. It is a hit that I will never forgive her for.

"Fine," I seethed back to her. "You can live in your fantasy as long as you like. If you don't want to come, you don't have to. But we're leaving. I'm heading to the mountains, and I'm taking Bree."

She snorted back derisively. "That's ridiculous. The bridges are blocked."

"I'll take a boat," I answer, prepared. "I know someone who will take us. He's got a speed boat and he'll take us up the Hudson."

"And how can you afford that?" she asked me coldly.

I hesitated, feeling guilty. "I traded my gold watch."

She narrowed her eyes at me. "You mean Dad's gold watch," she snapped.

"He gave it to me," I corrected. "And I'm sure he'd want to see me put it to good use."

She looked away from me in disgust, staring back out the window.

"Don't you get it?" I continued. "In a few more weeks, this city will be destroyed. It's not safe here anymore. This is our last chance to get out."

"And how's your father going to feel when he comes home and finds us all gone? When he discovers that we have all abandoned him?"

I stared at Mom, incredulous. She was really lost in her fantasy.

"He *left* us," I spat. "He volunteered for this stupid war. No one asked him to go. He's *not* coming back. And this is exactly what he'd want us to do. He'd want us to survive. Not to sit around some stupid apartment waiting to die."

Mom slowly turned and looked at me with her cold, steely-gray eyes. She had that awful determination, that same awful determination that I have. Sometimes I hate myself for being so much like her. I could see in her eyes, at that moment, that she would never, ever, give in. She had gotten it into her head that waiting was the loyal thing to do. And once she got something into her head, there was no changing it.

But in my view, her loyalty was misplaced. She owed her loyalty to *us*. To her children. Not to a man who was more devoted to fighting than to us.

"If you want to leave your father, go ahead. I'm not going. When your plans fall through, and you don't make it upriver, you can come back. I'll be here."

I didn't wait a second longer. I grabbed Bree by the hand, turned and strutted with her to the door. Bree was crying, and I knew I had to get out of there quick. I stopped one last time before the door.

"You're making a mistake," I called out.

But she didn't even bother to turn, to say goodbye. And I knew she never would.

I opened the door, then slammed it behind me.

And that was the last I ever saw Mom alive again.

THIRTY

I wake to blinding sunlight. It is as if the world is alive again. Sunlight streams in through the windows all around me, brighter than I've ever seen, bouncing off of everything. The wind has stopped. The storm is over. Snow melts off the window ledge, the sound of dripping water echoing all around me. There is a cracking noise, and a huge icicle crashes down onto the floor.

I look around, disoriented, and realize I'm still lying on the floor, in the same place I was last night, Logan's coat draped over me. I feel completely rejuvenated.

Suddenly, I remember, and sit up with a shock. Dawn. We had to get up at dawn. The site of the bright morning light suddenly terrifies me, as I look over and see Logan lying there, right beside me, eyes closed. He is fast asleep. My heart stops. We have overslept.

I scramble to my feet, feeling energetic for the first time, and roughly shake his shoulder.

"LOGAN!" I say urgently.

Immediately, his eyes open, and he jumps to his feet. He looks around, alert.

"It's morning!" I plead. "The boat. We're going to miss it!"

His eyes open wide in surprise as he realizes.

We both jump into action, sprinting for the door. My leg still hurts, but I am pleasantly surprised to realize I can actually run on it. I race down the metal staircase, footsteps echoing, right behind Logan. I grip the rusted metal railing, careful to pass over steps that are rotting away.

We reach the ground floor and burst out of the building, into the blinding light of snow. It is a winter wonderland. I wade into the snow, up to my thighs, and it slows my running, each step a struggle. But I follow Logan's tracks, and he plows through, making it easier.

I see the water up ahead and realize we are only a block away. To my great relief I see the barge docked at the pier, and can barely see its loading ramp being lifted, as the last of a group of chained girls is led on board. It looks as if the boat is about to leave.

I run harder, trudging through the snow as fast as I can go. As we reach the pier, still about a hundred yards away from the boat, the ramp is removed. I hear the roar of an engine, and a huge cloud of black exhaust exits from the back of the barge. My heart is pounding.

As we near the end of the pier, I suddenly think of Ben, of our promise to each other—to meet at the pier at dawn. As I run, I scan left and right, looking for any sign of him. But there is nothing. My heart sinks, as I realize that can only mean one thing: he didn't make it.

We close in on the barge, hardly thirty yards away, when suddenly it begins to move. My heart starts to pound. We're so close. Not now. *Not now*!

We are only twenty yards away, but the boat has departed from the pier. It is already about ten feet out into the water.

I increase my speed and am now running beside Logan, fighting my way through the thick snow. The barge is now a good fifteen feet off shore, and moving fast. Just too far to jump.

But I continue to sprint, right up to the very edge, and as I do, I suddenly spot thick ropes, dangling from the boat to the pier, slowly dragging off the edge.

The ropes stretch behind it, like a long tail.

"THE ROPES!" I scream.

Logan apparently has the same idea. Neither of us slows—instead, we keep sprinting, and as I reach the end, without thinking, I aim for a rope and leap.

I go flying through the air, hoping, praying. If I miss, it would be a long fall, at least thirty feet, and I would land in icy cold water, with no way back up. The water is so cold and the tides so strong, I'm sure I would die within seconds of impact.

As I fly through the air, reaching for the thick, knotted rope, I wonder if this could be my last moment on earth.

THIRTY ONE

My heart leaps in my throat as I reach out for the thick, knotted twine. I catch hold of it in the air, clutching onto it for life. Like a pendulum, I swing on it, racing through the air at full speed towards the immense hull of the rusted barge. The metal flies at me, and I brace myself for impact.

It is excruciatingly painful as I hit it at full speed, the metal slamming into the side of my head, ribs, and shoulder. The pain and shock of impact is almost enough to make me drop the rope. I slip a few feet, but somehow manage to hang on.

I wrap my feet around it, before I slip all the way down to the water. I cling to it, dangling there, as the barge continues to move, gaining speed. I look over and see that Logan has managed to catch his and hang on, too. He dangles there, a few feet away.

I look down and see the rough waters a few feet below me, churning white as the barge cuts a path across the river. Those are big currents below, especially for a river, strong enough to lift this huge barge up and down.

I look over to my right and see the Statue of Liberty towering over us. Amazingly, it has survived intact. Seeing it, I feel inspired, feel as if maybe I can make it, too.

Luckily, Governors Island is close, barely a minute's ride. I remember taking ferry rides there with Bree on hot summer days, and how amazed we were that it was so close. Now, I'm so grateful that it is: if it were any further, I don't know if I'd be able to hang on. The wet rope digs into my freezing hands, making every second a struggle. I suddenly wonder how I will get out of this mess. There is no ladder on the side of the boat, and once we reach the island, there will be no way for me to get out except to drop down off the rope, into the water. Which would surely make me freeze to death.

I detect movement and look over and see that Logan is slowly climbing his way up the rope. He has devised an ingenious method of lifting his knees, clamping the insoles of his feet tightly against the thick rope, then using his legs to pull himself up.

I try it. I raise my knees and clamp my feet into the twine, and am happily surprised to see that my boot catches. I straighten my legs and pull myself up a notch, and am amazed to see it works. I do it again and again, following Logan, and within a minute, the time it takes to reach the island, I'm at the top of the rope. As I reach the top, Logan is there, waiting, hand outstretched. I reach up and grab it, and he pulls me quickly and silently over the edge.

We both crouch down, hiding behind a metal container, and furtively survey the boat. Standing up front, their backs to us, are a group of guards, holding machineguns. They herd a dozen young girls, direct them down a long ramp lowered from the boat. The sight makes me burn with indignation, and makes me want to attack them right now. But I force myself to wait, to stay disciplined. It would give me temporary satisfaction, but then I would never get Bree.

The group starts to move, chains rattling, until they are all off the ramp and on the island. When the boat is emptied, Logan and I nod to each other and silently make our way off the barge, running alongside the edge. We hurry down the ramp, a good deal behind everybody else. Luckily, no one is looking back for us.

In moments, we are on land, and we hurry through the snow and take shelter behind a small structure, hiding out of sight as we watch where the girls are being taken. The slaverunners head towards a large, circular brick structure which looks like a cross between an amphitheater and a prison. There are iron bars all around its perimeter.

We run out, following their trail, hiding behind a tree every twenty yards, running from tree to tree, careful not to be seen. I reach down and feel for my gun, in case I need to use it, and see Logan do the same. They might notice us at any moment, and we have to be ready. It would be a mistake to fire—it would draw too much attention, too soon. But if I need to, I will.

They herd the slaves into the open doorway of the building, and then disappear in the blackness.

We both break into action, running inside after them.

It takes my eyes a moment to adjust to the darkness. To my right, around the bend, a group of slaverunners leads the girls, while to my left, a single slaverunner heads solo down a corridor. Logan and I exchange a knowing glance, and both silently decide to go after the stray slaverunner.

We run silently down the corridor, just yards behind him, waiting for our chance. He reaches a large iron door, pulls out a set of keys, and begins to unlock it. The metal clangs, reverberating in the empty corridors. Before I can react, Logan pulls out a knife, charges the slaverunner, grabs him by the back of his head, and slices his throat in one quick motion. Blood spurts everywhere as he collapses, a lifeless heap on the ground below.

I grab his set of keys, still in the door, turn it, and pull back the heavy iron door. I hold it open and Logan runs in, and I follow.

We are in a cell block, long, narrow, semi-circular, filled with small cells. I run down it, looking left and right, scanning the faces of all the young girls. Their haunted, hollow faces stare back at me, hopeless, desperate. It looks like they've been here forever.

My heart is thumping. I look desperately for any sign of my sister. I feel she is close. As I run through, the girls go to their cell doors and stick their hands through. They must realize we're not slaverunners.

"PLEASE!" one cries. "Help me!"

"LET ME OUT OF HERE!" another cries.

Soon, a chorus of shouts and pleas rises up. It is drawing too much attention, and it worries me. I want to help each one of these girls, but there's no way I can. Not now. I need to find Bree first.

"BREE!" I scream, desperate.

I increase my pace to a jog, running cell to cell.

"BREE? CAN YOU HEAR ME? IT'S ME! BROOKE! BREE? ARE YOU HERE!?"

As I race by a cell, a girl reaches out and grabs my arm, pulling me to her.

"I know where she is!" she says.

I stop and stare at her. Her face is as frantic as the others.

"Let me out of here, and I'll tell you!" she says.

If I set her free, she might draw unwanted attention to us. Then again, she is my best bet.

I look at her cell number, then look down at the keys in my hand and find the number. I unlock it, and the girl comes running out.

"LET ME OUT, TOO!" another girl yells.

"ME TOO!"

All the girls start streaming.

I grab this girl by the shoulders.

"Where is she!?" I demand.

"She's in the mansion. They took her this morning."

"The mansion?" I ask.

"That's where they take the new girls. To be broken in."

"Broken in?" I ask, horrified.

"For sex," she answers. "For the first time."

My heart plummets at her words.

"Where?" I demand. "WHERE IS IT?"

"Follow me," she says, and begins to run out.

I am about to follow her out, but suddenly I stop.

"Wait," I say, grabbing her wrist.

I know I shouldn't do this. I know I should just run out of here, focus on saving Bree. I know there's no time, and I know that helping the others can only cause unwanted attention and screw up my plans.

But something inside me, a deep sense of indignation, stirs. I just can't bring myself to leave them all here like this.

So, against my better judgment, I stop and turn back, running cell to cell. As I reach each one, I find the key and unlock it. One by one, I free all of the girls. They all come running out, hysterical, running every which way. The noise is deafening.

I run back to the first one I freed. Luckily, she is still waiting, with Logan.

She runs out and we follow her, racing down corridor after corridor. Moments later, we burst out into the blinding light of day.

As we run, I can hear the chorus of girls screaming behind us, bursting out to freedom. It will be only moments, I realize with apprehension, until all the soldiers catch onto us. I run faster.

The girl stops before us and points across the courtyard.

"There!" she says. "That building! The big old house. On the water. The Governor's Mansion. That's it! Good luck!" she cries, and turns and runs off in the other direction.

I sprint for the building, Logan right beside me.

We run across the massive field, thigh-deep in snow, on the lookout for slaverunners. Luckily, they aren't on to us yet.

I feel the wind burning in my lungs. I think of Bree, being taken somewhere for sex, and I can't possibly get there fast enough. I'm so close now. I can't let her be hurt. Not now. Not after all this. Not when I'm only feet away.

I force myself forward, never stopping to catch a breath, even as the wind burns my lungs. I reach the front door and am not even cautious. I don't stop to check, but just run into it and kick it open.

It bursts open and I continue running, right into the house. I don't even know where I'm going, but I see a staircase and my instinct tells me to go upstairs. I run right for it, and I sense Logan right behind me.

As I reach the landing at the top of the steps, suddenly a slaverunner bursts out of a room, his mask off. He looks at me, eyes open wide in shock, and reaches for a gun.

I don't hesitate. Mine is already out, and I raise it and shoot him point blank in the head. He goes down, the gunshot deafening in this contained area.

I continue to charge down the hallway and pick a random room. I kick the door open and am horrified to find a man inside, on a bed, having sex with a young girl, who is chained. It's not Bree, but still, the site sickens me. The man—a slaverunner without his mask—jumps up, looking at me in fear, and scrambles for his gun—but I raise my gun and shoot him between the eyes. The little girl screams as his blood splats over her. At least he is dead.

I run back down the hall, kicking open doors as I go, room to room, each filled with another man having sex with a chained girl. I move on, searching frantically for Bree.

I reach the end of the hall and there is one final door. I kick it open, Logan behind me, and charge inside. As I do, I freeze.

A four-poster bed dominates the room. On it lies a large, fat naked man, having sex with a young girl, chained to his bed. This man must be important, because beside him sits a slaverunner, standing guard.

I aim for the fat man, and as he turns I shoot him once in the stomach. He crashes to the ground, grunting, and I shoot him a second time—this time, in the head.

But I'm reckless. The guard aims his gun at me, and I can see out of the corner of my eye that he's about to shoot. It was a stupid mistake: I should have taken him out first.

I hear a gunshot, and flinch.

Somehow, I am still alive. I look over and see that he is dead. Logan stands over him, gun drawn, and I realize the gunfire was Logan's.

I look across the room and see, chained to the chairs, two young girls. They sit there, fully clothed, shaking with fear, clearly next in line to be brought to the bed. My heart soars, as I see that one of them is Bree.

Bree sits there, chained, terrified, eyes open wide. But she's safe. Untouched. I made it just in time. A few more minutes and I'm sure she would have been at the mercy of that fat man.

"Brooke!" she screams, hysterical, and bursts into tears.

I run to her, kneeling down and hugging her. She hugs me back as best she can with the chains on, crying over my shoulder.

Logan appears and, having grabbed the key from the dead slaverunner's belt, unlocks them both. Bree jumps into my arms, giving me a hug, her whole body shaking. She clings to me as if she'll never let go.

I feel the tears pour down my cheeks as I hug her back. I can't believe it: it's really her.

"I told you I'd come back for you," I say.

I want to hold her forever, but I know we haven't time. Soon this place will be overrun.

I pull her back and take her hand. "Let's go," I say, preparing to run.

"Wait!" Bree yells, stopping.

I stop and turn.

"We have to bring Rose, too!" Bree says.

I look over and see the girl beside Bree looking up at us, so hopeless, so lost. It is odd, but she actually resembles Bree; with her long black hair and large brown eyes, the two of them could pass for sisters.

"Bree, I'm sorry, but we can't. We don't have time and—"

"Rose is my friend!" Bree yells. "We can't just leave her. We can't!"

I look at Rose, and my heart wells up at the sight. I look at Logan who looks back disapprovingly—but with a look that says it's my call.

Bringing Rose will slow us down. And it will be another mouth to feed. But Bree, for the first time in her life, is insistent—and our standing here will only slow us down. Not to mention, Rose seems so sweet, and reminds me so much of Bree, and I can see how close they already are. And it is the right thing to do.

Against my better judgment, I say, "OK."

The four of us burst out of the room, and as we do, we meet two guards, charging us, reaching for their guns. I react quickly, shooting one in the head, while Logan shoots the other. The girls scream at the gunshots.

I grab Bree's hand and Logan grabs Rose's and we sprint down the stairs, taking them two at a time. A moment later we burst out the house, into the blinding snow. I see guards charging us from across the yard, and only hope we can find a way off this island before we are completely overrun.

THIRTY TWO

I look around frantically, trying to figure some way out of here. I scan for vehicles, but don't see any. Then I turn around completely, and find myself scanning the water, the shoreline. And that's when I see it: right behind the Governor's mansion, tied up to a solitary pier is a small, luxury powerboat. I'm sure it is reserved for the privileged few who use this island as their plaything.

"There!" I say, pointing.

Logan turns and sees it, too, and a moment later, we sprint for the shoreline.

We run through the snow, down to the shore, right up to it. It is a beautiful, shining, motorboat, big enough to hold six people. It bobs wildly in the rough water and looks powerful, like a thing of luxury. I have a feeling that this boat was used by that fat, naked man having sex with those girls. All the more vindication.

It is bobbing so wildly, I don't want to risk Bree and Rose trying to board themselves, so I lift Bree and place her into it, while Logan lifts Rose and places her in.

"Cut the rope!" Logan says, pointing.

I turn and see a thick rope tying it to a wooden pole, and run over to it, extract my knife and cut it. I run back to the boat and Logan is already standing inside, grasping the pier to keep it from floating away. He reaches out a hand and helps me down into it. I check over my shoulder and see a dozen slaverunners charging us. They are only twenty yards away, and closing in fast.

"I got them," Logan says. "Take the wheel."

I hurry over to the driver's seat. Luckily, I've driven boats all my life. Logan shoves us off and takes a position at the back of the boat, kneeling and firing at the oncoming soldiers. They duck for cover, and it slows them down.

I jump into the driver's seat and look down, and my heart drops to see there are no keys in the ignition. I check the dash, then check the front seats frantically, my heart pounding. What will we do if they aren't here?

I look over my shoulder and see the slaverunners are closer now, barely ten yards away.

"DRIVE!" Logan screams, over the sound of his gunfire.

I get an idea and check the glove compartment, hoping. My heart soars to find them there. I insert them in the ignition, turn the keys, and it roars to life. Black exhaust comes gushing out, and the gas gauge pops all the way. A full tank.

I hit the throttle and am jerked backwards as the boat takes off. I can hear the bodies falling behind me, and I look back to see that Bree, Rose and Logan were all knocked over by the torque, too. I guess I gunned it too hard—luckily, they didn't fall overboard.

We are also lucky because the slaverunners are at the shore's edge, just ten feet away. I pulled out just in time. They fire back at us, and because everyone hit the deck, their bullets whiz over our heads. One of the bullets grazes the wood paneling, and another takes out my side view mirror.

"STAY DOWN!" Logan screams to the girls.

He takes a knee at the rear, pops up, and fires back. In the rearview I see him take out several of them.

I keep gunning it, pushing the engine with all it has, and within moments, we're far away from the island. Fifty yards, then a hundred, then two hundred…. Soon, we are safely out of range of their bullets. The slaverunners stand on shore helplessly, now just dots on the horizon, watching us tear away.

I can't believe it. We are free.

*

As we pull away, deeper and deeper into the river, I know I should stay in the middle, far from either shore, and head upriver, getting as far from the city as I can. But something inside stops me. Thoughts of Ben come rushing back, and I can't let him go so easily. What if somehow he's made it down to the Seaport? What if he was late?

I just can't let it go. If by some chance he is there, I can't just abandon him. I have to see. I have to know.

So instead of turning upriver, I point the boat straight for the opposite shore—back towards the Seaport. Within moments the Manhattan shoreline rushes at us, getting closer and closer. My heart pounds at the potential danger that could be waiting—any number of armed slaverunners waiting on shore to fire on us.

Logan realizes I'm going the wrong way, and suddenly comes running up beside me, frantic.

"Where are you going!?" he screams. "You're heading back to the city!"

"I have to see something," I say, "before we go."

"See what!?"

"Ben," I answer. "He might be there."

Logan scowls.

"That's crazy!" he says. "You're bringing us right back into the hornet's nest. You're endangering us all! He had his chance. He wasn't there!"

"I have to check," I yell back. I am determined, and nothing will stop me. I realize that, in some ways, I'm just like my Mom.

Logan turns and sulks away, and I can feel how disapproving he is. I don't blame him. But I have to do this. I know that if it was Ben, he'd come back and check for me, too.

Within moments the Seaport comes into view. We get closer, 300 yards…200…and then, as we reach a hundred yards out, I could swear I spot someone, standing alone on the end of the pier. He's looking out at the water, and my heart leaps.

It is Ben.

I can hardly believe it. He's really there. He's alive. He stands there, in the snow, up to his thighs, shivering. My heart drops to realize that Ben is alone. That can only mean one thing: his brother didn't make it.

We are close now, maybe twenty yards out, close enough that I can see the lines of sorrow etched into Ben's face. In the distance, I see a caravan of slaverunner vehicles racing through the snow, heading right for the pier. There isn't much time.

I slow the boat and pull up to the pier; Ben, waiting, runs to the edge. We idle, rocking wildly in the waves, and I suddenly wonder how Ben will get in. It is a good ten foot drop from the pier. Ben looks down, fear in his eyes, and he must be thinking the same thing, trying to figure out how to jump.

"Don't jump!" Logan screams. "It might destroy the boat!"

Ben stops and looks at him, frozen in fear.

"Get on your hands and knees, turn around, and crawl down backwards," Logan commands. "Inch your way down. Grab onto the edge of the pier and dangle off it with your hands. I'll catch you."

Ben does as he's told and slowly slips and slides over the edge, until he's hanging by his hands. Logan, to his credit, reaches up and grabs him, lowering him into the boat. Just in time: the slaverunners are hardly fifty yards away, and closing in fast.

"MOVE!" Logan screams.

I gun the throttle and we take off, flying upriver. As we do, shots are fired out again, just grazing our boat, and sinking into the water in small splashes. Logan takes a knee and fires back.

Luckily, they are no match for our speed: within moments we're far from shore, in the middle of the river, out of firing range. I keep heading north, upriver, back in the direction of home.

Now, finally, there is nothing left to stop us.

Now, we are free.

*

We race up the East River and as we go, it is extraordinary to see the wreckage of the bridges up close. We race past the remains of the Brooklyn Bridge, its rusted metal sticking out of the water like a prehistoric thing. It towers above us, several stories high, like a skyscraper sticking out of the water. I feel dwarfed as we drive under it, and can't help wondering if any of this will ever be rebuilt.

Nearby is the wreckage of the bomber plane sticking out of the water, and I swerve to keep a good distance from that, too. I don't know what sort of metal might be protruding from these freezing waters, and I don't want to test it.

We soon pass the remnants of the Manhattan Bridge, then the Williamsburg Bridge. I hit the throttle, wanting to get us past all these horrific sights as soon as possible.

We soon race by what was once Roosevelt Island, its thin strip of land now a wasteland, like everything else. I fork left and find the 59th Street Bridge has been destroyed, too—along with the tram that used to connect the island to Manhattan. The tram, rusted and demolished, bobs in the river like a huge buoy. I have to be careful to avoid it as the waterway narrows.

I continue racing upriver, further and further, passing nothing but destruction, until finally, I fork left into the waterway of the Harlem River. This waterway is much more narrow, with land only fifty yards on either side of us. I feel much more on edge as we traverse it. I scan the shores, on the lookout for an ambush.

But I see nothing. Maybe I'm just being paranoid. If the slaverunners are going to mobilize after us—and I'm sure they are—we probably have at least an hour jump on them. Especially given all the snow. And by then, I'm hoping we'll be too far up the Hudson for them to catch us.

The Harlem River snakes through between Manhattan and the Bronx, and finally dumps us out onto the vast, wide-open expanse of the Hudson River. The Hudson, by contrast, is as wide as ten football fields, and I feel like we have just entered an ocean. Finally, I feel at ease again. Finally, we are back on the river that I remember. The river that leads us home.

I turn right and point us north, and we race back in the direction of home, towards the Catskills. In just two hours, we will be there.

Not that I plan on returning home. I don't. Going back now would be foolish: the slaverunners know where we live, and it is surely the first place they will look for us. I want to stop at home, to bury Sasha, to say my goodbyes. But I won't be staying. Our destination will have to be much further north. As far as we can get.

I think of the stone cottage I'd found, all the way up the mountain, and I feel a pang, as I feel how badly I wanted to live there. I know that one day it might make a great home for us. But that day is not now. It's too close to where we used to live, too dangerous right now. We have to let things cool down. Maybe, one day, we can come back. Besides, there are five of us now. Five mouths to feed. We need to find a place that can sustain us all.

As we head further upriver, I finally begin to relax, to unwind. I feel the tension slowly leaving my neck, my shoulders. I breathe deeply for the first time. I can't believe we actually made. It is more than I can even process. I feel the aches and pains and bruises all over my body, but none of that matters now. I'm just happy that Bree is safe. That we're together.

I take a moment to look around, to take stock and survey the others in the boat. I have been so focused on just getting us away from the city that I haven't even stopped to consider everyone else. I look over at Logan, sitting there, content, in the passenger seat beside me. I turn and see that the others are sitting in the rows behind me. Each person looks out at the water, each in his or her own direction, each lost in his or her own world.

I reach over and tap Logan on the shoulder. He turns towards me.

"Mind taking the wheel?" I ask.

He rises from his seat quickly, happy to accommodate me, and grabs the wheel as we switch places.

I climb over to the back of the boat. I'm dying to talk to Bree, and I'm also dying to talk to Ben, to find out what happened with his brother. As I head back, I see Ben sitting there in what looks like a catatonic state, staring out at the river. He looks as if he's aged ten years overnight, and I can see the grief etched into his face. I can only imagine what hell he's been through, the guilt he must have of not saving his brother. If it were me, I don't know if I'd be able to handle it. I admire him for even being here.

I want to talk to him, but I need to see Bree first. I climb over to the back row and sit beside her, and her eyes light up at the sight of me. She gives me a big hug, and we embrace for a long time. She holds me tight, clearly not wanting to let go.

After several seconds, I finally pry her off. Tears roll down her cheeks.

"I was so scared," she says.

"I know, sweetheart," I answer. "I'm so sorry."

"Are we going home now?" she asks, hope in her eyes.

Home. What a funny word. I don't know what that means anymore. I once thought it meant Manhattan; then I thought it meant the mountains. Now I know it's neither of those places. Home is going to have to be a new place. Some place that we haven't even been yet.

"We're going to find a new home, Bree," I say. "An even better one."

"Can Rose come, too?" she asks.

I look over and see Rose, sitting beside her, look up at me hopefully. They are already two peas in a pod.

"Of course," I say. "She's part of the family now."

I smile at Rose, and she surprises me by leaning over and giving me a hug. She clings to me, just like Bree, and I suddenly wonder where she came from, where her family us, where they captured her. I realize the hell that she must have gone through, too, and it hits home that we saved her, too. I think of an old saying: when you save a person's life, that person becomes your responsibility for life. I can't help feeling that somehow it's true, that I'm now responsible for Rose, too. In my mind, her and Bree are inextricably linked.

"Thank you," Rose whispers over my shoulder, into my ear.

I kiss her on the forehead, and she slowly pulls away. She reminds me of Bree in so many ways, it's scary.

"What about Sasha?" Bree asks. "Can she come?"

It is the question I've been dreading. I take a deep breath, trying to think of the best way to phrase it. I have to tell her the truth; after all she's been through, Bree deserves it.

"I'm so sorry, Bree," I say, looking down. "Sasha didn't make it."

Fresh tears rush to Bree's eyes, and she starts crying again, hysterical. Rose leans over and hugs her.

But after several seconds, to my surprise, Bree leans back, brushes away her tears, and looks back at me, red-eyed.

"I knew it," she says. "I had a dream. She was visiting me. Somehow, I already knew she was dead."

"This might cheer you up," suddenly comes a voice.

I turn and see Ben standing there. To my surprise, there is a slight smile on his face.

I look down and see that he is holding something. Something small, wrapped in a blanket. He's holding it out towards Bree.

Suddenly, a small dog pops its head out from the blanket. I can't believe it. It is a small Chihuahua, missing one eye. It shakes and trembles, looking terrified.

"OH MY GOD!" Bree and Rose both scream out at once, eyes open wide in surprise.

Bree grabs it and holds it tight, cradling it, and Rose leans in and pets it, too. They both lean down, and it leans up and licks their faces. They scream out in delight.

"I found it in the boat," Ben says. "I almost sat on it. I guess someone left it. Or maybe it crawled its way on."

I'm shocked. I hadn't seen the dog, and now that I think of it, I realize I didn't spend any time examining the boat at all. Suddenly I look around, wondering what else could be here.

I spot all the side compartments and hurry to each one, opening them one after the other. I am surprised and delighted as I begin to discover all sorts of surprises. I open a sealed crate and am breathless to see its contents: it is packed with chocolate bars, candy, cookies, crackers and delicacies of all types.

I reach down and grab a huge bag filled with chocolate-covered jelly rings. I hold open the bag for Bree, Rose, Ben and Logan, and they each, wide-eyed, reach in and grab a handful. I then grab a handful myself and stuff my mouth, chewing one after the other.

It is ecstasy, by far the greatest thing I've ever tasted. I feel the sugar rush race through my body, and feel like I've gone to heaven. I look over and see the others wolfing them down, too, eyes closed, chewing slowly, savoring each bite. All of us, ravished.

I reach back into the crate and discover bags of gummy bears and twizzlers. I am amazed. I never thought I'd see these again. These are like gold, and I know I should ration them.

But after what we've all been through, now is not the time to ration anything—and for once, I let my emotions overcome my rational side. I throw the small bags to everyone in the boat, distributing them equally, and each person catches them in the air with a cry of joy and surprise. As Logan catches his, taking his hand off the wheel, the boat swerves a bit, then quickly straightens out.

I tear open my bag of gummy bears and finish the whole thing in just a few seconds, shoveling them into my mouth. Then I turn to the twizzlers. I try to take my time with these, forcing myself to chew each one slowly. I've barely eaten in days, and it is a shock to my stomach. It screams out in pain, and I force myself to slow down.

I spot a small fridge in the back of the boat, and hurry over and open it. I can't believe it. It is stocked with everything from juice to champagne. The inequality of it all infuriates me: here we are, starving to death, while these fat slaverunners have been guzzling champagne. At least now it's time for revenge.

I grab a bottle of champagne, twist off the wire, and pop the cork. It goes flying through the air, overboard, and into the river. Everyone turns at the sound and sees me standing there, holding the bottle as foam sprays out the top and over my hand. It is icy cold, but I don't care. I put it to my lips, and take a swig. It goes right to my head.

I know I shouldn't, but after everything they've been through, I offer it to Bree and Rose; they each take a small sip, giggling. I then reach over and hand it to Ben, and he takes several swigs without stopping. He hands it back to me, but still won't look at me. He keeps his eyes fixed somewhere on the water. I wonder if he is ashamed to look at me, ashamed for having not saved his brother.

I study him as he looks out over the water. His eyes are red, and I can see he's been crying. He reaches up and rubs one of them, wiping away a tear. I can hardly imagine what he's been through.

"Do you want to talk about?" I ask.

He shakes his head no.

I understand. If it were me, I wouldn't want talk about it either. He looks like he wants space, and I don't want to press him.

When he's ready, I think to myself.

I climb back to the front of the boat, sit in the passenger seat, and pass the bottle over to Logan. He takes a twizzler out of his mouth, grabs the bottle, takes a long swig, then hands it back to me, never taking his eyes off the water. He then inserts another twizzler into his mouth, chewing slowly.

I sit there in the plush leather passenger seat and lean back. We drive for a few minutes in silence, the only sound that of the whining engine. Finally, Logan turns to me.

"So, where to?" he asks.

I stare out at the water, thinking. I think about what Logan said before, about that perfect town, somewhere in Canada. And for the first time in as long as I can remember, I feel hope. I wonder if maybe he's right, if maybe there could be some place left in the world that isn't ruined. I wonder if maybe it's good to dream.

I turn to him.

"I'm thinking Canada," I say.

He looks at me and his eyes open wide in surprise. He must realize what I'm really saying: *Maybe you are right.*

Slowly, he breaks into a smile, and I can't help smiling back.

He reaches down and leans on the throttle, and I feel the boat accelerate just a bit.

"Canada it is," he says.

I lean further back, starting to relax for the first time. For some reason, I think of Dad. I wonder if he's up there, looking down on us. If he is, would he be proud? I feel that he would. I can almost hear his voice: *Brooke, you're in charge now. Do whatever you have to to keep them alive. Don't rest on your heels, soldier.*

It will be a long road ahead of us, I realize that. Soon, we'll run out of fuel. Then out of food. It will get dark, colder. The Hudson will turn to ice, and we'll have to find shelter. The slaverunners will be after us, and if we don't keep moving, they'll find us.

But I also realize I can worry about all of this later. For once in my life, I can just sit back and enjoy *right now.* The present moment. For the first time in my life, I finally realize that that is what really matters. Not later today. But right now.

I lean back in the plush leather seat and take another swig of champagne, and it goes right to my head. I haven't had a decent meal in days, and I know I shouldn't drink. But right now, I don't care. We're cruising up the Hudson, it's a sunny, beautiful morning, and for the first time in as long as I can remember, everything is good in the world. I look over and, surprisingly, see a patch of bright purple flowers, somehow surviving, sticking up in the snow. They are the most beautiful flowers I've ever seen, glowing in the sunlight. I wonder how they can even be real.

If these can survive, I think to myself, *so can we.*

I close my eyes and feel the salty air on my face. And for the first time in as long as I can remember, I think: *this feels good. It feels really good.*

COMING SOON...
Book #2 in the Survival Trilogy

ACCLAIM FOR MORGAN RICE'S BOOKS

"Grabbed my attention from the beginning and did not let go....This story is an amazing adventure that is fast paced and action packed from the very beginning. There is not a dull moment to be found."
--Paranormal Romance Guild {regarding *Turned*}

"A great plot, and this especially was the kind of book you will have trouble putting down at night. The ending was a cliffhanger that was so spectacular that you will immediately want to buy the next book, just to see what happens."
--The Dallas Examiner {regarding *Loved*}

"A book to rival *Twilight* and *The Vampire Diaries*, and one that will have you wanting to keep reading until the very last page! If you are into adventure, love and vampires this book is the one for you!"
--vampirebooksite.com {regarding *Turned*}

"An ideal story for young readers. Morgan Rice did a good job spinning an interesting twist on what could have been a typical vampire tale. Refreshing and unique, has the classic elements found in many Young Adult paranormal stories."
--The Romance Reviews {regarding *Turned*}

"Rice does a great job of pulling you into the story from the beginning, utilizing a great descriptive quality that transcends the mere painting of the setting....Nicely written and an extremely fast read, this is a good start to a new vampire series sure to be a hit with readers who are looking for a light, yet entertaining story."
--Black Lagoon Reviews {regarding *Turned*}

"Jam packed with action, romance, adventure, and suspense. This book is a wonderful addition to this series and will have you wanting more from Morgan Rice."
--vampirebooksite.com {regarding *Loved*}

"Morgan Rice proves herself again to be an extremely talented storyteller....This would appeal to a wide range of audiences, including younger fans of the vampire/fantasy genre. It ended with an unexpected cliffhanger that leaves you shocked."
--The Romance Reviews {regarding *Loved*}

ABOUT MORGAN RICE

Morgan Rice is the #1 Bestselling author of THE VAMPIRE JOURNALS, which has sold over 100,000 copies and has been translated into six languages. Morgan lives in New York City.

Please visit Morgan's site, where you can join the mailing list, hear the latest news, see additional images, and find links to stay in touch with Morgan on Facebook, Twitter, Goodreads and elsewhere: www.morganricebooks.com

Also by Morgan Rice

TURNED (Book #1 in the Vampire Journals)
LOVED (Book #2 in the Vampire Journals)
BETRAYED (Book #3 in the Vampire Journals)
DESTINED (Book #4 in the Vampire Journals)
DESIRED (Book #5 in the Vampire Journals)
BETROTHED (Book #6 in the Vampire Journals)
VOWED (Book #7 in the Vampire Journals)

CPSIA information can be obtained at www.ICGtesting.com
Printed in the USA
LVOW090800210512

282587LV00001B/55/P

9 780984 975310